What So Proudly We Hailed

James Howard

Author's Note

On October 31st, 2006, at 12:15am, I experienced a disturbing dream. In it my son and I were on our way home from a store at night and saw a large glow in the sky to the north. I also saw a long contrail illuminated in the glow where a missile had passed. In the dream I knew that a nuclear attack had begun. (The details of this dream form the opening chapter of this novel.) I awoke stunned with fear, and with a question ringing in my head, "What would you do? What would you do?"

The question did not imply, "What would you do if you had thus and so?" But rather, "What would you do with what you have in your possession *right now?*" As I thought out the implications, I got up and began taking notes and outlining themes. Two hours later, I had the framework for what would become this novel.

I make no claim to divine intervention, inspiration, or prophecy. All I know is that I have felt an ongoing urgency to write this novel, and get it into as many hands as possible. For some it may present a new way of looking at world events, and for others it may serve as a wakeup call to prepare, still others may enjoy it purely as entertainment. I welcome you to read it and draw your own conclusions. God bless you.

James Howard
February 26, 2010

Praise for *What So Proudly We Hailed* -

James Howard has taken some incredibly deep and complex Bible prophccy and with a masterful touch of the pen has unpackaged them in a gripping, modern day story that makes the concepts easily digestible and palatable to today's readers.
> Michael Lewis, Senior Pastor, Cathedral of Praise church, Charleston, SC

I recommend this book...excellent story...timely and well thought out.
> Kirk Lowe, Screenwriter, Vice President of the Lowcountry Christian Fiction Writers

James Howard has an amazing way of holding a person's interest. *What So Proudly We Hailed* is superbly written. I recommend it to anyone and everyone.
> Mike Lowry, Associate Pastor, Northwoods Assembly Church, North Charleston, SC

I started Chapter 1 and was totally hooked... I had to force myself to put it down.
> Robin Summitt, Instructor, Gaston College, Gastonia, NC

I was on the edge of my seat. As I read it I kept wondering, *if this really happened, what would **we** do?*
> Barbara Haile, author and inspirational speaker, Greenville, SC

I am amazed by this book. From a secular perspective or a Christian one, it was just a great story.
> Don Bantz, Iron Man Competitor, Summerville, SC

It's a definite page-turner. This book has an anointing.
> Danyl Bean, Professional Musician, Summerville, SC

This book should make anyone think about the principles upon which this nation was founded – and cling to them.
> Rep. Mike Pitts, S.C. House District 14, Laurens, SC

James Howard's talent for storytelling is superseded only by his faith.

Amanda Capps, author/editor/publicist, Greenville, SC

A suspenseful adventure… beautifully written and well detailed.

Kristin Threet, Student, College of Charleston

This story is amazing …

Shannon McNear, Novelist and Zone Director, American Christian Fiction Writers

What So Proudly We Hailed

Chapter One

"An alien sun rising in the north."

Jason Ribault stood up straight and stepped back from
the hull of his boat where he had been sanding a patch of
fiberglass repair material. He stretched, arching his back to
loosen the stiffness, and groaned. Looking down the hull
along the waterline he surveyed the four other sanded
patches and the corresponding piles of white powder on the
ground below. He sighed and wiped the sweat from his
brow, leaving a streak of white across his forehead. Around
him the shadows were beginning to lengthen and the chorus
of insects in the woods beside his home was getting louder.
A cicada buzzed from a nearby tree.

From the house Jason heard the screen door slam shut
and turned to see his fifteen year old son Brian leap down
the front porch steps and walk across the yard toward him.
The young man's jeans and tee shirt accentuated his narrow
frame and he jerked his head to clear the long hair from his
eyes before he spoke.

"Mom wants to know if you'd take me to the store to get
some stuff for school."

Jason sighed again and looked down at his white
powdered legs and feet. "Can't she take you?"

"She's making dinner."

Jason nodded. "All right. What do you need anyway?"

"A poster board and some other stuff for a project."

1

"A project? They've got you doing projects already? School's just started."

"I know, right?"

"When's it due?"

"Tomorrow."

"Tomorrow? Why did you wait until the last minute?"

"I didn't. It's all done. I just have to mount it on the board." Brian smiled and jerked his head again. "When I get my license I'll be able to drive myself to the store."

"I can't wait," Jason said, rolling his eyes. "Let me get cleaned up."

As Brian returned to the house, Jason gathered his sandpaper and tools and canteen and headed for the garage. At the deep sink he washed the dust from his arms and neck. The door to the kitchen opened and Jason's wife Valerie stepped down into the garage.

"Thanks for taking him," she said. "I hated to ask, but I can't leave the dinner on the stove for that long."

"That's okay. It smells good."

"You've got something on your forehead," Valerie said, tapping her own forehead with her index finger.

Jason rubbed his face, and then glanced at his wet hand before rinsing it again. "Thanks." He took a nearby towel and began to dry himself.

"Hey," she said, "what's my Penguins towel doing out here?"

"I don't know. Someone took the one I had here before."

"Hand it here. I don't want it to get filthy."

"Huh!" Jason handed her the towel. "You act like they won the cup or something."

"They did. How's the boat coming?"

"Slow, as usual. With the days getting shorter, there aren't enough daylight hours after work to get anything done." Jason looked out past the garage doors to where the cabin cruiser lounged on its trailer in the front yard. "It's already September and I still haven't got it painted, yet. Another summer gone and we've never camped out in it even once."

"I'm sure you'll have it done by next summer."

"Yeah, but who'll be here to go out with us? Kathy's always on the go with work and school. Jeremy's always at

2

Ruth's. Before you know it Brian'll have his license and will be gone as well."

"I'm not going anywhere," Valerie said, "so you have at least one crew aboard."

Jason looked up at her. "I am glad for that."

Valerie came down the steps and stood next to him as she studied the boat, now becoming a shadow against the backdrop of trees. "I think once you get the boat in the water, they'll make time to come camping with us."

"Yeah. Maybe I could kidnap Ruthie aboard. That'll bring Jeremy."

Valerie started to reply when Brian came down the steps. His hair was neatly brushed, he wore a new shirt, and an aroma of aftershave wafted in his wake. "I'm ready. Let's go."

Valerie exchanged a glance with Jason and said, "Youins hurry back. Dinner will be ready in about twenty minutes or so."

*

Jason adjusted the ball cap on his head as he steered his extended cab truck down the road. Above him the stars began to twinkle across the darkening sky and scattered clouds. He dimmed his headlights for an oncoming car, then said to Brian, "Are you meeting someone at the store?"

"No," Brian said, with unmasked irritation. "I just don't like to go someplace, like, all sweaty and everything."

Jason suppressed a smile. "Sorry if I look kind of ratty. I just thought it would be a quick trip."

"It's not about you, all right?"

Jason sighed aloud. Here we go, he thought. He pulled into the parking lot of the large discount store and found a place not too far from the front entrance.

"Are you sure this poster board is all you're going to need?"

The kid flung his hair to the side with a jerk of his head. "Yes, that's it."

"You don't need any tape, or glue, or anything like that?"

3

The son drew in a breath to speak, paused, and said, "I'm not sure about the tape. I might need some tape, too."

Jason nodded. "Let's just get whatever you think you need now." He removed the keys and unlocked the door. "I don't want to have to come back out."

"All right."

They headed for the store entrance and briskly made their way to the aisle where the school supplies were. As Brian thumbed through the poster boards, Jason stopped to look at the pens on display. He looked up when a woman with a shopping cart came around the far end of the aisle and called to him.

"Hey, Jason!"

"Hey, Pam. How are you doing?" They met with a friendly hug. "Where's Derek?"

The two spoke for a few moments as Brian collected what he needed. Then he carried his supplies over to where a couple of teens were looking at a display of DVD's.

"Are you and Valerie involved in any groups at the church?" Pam asked Jason.

"We're kind of taking a break right now," Jason said, "But we plan to join another group in January."

"Let us know which one and we'll join it, too."

"Will do." Jason glanced at his watch and looked around him. "Well, I guess I'd better get... Where did he go?"

"I think he's over there," Pam said, pointing.

"Ah," Jason said. "Well, give Derek a hug for us and keep in touch."

"I will. Take care!"

Jason walked quickly over to the DVD rack. "Come on son. We've got to go."

Brian parted company with his friends and followed his dad to a nearby register. They paid for the items and headed out of the store. They put the items in the backseat of the truck and drove out onto the road.

"Who were those kids you were talking to?"

"Just some kids from school."

"What were they talking about?"

"Nothing. Just school stuff."

The two rode in silence as the road passed through a wooded area. In the absence of streetlights and businesses,

4

something caught Jason's attention in the sky. He turned his head left and saw, through the trees, a vivid, unnatural yellow light that grew rapidly in intensity, as if an alien sun were rising in the north.

"What's that?" Brian asked, staring out the driver's side window.

Jason didn't answer. He divided his attention between the strange light and the road, and as the trees thinned, he saw that it was brightest toward the horizon. Then suddenly it began to fade. Before the light was completely gone, he noticed a single contrail, a gash across the sky from the southwest to the center of the glow at the horizon. Jason could tell by the thick, puffiness of the contrail that it had not come from a jet flying at high altitude, but rather by an object entering the earth's atmosphere.

A prickly feeling spread across Jason's scalp.

Then the light faded completely, and the sky grew black once more.

"What the heck was that?" Brian asked again.

Jason knew. Though his eyes returned to the road, his mind reeled with the implications. The contrail had explained all.

"Dad?"

"Uh," Jason said. "We need to go home and check the news."

"Was it the mill?"

Jason drew in a breath to speak, but only shook his head and exhaled again.

*

Ten minutes later, Jason pulled into the driveway of their home and parked the truck next to his boat trailer. The house brooded darkly against the backdrop of woods except for the glimmer of a single candle in one of the front rooms. A wavering flashlight beam shone from the front door. Leaving Brian to gather his supplies from the backseat, Jason got out of the truck and jogged across the front lawn. Valerie, her face a pale blur against the black of her hair, directed the flashlight beam toward Jason's feet as he came up the steps.

"How long have the lights been out?" Jason asked.

5

"About ten minutes or so. I nearly broke my neck trying to find a flashlight."

"Did you see that weird glow in the sky?" Brian asked, coming up the steps.

"No. What glow?"

They all stepped inside where the smell of dinner on the stove still hung in the air. Jason went to the television set out of habit and pushed the power button. Then he sighed loudly and turned to Valerie. "We need to get a radio on."

"What's going on?"

"We were coming home and saw this bright yellow glow in the sky," Brian said.

"Glow?"

Jason moved into another room. "Do we have any more candles?"

"Yes. Wait! What's going on?"

Jason picked up the lit candle on the dining room table, but as he did so the power restored and the rooms became bright once again. He waited to see if the lights would stay on, then brought the candle into the living room and placed it, still lit, on the mantle above the fireplace. He turned to face Valerie. "We need to get the TV on."

"Honey, first stop and tell me what's going on." She grabbed his arm as he reached for the TV remote. They both sat on the couch.

"Um, I'm not sure." He bit his lower lip. "There was this glow in the sky, like a bright, searing yellow. And above us I could see a contrail where something had passed overhead, in a line straight to the glow."

"Like a plane?" Valerie asked.

"No, like a...." He hesitated. "Like maybe a missile or something."

"A missile?"

"You mean a nuclear missile?" Brian asked.

"Maybe."

"Are you sure?" Valerie asked.

"No. We need to turn on the news." He switched on the television and the satellite receiver and went to the program guide. He tried the main news channels, but most of them were running their regularly scheduled programs recapping the news of the day.

6

"Try Fox," Valerie said, and he did so. On that channel a blonde woman was talking to a person by phone line.

"...so while we have no estimate of damage or casualties at this time, the hope is that because it was a semi-rural area the loss of life might be limited."

"And how widespread is the power outage?"

"From what we can tell right now, the southern and central portions of the state are completely without power."

"So cities like Miami, Tampa, and Orlando and their surrounding areas are blacked out?"

"Yes, that's correct."

Valerie pointed to the screen. "Look at the words on the bottom."

At the bottom of the screen scrolled, "At six forty-seven p.m. EST a large explosion occurred in Central Florida causing power outages throughout the state."

"That's what you saw?" Valerie said.

Jason shook his head. "What we saw was to the north."

The newscaster concluded her phone call, then spoke to the viewing audience. "For those of you just joining, there are reports of a massive explosion that occurred in northern central Florida. We have no details as to the cause of the blast, nor of the extent of the damage, but the explosion seems to have triggered power outages across the state." She paused as she read from a monitor at the desk. "Uh, this just in. Moments ago a similar explosion was reported outside the city of Charlotte, North Carolina. Widespread power outages are occurring in that state as well."

"Is this a nuclear war?" Brian asked, his voice anxious.

"I don't know," Jason said. "I'm not sure what it is or who's doing it, or why. But I'm worried this may be just the beginning." He stared at the screen. "And if it's just the beginning, we've got to prepare. Right now."

"Prepare?" Valerie asked. "How do you prepare for something like this?"

"We go out and prepare as if a hurricane was coming. Water, canned goods, etc."

Just then the front door opened and a slender young woman dressed in the black pants and white blouse of her work outfit walked in. She tossed back her long brown hair and set down her purse and bottled drink. "Have you guys heard anything about some explosions going on? We lost power at work and...."

"Shhh!" Jason gestured with his hand. "It's on right now, Kathy. Watch!" The young woman sat on the couch with the rest of the family.

The newscaster continued. "At this time we are going to join our affiliate station in Charlotte to see what is going on there." A man's picture came on the screen. "Patrick, can you tell us what is happening in the Charlotte area?"

"Charlotte?" Kathy exclaimed.

"Shhh!" Valerie said.

A man's voice, crackled with static, came over the speakers. "Yes. We've been speaking to several eyewitnesses who saw the blast and all of them describe what appears to have been a nuclear detonation. They saw an extremely bright flash of light followed by the sound of a thunderous explosion and a telltale mushroom shaped cloud. There are many reports of blindness caused by the flash of light, and also many people reported feeling a blast of hot air many miles from the explosion."

"Was it a direct hit on the city?" the newscaster asked.

"No. The city itself was spared the brunt of the explosion, but, unfortunately, some of the outlying towns and suburbs have been destroyed."

"Oh, my God," Valerie whispered.

"What about Uncle Terry and Aunt Rhonda?" Brian asked.

"We've got to make preparations," Jason said. "We've got to get ready."

"What about Uncle Terry and Aunt Rhonda?" Brian asked again, more insistent.

"Oh, that's right!" Kathy said. "Uncle Terry and Aunt Rhonda live there! What's going to happen to them?"

"Kathy, listen!" Valerie said.

Just then the power blinked, but came on again. Jason looked up at the lights, then he stood and shut the television off. "We've got to go right now. We can't wait." He turned to face his family. "I'm sure Uncle Terry and Aunt Rhonda will be all right. We don't know what area was hit. You know Terry. He'll take care of them both well enough. And that's just what we're going to do." He pointed to Valerie.

"Get your purse. Let's go." He turned to his daughter. "Kathy, get on the phone and call our relatives. Don't stay on long, just check in and see if they're all right. The numbers are in my Palm Pilot on my desk. Let them know we're okay. Tell them they should prepare as if for a hurricane. Brian, come with us."

Valerie grabbed her purse and the three of them headed for the door. Jason called back, "Keep the TV off until you make the calls." Then they went out to the truck.

Chapter Two

"Is this Armageddon?"

Out on the road, Jason hit the gas hard until he was just above the speed limit. The darkened road made him remember the glow and his scalp prickled over again. *God, please help me protect my family.* He adjusted his ball-cap and accelerated a little more.

"Not too fast, please," Valerie said, jotting on a small notepad.

"We need to make a list," Jason said.

"I'm on it."

"Water," Jason said, "and canned foods."

"I've got those already."

"Brian and I will go get a few of those five gallon jugs of water. I've got a pump for them at home, and I can fill the one we already have. I'll pick up some of those five gallon gas cans for the generator, as well."

"Okay. Now let me write my stuff down," she said.

"I guess I didn't need the tape after all," Brian said in a gloomy tone.

Jason glanced at him in the rearview mirror and then pulled into a parking space at the store. As they all got out he said, "I can take Brian with me unless you need him."

"He can help you. I know what I need."

They hurried into the store and grabbed two shopping carts. "Meet you in the grocery section when I'm done," Jason said. He headed toward the opposite side of the store

10

with Brian in tow.

The store seemed eerily empty. Here and there a few people lazily picked through the racks and shelves, but the bulk of the shoppers were Mexican families in the grocery aisles. Jason and Brian headed for the sporting goods section at the back of the store and behind the counter stood an older man with a crew cut and thin gray mustache. Counting through a small stack of papers, he looked up as Jason approached.

"Can I help you?"

Jason studied the gun cabinet behind the man and pointed to one of the pump shotguns. "Could I have a look at that 870, please?"

The man unlocked the cabinet and took out the gun, opening the chamber as he handed it over. Jason sighted along the barrel and inspected the simple mechanisms. It was plain in appearance and uncomplicated in function. He handed the shotgun back.

"I'll take it," Jason said.

The man turned to relock the cabinet. "I'll need to get a copy of your driver's license, please."

"You're buying a shotgun?" Brian asked.

Jason nodded, handing the man his driver's license. "Why?"

"I've always wanted one." He tried to force a smile.

The man placed a form in front of him. "Fill this out, please."

Jason filled out the paper while the man made a copy of the driver's license. He handed it back to Jason and said, "Do you want to make the purchase now or when you come back to pick it up?"

"Come back?"

"Yes. I have to wait for your background check to come through."

"How long will that take?"

"Half an hour, maybe less."

Jason looked at his watch. "I'll come back."

"I close this register at nine."

"Thanks." He turned to Brian. "Let's go."

The two went to an aisle with water coolers and loaded five large jugs of water, emptying the shelf. Next they went

11

to the automotive section and stacked empty five-gallon gas cans atop the water jugs before heading for the camping gear. In eight minutes they rejoined Valerie, her cart full to the top. "Did you get everything?" Jason asked.

"Everything except...."

Just then the lights dimmed and began a staccato flickering, but a second later they were burning fully again.

"...ice," she continued.

"We'll get that at the front," Jason said. "We need to go now."

At the front of the store, they found a register with only one person ahead of them and got in line. Valerie pulled her wallet out of her purse and drew out a debit card. "This okay?" she asked Jason.

Jason shrugged. "Yes, and get cash back."

"How much?"

"As much as you can."

When it was their turn the cashier began ringing up their items. About halfway through the checkout the lights blinked out again for a split second.

"What is going on tonight?" the cashier said, looking up at the lights. She glanced over at the cash register. "I guess we're still on." She continued ringing up the items and as the water jugs came on the belt she smiled and said, "Is there a storm coming that I don't know about?"

"Get ready for one," Jason said. "As soon as you can."

The girl paused. "There is a storm, for real?"

"Not a hurricane, but yes, a storm."

The cashier looked at her watch. "I go on break in about fifteen minutes."

"Prepare as soon as you can," Jason repeated. They finished their checkout and pushed their two carts toward the front of the store.

"Dad," Brian said, "is it possible you scared that girl for nothing?"

Jason opened his mouth to reply, but as they stepped through the doors he saw he didn't need to. The traffic in the parking lot had increased and people were already heading for the doors to get in. "I don't think so," he said as they threaded their way to their truck.

At home, Jason held the front door open with his foot as Valerie carried several grocery bags inside. "Give us a hand, Kathy."

"No, wait!" Kathy pointed to the television screen. "Come in and watch this!"

The three set their bundles on the living room floor. Brian sat on the couch.

"There have been two more hits, in the Midwest," Kathy said. "The White House is holding a press conference. There's some guy from the Air Force on right now."

The screen showed the White House pressroom where several uniformed people stood along the wall behind the podium, flanked by civilian officials in suits. The headliner at the bottom of the screen described the two hits in the Midwest. A general at the podium fielded questions from reporters. He spoke calmly and clearly, despite the intermittent camera flashes.

"No. As I said before, we believe these missiles were not of the intercontinental ballistic type. They appear to be a medium or long range type."

A flurry of questions followed about responsibility.

"The president has already spoken to the leaders of the Russian Federation and the People's Republic of China, and both nations deny any involvement in the attacks. China's two ballistic submarines are home ported, and all of Russia's submarines are accounted for. None of them are currently operating in the Gulf of Mexico."

Another burst of questions.

"Yes, we have tracked the missiles to a point somewhere off the coast of either Florida or Alabama. U.S. Navy anti-submarine aircraft are searching the area now, along with a destroyer from the Royal Navy that happened to be in the area."

Questions about missile defense were heard.

"The nation's patriot missile batteries are not usually kept on alert status, but they are being mobilized at this time."

There was another volley of questions, but this time one man's voice in particular was heard above the rest. "Are there still more missiles being launched?"

"We don't think so," said the general.

The voice boomed in again. "How many are in flight right now?"

The general paused a moment, looking at the man. "I am not at liberty to discuss that at this time. This conference is adjourned. Thank you." Then the general moved away from the podium amid a vigorous barrage of questions and photoflashes.

"Oh, my God," Valerie whispered.

"Is this it?" Kathy asked, standing abruptly. "Are we all going to die? Are we?"

"I don't want to be in Armageddon," Brian said.

"Are we going to die?" Kathy screamed. "Why don't you answer me?"

Jason grabbed the remote and jumped to his feet. He switched off the TV and held Kathy tightly. "No one here is going to die. If Charleston had been a target we would have been hit by now."

"Is this Armageddon?" Brian asked.

Valerie shot a glance at Jason, who spoke calmly and patted his son's shoulder. "No, son. I don't think so, just yet." He looked down at Brian and tried to smile. "Besides, Armageddon is in Israel." He released Kathy and said, "Did you call our relatives?"

"I tried but the lines were jammed," she said.

"Has anyone heard from Jeremy?"

"He went to Ruth's to study," Valerie said.

"I tried his cell phone but those circuits are jammed also," said Kathy, returning to the couch.

"Try again." Jason turned to Valerie. "We've got to do something. Quick."

"I thought we already did," she said, gesturing toward the groceries.

Jason shook his head. "Something's not right. We need to go someplace safe."

"But you said we wouldn't be hit again," said Valerie.

Jason turned to Kathy. "Call Jeremy now. Use your cell phone. Keep trying until you get him." He took Valerie by the hand and led her into the kitchen. "I don't think we'll be hit again. But I wonder what the ramifications from all this

14

will be. Remember how it was in New Orleans after Katrina, the looting and lawlessness? Well, imagine that happening across the whole US."

"Why should that happen now?"

"Because the law enforcement agencies, as well as the National Guard and all other services, will be overwhelmed. Remember the St. Pete, Florida riots back in 1996? Matt said they were calling in police from the entire Tampa Bay area. But this time, all of the other areas will be overwhelmed already. No one will be able to send any help when everything's breaking loose all around them, too."

"Don't you think that most people will just sit tight? They're probably scared."

"Yes, for now, but what about when food starts running out? How long will people sit quietly then? This house was without power for twenty-one days after Hugo hit, and that was with crews coming in to make repairs from all over the country. Well, this time you can be sure they're not coming. They'll be trying to get their own power back on. Remember," he added, gesturing to the TV set, "this isn't done, yet."

Just then, as if to underscore his words, the lights dimmed again. It seemed much longer for them to return this time. They held still, their upturned faces frozen in the flickering yellow light. After what seemed like several seconds the power was restored once more and they let out a sigh of relief.

"I think we need to go someplace safe," Jason said, more softly this time.

"We can go to my parents place in West Virginia," Valerie said. "I know of people up there who have been preparing for this kind of thing for years."

"Sounds good. But for now, we need to get all the gas cans filled while we still have power. Take Brian and get the gas cans filled. Fill the truck, too." He turned to the living room. "Kathy, what about Jeremy?"

"The lines are still jammed."

"Keep trying. Tell him to come home." Jason looked at his watch. "Hurry and go right now. I've got to go back to the store. Kathy, I need to borrow your car."

Chapter Three

"Blink the lights a couple of times and people start a panic."

Jason considered himself lucky to find a parking place
near the end of one of the center aisles. Cars filled the lot
and few people seemed to be leaving. He looked at his watch
again and saw that he still had a little more than five minutes
left before the sporting goods register closed. He hurried
through the doors.

Inside the store, chaotic crowds jostled and bickered,
arguing over shopping carts or racing to get in the checkout
lines. It reminded him of Christmas Eve, only twice as rude
and laced with panic. One woman nearly hit him with a cart
as she tried to snatch it away from someone else. Pallets of
water and canned goods had been rolled out into the main
aisles, and people were greedily filling their carts from them.
He skirted past the crowds, darting through the smaller aisles
of clothes and housewares until he came to the sporting
goods section.

The man behind the counter looked up at him as he
approached, and then looked at his watch. "I thought you
might not make it back," he said.

"Sorry. I know you're getting ready to close and I came
back as quickly as I could," said Jason. He could see the
shotgun in its original box leaning against the gun cabinet.
"How did the background check go?"

"I'm still waiting," said the man, glancing at the
computer monitor. "But it's got to come through any second

16

now. Did you want to go ahead and ring everything up?"

"Yes, please."

"What kind of shells do you want?"

Just then a man hurried up to the counter. He was pushing a shopping cart full of canned goods, water, and other supplies. "Do you have kerosene lanterns?"

The man behind the counter turned toward him and sighed. He pointed and said, "Third aisle over, toward the back, if there are any left. The flashlights are there, too."

"Can I ring this stuff up here?" asked the shopping cart man.

Careful not to let his eyes fall to the mound of stuff in the man's cart, the man behind the counter cocked his head sympathetically and said, "I'm sorry, sir, but this register is closed. As soon as I finish this paperwork with this customer I have to report to another part of the store."

The shopping cart man snorted and pushed his cart away.

The man behind the counter shook his head. "It's been like that for the last hour or so. Blink the lights a couple of times and people start a panic."

Jason made no reply as he took out his wallet. He opened it and looked over its assortment of cards and cash, then he took out his credit card and put the wallet back into his pocket. "Where are the shells?"

"Small game shells are on that shelf over there, and I have the larger game shells behind this counter."

"Please give me five packs of twelve gauge slugs, ten boxes of double-ought buck, and ten boxes of number one shot shells," said Jason as he went to the shelf and gathered several boxes of the small game and bird shot shells. He placed them on the counter next to the gun.

The man shook his head and retrieved the shells Jason had requested. "I don't suppose you'll be needing a hunting license?"

"No," said Jason.

"So, you're swept up in all this panic, too?"

Jason bristled for a moment, then said, "You have no idea what's going on, do you?" The man stared at him. "Before you leave, go to the electronics section and see what's happening on the TV." He gestured toward the gun

17

and shells. "Please ring this up now."

The man rang up the shotgun and all of the shells in thoughtful silence. "Six hundred ninety-eight dollars and forty-three cents," he said.

Jason swiped the credit card and returned it to his wallet as the man bagged the items. He stared at the small screen while he waited for the authorization. The man finished bagging and looked at the register as the words "Transaction Cancelled" appeared. "Oh, what now?" Jason said sharply.

"Let me try to run it through from here," said the man. Jason handed him the card and the man swiped it at the register. He handed it back and they both waited again. Then the man shook his head. "It's just not taking it. Do you have another card you'd want to try?"

Jason reached for his wallet just as the lights went out again. This time there was no flicker, only sudden blackness, then the pale glow of emergency lights. A rising tumult of frightened voices swelled throughout the store and toward the front a woman screamed. In the dim light he could see the older man's face looking up toward the ceiling. Jason opened his wallet and tilted it to look inside. He knew he couldn't have much more than three hundred dollars in cash. "Can I just get the gun and one box of shells?"

"Not without the background check," said the man. "Sorry." He took the bag of shells off of the counter and placed the shotgun on the floor against the cabinet.

"Come on, man. I have cash. You can ring it up later."

The man took out his keys to unlock the cabinet. "Come back tomorrow."

Just then there arose a sound of shouting and arguing and broken glass a few aisles over. The man came out from behind the counter and headed for the sound, which was growing in intensity. In the dim light Jason stared at the shotgun, standing just out of reach next to the bag of shells. Behind him he could hear a patter of running feet and a woman's voice yelling out for someone to call the police. Still staring at the gun he wavered, then took a deep breath and shook his head. He turned away from the counter and headed out of the store.

*

Jason pulled into his driveway and saw that the house was without power again. Candlelight flickered in several of the windows and he saw his older son's car parked next to the boat. He stopped the car and headed for the front door, taking care not to trip while going up the darkened steps. Kathy met him at the front door with a flashlight.

"Dad, I'm glad you're back," she said.

Jason stepped inside. "Was there any more on the news?"

"No. The news station went out a little before the power did. It hasn't come back on at all since."

Jason stopped in the living room. "Were you able to call of anyone in the family?"

"No, the lines are still jammed."

"Where's Jeremy?"

"On the phone with Ruth."

Jason raised his eyebrows and cocked his head toward her as if to point out the contradiction.

"The long distance lines were jammed," she clarified. "He kept dialing locally until he got through. The cell phones have come and gone with the power."

Just then Jeremy came down the hall from the bedrooms. He held the cordless house phone receiver in one hand and his cell phone in the other. He was using the cell phone to light his way down the hall. "Hey, Dad."

"Jeremy, I'm glad you're here. How's Ruth's family?"

"They're all right. Ruth's wigging out. I was just on the phone with her." He closed his cell phone as he came into the candle lit room, replacing the cordless phone on the dead receiver. His linebacker's shadow appeared magnified on the wall behind him. "What's going to happen to us?"

"We need to talk about that when your mom gets back." He took one of the tea light holders from the top of the TV cabinet. "I want you guys to start packing your things. Pack as if we were going on a long vacation."

"Ruthie's dad is calling a meeting at the church for all members," Jeremy said. "He wants to pray and touch base with everyone."

"When?" Jason asked.

"In about an hour."

19

"Pack first." Jason went to the master bedroom and set the candle on his chest of drawers. In the dim glow he found a flashlight and grabbed a plastic case out of the closet. Placing it on the bed, he unlocked and opened the case and assessed the weapons inside. The thirty-eight special government surplus revolver was loaded, as was its speed loader. The twenty-two-caliber single action revolver and the twenty-two-caliber semi-automatic pocket pistol were not loaded. He chambered the revolver for twenty-two magnum and loaded them both. He had just replaced the guns in the case when he heard the front door opening. He left the guns and the candle and brought the flashlight with him to the living room.

Valerie and Brian had come in. She was sitting on the couch, and Brian was using a flashlight to rummage through the refrigerator.

"Brian," Jason said, "you're letting all the cold air out."

"I'm looking for a drink I had in here."

"I drank it," Jeremy said, coming into the living room carrying a load of dirty clothes in a basket. "Sorry."

Brian slammed the refrigerator door. "Thanks, Jeremy."

"I'll get you another one."

"Where are you going with those?" Jason asked.

"I need to do a load of clothes before I can pack." Jeremy took a few more steps, then turned around and dropped the basket of clothes on the floor. "Oh, great! How am I supposed to do laundry with no power?"

"You've nothing clean you can bring?" asked Jason.

"Nothing I'd want to be seen in." He started back to his room.

"Just bring something comfortable," said Jason. "And don't leave your dirty clothes in the kitchen."

Jeremy sighed and walked back to the laundry basket. He picked it up and headed back to his room. "I don't see why we have to pack anyway," he said. "Where are we supposed to go?"

"We were just going to discuss that," Jason said. He turned to Valerie and could see her eyes fixed on him in the candlelight. "Were you able to fill all of the gas tanks?"

"Yes," she answered. "We filled up the truck, too. It came to a hundred and fifty-seven dollars. I put it on the

20

debit. I hope that's all right."

"Yes. I don't think it will matter in the morning."

"Why's that?" Kathy asked.

"Because the power's out," Jason said. "The banks won't be open."

"Well, what about when the power comes back on?" Jason looked at her. "I'm thinking the power may be off for some time."

"What, so we won't be banking anymore? What did you do after Hugo?"

"Most places were without power for about a week. Some ran off generators. But I think this may last a lot longer," Jason said. Then, without giving room for another question he said, "Which brings me to the subject of our destination. I'm not sure about us going to West Virginia."

"Why?" Valerie asked.

"Well, first of all, if the Charlotte area was hit, then the interstate may be impassable. I-77 goes right through the city. If the blast was north or south of Charlotte then the interstate may be gone completely. But even if the interstate wasn't hit directly, I still have no desire to be driving through a major city during a crisis like this."

"Why not?" Kathy asked.

"Because people can get weird during blackouts. I would rather stay here than get caught up in some civil disturbance in a strange town."

"So, you think we'll be okay staying here after all?" Valerie asked.

"No. People are bound to get weird here, too. But I did have something else in mind." He looked at each one of them, building their expectation. "I've been thinking, maybe it's time we gave our live-aboard dream a go."

"The boat?" asked Valerie.

"Sure. It would hold us all comfortably."

"I didn't think it was finished."

"Cosmetically, it isn't finished. But the engine and stern drive have been rebuilt. I've already changed out the bad piping, and I've done most of the electrical work. The boat is functional, if not pretty. Besides, we can continue with the cosmetic stuff while we're aboard."

"Are you talking about the boat?" Jeremy asked,

21

entering the room.

"Dad wants to go camp out on the boat until this blows over," Kathy said.

"For how long?" Jeremy asked.

"At least until we know what's going on," Jason said.

"Is there enough room for all of us?" Valerie asked.

"Yes. There's the master bunk for us, and forward is the salon where two can sleep on the bench cushions. When the table is lowered the third cushion goes on top of it so that three can lie side by side. And if someone wants to use it, there's the cushioned bench that's topside. I don't have the enclosure but we could rig up the tarp like an awning."

"You've got to be kidding," Jeremy said.

"Why?" Jason turned to his son.

"You expect us to stay cooped up on a twenty-five foot boat for God-only-knows how long?"

"Twenty six feet," Jason said.

"Whatever," Jeremy said. "We'd be at each other's throats in no time."

"We wouldn't have to stay on the boat all the time. We've got the tent, as well. We could anchor next to a small barrier island and camp ashore. It would be like a vacation."

"Not," Jeremy said. There was silence for a moment, and then Jeremy said, "I don't see why we have to go anywhere."

"Yeah," Kathy said, "Shouldn't we just be staying home and listening for emergency broadcasts on the radio, or something?"

"Listen to me. I know it's hard for you kids to understand, but your mom and I know what we're talking about. We grew up during the Cold War. We've seen the movies and read the books about nuclear holocaust. I even worked around nuclear weapons in the Navy. But as bad as everyone thought that would be, I think that this time the real thing will be worse. In the old scenarios, the major population centers were destroyed, but in this scenario the population centers are left intact and we will eventually destroy ourselves."

"And why is it necessary that we destroy ourselves?" Kathy asked.

Jason looked at her. "Can't you feel it?" He looked around at each one in the room. "Can't you feel, day after

22

day, the lawlessness and chaos that writhes under the surface of the law and order we live in? Look in the papers, watch the TV news, and look at the bumper stickers, read the tee shirts. It's all around us, waiting to explode. Nobody cares for his country or his fellow man anymore. We're awash in selfishness and that attitude is going to explode now. The thin veneer of law and order that has kept a lid on it, and has protected a normal way of life, has been stripped away. It's every man for himself and to hell with everyone else." He paused, letting his words sink in. Then he said, "What we do in the next six hours will decide whether or not we survive the next six months."

Everyone remained quiet for a few moments. Then Jeremy spoke, his eyes averted from Jason. "Well. I've got to go to this meeting at Ruthie's church. My suitcase is on the bed, and I'm almost packed. I'll finish when I get back." He turned and headed for the door.

"Did you hear anything I just said?" Jason asked.

"Yeah, Dad, I heard it. But I've already told Ruthie's dad I'd help him usher the meeting. I'll talk about it more with you when I get back. If I don't go now I'll be late."

"Drive careful," Valerie said. But Jeremy left without saying anything more.

Jason exchanged a glance with Valerie and shook his head. Then he pointed to Brian and said, "Did you get all of the ice in the cooler?"

"Yes, except for one bag that wouldn't fit. I put that one in the freezer."

"Very good." From the front yard he could hear the sound of Jeremy's compact car starting up.

"Are you sure about this boat idea?" Valerie asked.

Outside a police car sped down past the house, siren blaring. Through the front screen door a single flash of blue light illuminated a wall of the darkened living room before the siren faded away down the road. Then they heard the sound of Jeremy's car accelerating out of the driveway. Jason turned to Valerie.

"I think the boat is our best bet for remaining safe until this whole business settles down. Once it does, we can see how everything is and then decide what to do from there." He glanced around at his family. "All right. First, let's pack our personal things, one suitcase each. Try to bring comfortable clothes. Remember your toothbrushes and other toiletries. Bring only what you need, but pack as if for a long vacation. Bring some books or your MP3 players or things like that for leisure items. We don't have room for the kitchen sink."

He finished speaking and everyone stared at him. He clapped his hands twice and said, "Let's go!" Everyone got up and headed for the bedrooms. "Brian, help me get the suitcases out of the attic."

Chapter Four

"Why am I the only one who senses danger in all this?"

Fifteen minutes later Jason had his suitcase opened on his bed and was hurriedly loading clothes into it. A few more candles had been lit and his eyes had adjusted well to the low light. Valerie had her suitcase opened opposite of his, and she was carefully selecting clothes and folding them compactly into it.

"I'm wondering if I should bring my flip-flops," she said.

"I don't know where you'll be wearing them," said Jason. "We'll probably be barefoot on the boat most of the time. But do be sure to bring an old pair of tennis shoes."

"I keep visualizing us being on a beach somewhere."

"We might see some beach, but mostly we'll be in the salt marshes, I imagine."

"Mom," Kathy said, stepping up to the doorway. "I guess we'll need to share a curling iron and hairdryer. Do you want to take yours or mine?" She held the items up before her.

"Where are you going to plug them in?" Jason asked.

"I thought you had lights and stuff on the boat."

"Twelve volts DC. Those things run on one hundred ten volts AC. I hadn't bought an inverter, yet."

Kathy let the devices fall to her side. "How am I supposed to do my hair?"

"Well, I guess you can wash it and brush it and tie it up

in a ponytail."

"Dad!"

"I'm serious. We've got to make do with what we have."

"What about my laptop?"

Jason spread his hands, raised his eyebrows, and cocked his head toward her. Kathy sighed loudly as she turned and headed down the hall. "I guess we'll just go back to living in the Stone Age."

Jason drew a breath to speak, but checked himself. The phrase "bomb them into the Stone Age" came to mind and the prickly feeling spread across his scalp again. He looked back across the bed and his eyes met Valerie's. He shrugged and said quietly, "We're not going to have power here, either."

Valerie nodded and continued packing.

Brian came down the hall dragging his wheeled suitcase behind him. "Where do you want me to put my suitcase when I'm done?"

"Do you have your toothbrush, comb, shampoo, things like that?" Jason asked.

"I'm about to get them out of this bathroom, now."

"All right. When you're done, put the suitcase in the foyer, then I want you to get all of the fishing stuff and put it out by the boat. Tackle box, rods, cast net, anything you can think of for fishing."

Brian smiled. "Okay." He set his suitcase down and went into the hall bathroom.

Jason turned to Valerie and said quietly, "Please take a look in his suitcase and make sure he has everything." Valerie nodded. Then Jason took a book off his nightstand and put it into his suitcase. This was followed by a small flashlight and several batteries from his nightstand drawer, as well as the extra ammunition for the handguns. Then he picked up the small flashlight again and turned to the door. "I'll be right back."

He went to the bookshelf in his study and took an old copy of *Chapman's Book of Seamanship and Small Boat Handling*, as well as his favorite Bible. He considered the other books, and then grabbed a one on ancient Roman history and another one on American history. Scanning the shelves with his flashlight he saw several other titles that he

26

wanted to bring, but he knew he would have neither the room to keep them nor the time to read them. But then his little ten-dollar short wave radio receiver caught his eye, still in its protective black pouch. He grabbed it and returned to his room.

*

An hour's passage found them all outside loading things into the boat by flashlight and by the boat's cabin lights. The stars shone brightly in the absence of the city's light haze. They had already stowed away their suitcases and the canned food, along with the jugs of water, the fishing gear, the guns, the extra cans of gas, the thirty-six quart cooler of ice, a camping tent, a tarp, and the linens for the beds. They had just stopped to figure out how to get the eighty-five pound generator up on deck when Jeremy drove up and parked his car next to the boat. The young man got out of the car along with his girlfriend Ruth. She looked over at them and gave a tired smile.

"Hello, Ruthie," Jason said. "Some night, huh?"

"Yes, sir," she said with a nod. "I'm sorry we're so late. We were helping my dad lock up the church."

Jeremy looked the boat over. "You guys are really going to do it, aren't you?"

"Yes," Jason answered. "I'd like to be out on the water by dawn. Would you give us a hand with this generator?"

"Yeah. But, first, uh...." Jeremy paused a moment, looking down at a tuft of grass he was pushing at with his shoe. "Dad, I'm not going with you guys."

"What?" Jason said, staring at his son.

"Ruthie's parents said I could stay with them if I wanted to."

"Well, that's very nice, but I don't believe it's an option."

"Jason," Valerie said, as if asking him to use restraint. Jeremy continued. "I don't want to go hide out on the boat. Pastor Rick says we need to stick together. He says we need to look out for one another right now. He said that this crisis might be the church's finest hour."

"Jeremy, this situation could get ugly. It could be

downright dangerous."

"That's why we need to stick together. We'll network to help each other. And if worse comes to worst, we can all stay at the church."

"Like the Alamo?"

"Jason," Valerie cautioned again.

Jeremy sighed and shook his head. He turned around to face Ruth, and it was she who spoke next. "My dad says you guys are more than welcome to join us. We know you are a bit of a drive away from your own church, and we'd welcome you as a vital asset to our network."

Jason held up his hand and closed his eyes. "Ruth, I really do appreciate what you're saying, and I'm sure you all are doing the right thing, but I just...." He looked at her again and took a deep breath, letting his hand fall to his side. "I'm just extremely concerned for my family's safety right now. I can't explain it, but I just feel that we all need to get someplace safe for a little while, if only just to see how all this is going to work out. If nothing happens, then we'll come back looking foolish. I would just rather err on the side of caution. That's all."

Jeremy turned around again. "But shouldn't the Lord be our safety? Shouldn't we rely on Him for our protection? Isn't that what you taught us?"

"Yes. And the Lord has provided a way of protection." Jason patted the hull of the boat. He looked at both of them. "Why am I the only one who senses danger in all this?"

"You're not," Jeremy said. "It's just that not everyone feels the need to run."

"Well, call it what you like, but I'm you're father, and I'm telling..."

"And I'm eighteen!" Jeremy interrupted. "I'm old enough to make my own decisions. I'm not going with you."

Jason stood quietly in the dark for a few minutes, feeling a flush of anger spread across his face. Then he abruptly turned away and bent over the generator. "Brian, get that end. Valerie, will you help him? Let's get it up on the swim platform."

The three bent over to lift the awkward generator. As it came off the ground Jeremy rushed over and lent his strength to the lift. They placed the generator on the swim platform, and then the stocky eighteen-year old scrambled up onto the platform and took a new hold of it. "Come on up, B," he said, and Brian similarly scrambled up. Before Jason could climb up, the two boys had lifted it up onto the top of the transom. Then they stepped into the boat in turn and carefully lowered the generator onto the deck.

Jason stood amazed for a few moments, looking at his two strong sons looming tall in the stern of the boat. They were breathing hard from the exertion and stared at him, as if waiting for his next order. Then he looked over at Valerie, who was starting to cry. He stepped toward her and put his arms around her. As he fought back his own tears, he realized that he hadn't taken into account his own family's fears and uncertainty. He hadn't even given thought to his own, other than to plan and act quickly. Valerie seemed to settle down somewhat, and he drew back to look her in the face. She said nothing, but her teary eyes registered a questioning look. He could see the beginning of doubt for the boat idea in her mind, especially now that it was splitting up their family. He tried to think of something to say, but in the absence of words he just looked to the ground.

Behind him a car pulled into the driveway. It was a small hatchback and its tires crunched on the gravel as it parked next to Jeremy's car. Jason looked up and saw Ruth wave to the driver as the engine shut down.

"It's Julie," Kathy said, as she walked over to the car. A young woman got out of the car and embraced Kathy in greeting. "Are you all right?"

"Yeah, I guess so," Julie said, drying her eyes with a tissue as the two walked over to where Jason and Valerie stood. They turned to face her. "I was watching all this stuff on the news, and I got really scared. I tried to call my mom, but I couldn't get through. One of those blasts hit right where she lives." She looked around at everyone as she spoke, her eyes swollen with tears. "Then the lights went off and I started freaking out, and I didn't know what to do. I was just sitting there in my apartment crying in the dark alone, and then I thought about you guys. I hope you don't mind my coming over."

"Not at all," Jason said. "It's fine."

"Thanks. I didn't know what I should do, but I knew that

you would know what to do." She looked at Jason when she said this. "I knew that you all would be doing the right thing whatever it was, so I came right over."

There was an awkward silence at this. Jason looked at Valerie and drew in a breath to speak, but his daughter spoke first.

"We're getting ready to go out on the boat. My dad feels like we should keep out of the way until all this blows over."

"Oh, that's right," Julie said. "I heard a guy on the radio say that people need to be ready and prepare for the worst. He said that the attack may be over, but the real fight for America is just beginning. I wasn't exactly sure what he meant, though." She looked up at the boat. "Where will you guys go?"

"I was thinking of just going up the coast a little ways," Jason said slowly. "I thought we might camp out on one of those uninhabited barrier islands and wait to see what happens."

"Oh, that sounds so good," Julie said. "I don't know what I'm going to do."

"You can take my place," Jeremy said from the deck of the boat. "I'm going to be staying behind with Ruthie and her family."

"Really?" Julie said, her face brightening. "I don't want to impose."

Jason looked up at Jeremy. The eighteen year old gave a half smile and a single nod and Jason's heart sank.

"Of course it's no imposition," said Valerie. "You've been like a daughter to us anyway." She touched Jason on the arm, but his eyes were fixed on Jeremy's face, high above him on the boat's deck, out of reach.

"I'll be all right, Dad," said Jeremy. "They need me there."

Jason only nodded vacantly, and then looked down. He recovered himself and took a long breath. "Yeah, that'd be fine," he said to Julie.

The young woman glanced up at Jeremy, then back at Jason. "Are you sure?"

Jason nodded. "Yes," he said, smiling weakly. "It wouldn't seem right leaving you here."

"Good," Kathy said. "Let's go to my room and find

some things for you to wear." She took Julie by the arm and led her toward the house. Then she stopped abruptly and turned back to Jason. "Hey, Dad, if we're bringing the generator, can I bring my hairdryer?"

Jason lifted his hand in defeat and let it fall again. "Why not?"

Kathy turned around excitedly and continued with Julie into the house.

"I'd better get my stuff, too," Jeremy said, and the two boys climbed down from the boat. Once on the ground Jeremy stood in front of his father. The two stared into each other's eyes for a few moments, and then embraced. Jason squeezed his son tightly and felt burning tears well up in his eyes. When they broke away Jeremy looked into his father's face, and Jason could see tears in his son's eyes as well.

"Be praying for us, Dad. I know we'll be all right if you're praying for us."

"I will, son. You be praying for us, too."

"I will." Jeremy patted his dad on the shoulder and then turned to Ruth. "I'll be right back. My stuff is already together."

"Okay," Ruth said. Jason watched as his son headed for the darkened house. Ruth stepped over to him. "My parents wanted me to ask you if there was anything valuable you'd like them to hold onto for you."

Jason shook his head. "You've already got it." Her eyes looked toward the house, and then looked to the ground. "No," Jason said. "I'm sorry. Come here." He reached out to her and hugged her. Her arms remained by her side. He kissed her on the side of the head and said, "Just take care of him. And, please, tell your parents I said thanks."

"I will," she said, nodding.

He let her go and Valerie embraced her. "And tell them that this house and everything in it is theirs to use if they need it. The cars, too."

"Thank you," Ruth whispered.

"We'll try to keep in touch as best we can," Jason said. Ruth nodded.

Jeremy came out of the house with his suitcase and a book bag. He walked past them to his car and put his things in his trunk. "That's it," he said to Ruth. She nodded and

31

moved toward the passenger side of the car.

Jason held up his hand. "Hold on a second." He climbed up onto the deck of the boat and went into the cabin. He came out again quickly carrying his small gun case. He climbed down and stood before Jeremy and opened it. "Take one of these."

"No, Dad. I won't need it."

"Take one. Take the thirty-eight."

"Dad, really. I don't want it."

"Son, please. I'll feel much better knowing you have something to protect yourself."

Jeremy sighed and took the little twenty-two caliber semi-automatic pistol. He slipped it in his pocket and turned away.

Jason closed the case and patted his son on the back. "I love you, son."

"I love you, too, Dad, Mom."

Valerie hugged him, and then he got in the car and started it. "You guys stay safe," he said through the open window. Then he put the car into gear, backed up, and then pulled out onto the road.

"I can't believe you let him take the automatic," Brian said.

Jason turned and patted his son's shoulder. "Let's get this boat hitched up."

"After that can I get something to eat? I'm hungry."

Jason looked at his watch. "Yeah, I guess so. It's almost three and we've been hitting it pretty hard. I'm not sure what's there to have, though."

"There's all that frozen breakfast stuff in the freezer," Valerie said. "I didn't think we'd have use for it in the boat with no microwave."

"Breakfast stuff?" Jason asked.

"Yes. Those sausage biscuits, and the frozen pancakes, and those ham and cheese croissant things."

"But we've already got the generator in the boat," Brian said.

"I know. We'll hitch the boat up and pull it close to the house. Then we can run an extension cord inside to the kitchen." Jason faced Brian and tried to sound enthusiastic. "Sausage biscuits, eh?"

"I'll go and get it ready." Valerie said.

Chapter Five

"I hope I'm not doing something stupid, here."

By the time Jason's watch beeped in the four a.m. hour they had finished their meal, coiled up the extension cord, shut up the house, and gathered next to the truck. Before they got in Valerie said, "We need to pray."

Jason took off his ball cap and placed it on the vehicle's roof. The family formed a circle and joined hands. Valerie stood to his right and Julie stood to his left. He took their hands and said, "Heavenly Father, thank you for watching over us during this dangerous time. Thank you for preserving us from these missiles. Thank you for all you have provided for us in this desperate time. Lord, there will still be danger all around us, and we ask for your protection as we leave our home to find safety on the water. Please be in the boat with us, Lord, as you were in the boat with the disciples. Guide us, Father, on the water." He felt a lump rise in his throat. "And Father, please go with Jeremy, too. Please protect him, and Ruthie and her family, until we are all safely reunited."

"And Father," joined Valerie, "please protect our home while we're gone. Please post your angels all around it, in Jesus' name."

"And Lord," continued Jason, "please be with our country during this time. Please help us to get through this crisis, help our leaders to know what to do, and help us to get back to where we were." He felt a sadness grip his heart.

34

"We're sorry, Lord, for how bad things have gotten. We're sorry for how we've let this country slide into immorality and lawlessness. Please forgive us. In Jesus' name we pray. Amen."

They all repeated the "amen," then released each other's hands. Jason replaced his ball cap on his head and they all slowly got in the truck. Jason started the engine.

"Bye, house," Kathy said.

Jason took one last look at the darkened house, then put the vehicle in gear and eased out onto the road, the big boat trailer creaking behind him.

*

They drove in silence over the deserted roads to the darkened town of Goose Creek. Jason had to slow down at every intersection on Highway 52 because all of the streetlights were out. The absence of working lights at the gas stations, shops, restaurants, and billboards made for an eerie passage through town, but soon they were on I-26 and were headed toward the peninsula of downtown Charleston. They saw few cars on the interstate.

As they neared the city Jason began to fiddle with the radio. "Julie, what station were you listening to earlier?"

"I don't remember, but there seemed to be several of them on."

"Most of them probably switched off to conserve fuel in their generators," Jason said. "I was wondering if there was any more news." He switched off the radio.

Soon they came to the Cooper River Bridge and the truck began to slow as it took the strain of pulling the boat up the long incline. As they topped the overpass the whole vista of Charleston and the harbor spread out before them. Darkness covered the peninsula except for the flickering orange glow of a fire near the Battery. Beyond the harbor, black against the dark sky, Jason could see James Island, Sullivan's Island, and Mount Pleasant without lights of any kind. Even the lighthouse on Sullivan's Island was out. Only the harbor itself was lit up as normal. The channel markers and buoys, powered by solar batteries, glowed green or red or flashed white. Even the long private docks glowed under

35

solar powered lamps that lined the handrails. The stars over the ocean seemed brilliant by contrast, and Jason pointed out Saturn high above the horizon.

They crossed the bridge into Mount Pleasant and then continued on to the Shem Creek public boat ramp. Jason stopped the truck in front of the ramp and everyone got out to prepare the boat for launch. In ten minutes the boat floated next to the dock, its engine idling to warm up. Jason drove the truck and trailer to the parking area and got out and locked the doors. He took a deep breath and sighed as he patted it on the roof and headed back to the boat.

He walked past the small cluster of town homes across from the boat ramp and something made him look up. In the moonlight he saw a window where the curtain was pulled slightly open to one side. Someone was watching him, but as he stared up at it the curtain abruptly closed again.

Jason walked down to the boat, his clanging footsteps on the metal dock obnoxious in the quiet of the morning, but as he climbed into the boat the gentle hum of the boat's engine merged with the stillness. He went to the wheel and everyone climbed aboard. "Brian, will you cast us off?"

Brian jumped onto the dock, released the lines, and jumped back aboard as the current from the ebbing tide eased the boat out into the creek. Jason switched the running lights on and put the motor into gear, easing forward on the throttle. The pattering sound of the ripples against the hull and the briny scent of the exposed pluff mud made him smile inside.

They passed under the low Shem Creek Bridge, and ahead in the darkness Jason heard the blowing of a mother dolphin and her calf feeding in the falling tide. The shops and restaurants hung dark and still over both sides of the waterway. Valerie stepped up next to him.

"It's strange seeing everything so quiet," she said.

"I know," Jason said. "Even the shrimp boats are shut down."

"It is a pretty morning, though," Valerie said, looking up at the sky.

"Yes, it is."

"What's that noise?"

"It sounds like a generator," Jason said. "Maybe

someone's in the icehouse."

But as the cruiser passed the icehouse they realized that the sound came from a row of opulent homes beyond it. One of them, with a large sport fishing boat docked in front of it with the words "Objection Overruled" painted on the transom, had a generator outside running continuously. Not a light could be seen in the house. Burn that gas, Jason thought, shaking his head.

When they reached the end of Shem Creek Jason steered left to follow the channel behind the crab bank island in the harbor. Out over the ocean the sky was beginning to lighten with the coming dawn and a light breeze, cool and damp, blew across the water. Waves lapped the far side of the bank where birds fed, darting about and probing the sand every few paces. Jason noticed Valerie studying the fancy homes that lined the channel. They were set back from the water's edge behind a salt marsh, and each one had a dock that stretched out to the deep water of the channel.

"Nice, huh?" Jason said.

"Yeah."

As they reached the end of the channel Jason turned left again and entered the Intracoastal Waterway heading northeast. To the right Sullivan's Island filled the horizon and beyond it the Atlantic Ocean. Ahead and to the left of them the endless salt marshes that separated the barrier islands from the mainland stretched away into the distance. They came to a small creek that wound its way back toward the mainland, and planted against the left bank Jason saw a large sailing yacht. It had apparently broken away from its mooring and had come to rest in the shallow mud of the creek bottom. Jason ran his eyes along the elegant traditional style hull.

"Hey, Dad," Brian called, "look at that boat."

"I see it," Jason said. "Pretty, isn't it?"

"Could you sail one that big?" Julie asked.

"I'm certified to sail one up to thirty five-feet long, but I'm pretty sure I could handle one that size, too."

"It's a shame to leave something like that just sitting there."

"Uh-huh," replied Jason.

They motored slowly along and soon Sullivan's Island

37

fell away behind its own buffer of salt marsh. Here the Intracoastal Waterway had been dredged out as straight as an arrow and Jason could allow himself to relax a little. Once they passed the Ben Sawyer Bridge the girls went below to take a nap on the salon cushions.

Valerie stood next to him looking over the water. "How far you planning to go?"

"Copahee Sound, or behind Pine Island, I guess. We'll see what looks good."

Valerie yawned. "I think I'm going to go lie down for a bit. You'll be okay?"

"Yes."

She patted his arm and then disappeared down the companionway. Brian took her place on the cushioned bench and curled up to go to sleep. Jason glanced over at the teen. A long night of excitement and toil had combined with the dull hum of the motor to produce an irresistible drowsiness in everyone. Jason could feel it, too, but he knew that he would never be able to go to sleep until the boat was riding safely at anchor.

The sun rose above the horizon now and the sky brightened steadily. He passed under the Isle of Palms Connector, and the salt marsh thinned out on the landward side of the long island. Expensive homes, each one with a dock, lined the water's edge to his right. On the opposite bank were the houses and docks of Goat Island. In the growing light he could see no one around, and an uneasy feeling began to disturb him

"Father, I hope I'm not doing something stupid, here," he said aloud. "I just want to protect my family."

Soon the boat came to a place where the channel opened into three parts. Ahead the Intracoastal Waterway widened and continued up the coast. To the right lay an inlet between Isle of Palms and Dewees Island that continued out into the Atlantic. The channel to the left curved back toward the mainland and divided into myriad smaller, winding channels. Jason steered left and headed for a place where a large creek joined the main channel from the right. He yawned and steered up the narrowing creek. It curved left toward the mainland, and he followed it until he came upon another smaller creek to the right. He steered into the creek and followed it as far as he thought the boat's draft would allow. The water depth was at its shallowest now and would only get deeper as the tide came in. Glancing back, Jason saw that the boat was now out of sight of the main channel. He powered back on the motor, reversing just long enough to stop the boat's way, then cut the engine and opened the windshield.

"What's wrong?" asked Brian.

"Nothing. Just anchoring."

Jason stepped up onto the foredeck and released the anchor. The drifted slowly backward with the wind until Jason cleated the line and the anchor dug into the mud. Once satisfied that the anchor was holding, he headed back to the bridge deck.

"Is this where we're staying?" Brian asked.

"Maybe. I'm not sure yet," Jason said. "I just need to catch a few zzz's."

Jason studied the area. They floated in a narrow creek about four or five boat lengths wide. The banks were steep and soft, but farther up the creek veered to the left and exposed a wide shelf of gray sand and shells. Beyond the shelf the land rose to a small dry island where some tightly packed trees stood at the far end. The low-tide smell of the pluff mud was strong here and on the near bank Jason could see fiddler crabs moving in and out of their holes. The gray sky was overcast and the air was humid despite the breeze. He yawned again.

"Don't sleep too late in this sun," he said to Brian. "You'll burn and not even know it. Here." Jason handed a towel to Brian. "Drape that over you to keep the sun off of you as you sleep. We'll rig an awning later."

Jason sat down on the deck and stretched himself out to go to sleep. His feet were up against the generator so he shifted himself diagonally across the deck, the life preserver under his head for a pillow.

"Do you want to sleep up here?" Brian asked.

"No, thanks. I'll be fine." Jason covered his face with a towel and was soon fast asleep.

Chapter Six

"Whoever hit us really knew what they were doing."

Jason's clothes were fully soaked by the time the sound of the rain hitting the deck and the creek had awakened him. He pulled the wet towel from his face and sat up just in time to see Brian scrambling down the companionway into the cabin. Jason got up and quickly scrambled through the companionway, shutting the door behind him.

Once inside he stretched to loosen the soreness from sleeping on the deck, crowding Brian up against the sink.

"Brian!" Kathy said. "You're dripping on the cushions!"

"Well, what do you want me to do about it?"

"Sorry, Brian," Jason said. "There're some more towels in that bag by your feet."

Valerie's head appeared around the corner of the stateroom bulkhead. "Is that rain I hear?"

"Yes," Jason said. "Hand us up a couple of those towels, would you?"

Valerie handed up the towels, and Brian wrapped one around him. Julie sat up and made room for him on the bench. "Brian, you can sit over here." The teen eased around the table and sat down.

"Let me come out, Jason," Valerie said. "I've got to stand up."

Jason backed into the door to the head and Valerie stood up next to him beside the sink. She stretched her back.

"That's better. Kathy, there are more towels in one of

those bags behind you."

Kathy fished through the grocery bags and said, "I'm kind of hungry," she said. "What time is it anyway?"

Jason looked at his watch. "It's almost noon." He looked at Valerie. "I'd like to give Jeremy a call."

"I'll call him," Valerie said. "You dry off."

Kathy put the extra towels on the table. Brian and Jason each took one to dry their hair. The rain outside slackened.

"I can't get a signal," Valerie said, looking at her phone. Kathy instinctively checked her phone, then put it back in her purse.

"I guess we'll have to try again later. How about some lunch while we listen to the radio to see what's going on?" Jason asked.

"There's bread in the grocery bags behind you, Julie," Valerie said. She looked at Jason. "The lunchmeats and cheese are in the cooler on deck."

Jason nodded. He handed her the towel and stepped through the door and back into the drizzle. He went to the cooler, grabbed the items and quickly returned to the cabin. Valerie draped the towel over his back as he turned and shut the door.

"I tried the radio but it wouldn't come on," said Julie, gesturing toward the console that held the AM/FM/cassette player.

"It's not hooked up," said Jason. "It's so old I'm not sure it even works anymore. I'll get my little radio out of my suitcase."

Jason squeezed past Valerie and knelt down into the crawlspace that formed the head of the bed in the master stateroom. He unzipped his bag and rummaged around in it until he found his tiny AM/FM/Short-wave receiver. Then he backed out into the salon and stood up. Everyone else was seated at the table.

"What do you want on your sandwich?" Valerie asked.

"One of everything. Thanks." Jason took the radio out of its pouch and found a station immediately. Apparently the radio station was broadcasting the audio portion of a television program. A female announcer was interviewing someone.

"And these control area operator centers control the flow

41

of power across the grid?"

"Yes," the man being interviewed said. "As the demand for power fluctuates across the various regions of the country, these control area operators route power through the various distribution stations and transmission lines to support that demand. If, for instance, the Northeast is experiencing a heat wave, and the demand for power is increased because of the increased need for air conditioning, power can be routed from other areas where milder temperatures are allowing a decrease in demand. The power demands across the grid are fluctuating constantly and these CAO's monitor and adjust the flow accordingly."

"How many of these CAO's are there?"

"There are over one hundred of them across the continental U.S."

"Well, how is it that sixteen nuclear missiles were able to knock out power across eighty percent of the country?"

"Sixteen nuclear missiles?" Kathy exclaimed.

"Shh," said Jason, putting his index finger to his lips. Valerie handed him his sandwich and he started to eat.

The man continued. "Well, first of all, in some places the CAO's were close enough so that two or even three could be destroyed with one nuclear detonation. And for each Control Area Operator hit, there was a power distribution station destroyed also. In some places, the Ohio River Valley for instance, there is such a high concentration of CAO's, as well as power stations, that the Electro Magnetic Pulse from a low altitude air burst, like the ones we saw last night, might disrupt control room operations for miles. Everything is run by computers, and computers are very sensitive to EMP."

"So, do we know how many CAO's were hit?"

"The latest figure is twenty-six CAO's damaged or destroyed. But we should keep in mind that even though that is only about a quarter of the total, some of the CAO's are more strategic than others. As you can see from this map of the power grid, one particular CAO might be destroyed that was an important link between two regions. Hitting two or three such places could isolate and shut down ten others."

"How did we build a power grid with such vulnerable choke points?"

42

"Well, we must remember that our power grid was not planned out and built all at once into its present state. It started out small, providing power only to the larger metropolitan areas. From there it grew and developed as America's population expanded and its economic and commercial centers shifted. Various regions of the country were linked up with the building of high-tension power lines. The system we call the power grid is an ever-evolving work in progress. These strategic choke points evolved as the power needs evolved."

"Dr. Friedman, one more question, please, and I think this is the foremost question on the minds of our viewers. How long do you estimate it will take to get the lights back on across America?"

"That is rather difficult to say. First, we are still not sure of the extent of the damage. But even more importantly, the types of electrical components destroyed were highly specialized pieces of equipment. They are typically custom fabricated to order and are purchased only for new construction contracts or for large scale system upgrades."

"Not items one could buy off the shelf at the neighborhood hardware store."

"Exactly right. I'm sure there are some components on hand, but it's unlikely there would be enough to fill the present repair need. Complicating matters further is the fact that the industrial facilities that make the devices will most likely themselves be without power."

"I suppose the sites that were hit will still be radioactive for some time."

"Oh, yes. That, too, will delay repairs."

"Hmm," said the announcer. "Whoever hit us really knew what they were doing."

"They had done their homework well. Yes."

"Dr, Friedman, thank you so much for your time."

"You're very welcome."

"That was Dr. Eric Friedman, Chairman of the Economic Planning and Development Board of the U.S. Department of Energy."

There was a pause and a sound of shuffling of papers heard over the radio. Jason sat on the companionway steps as he ate, holding the radio in one hand and his sandwich in the

43

other. The announcer continued.

"They had done their homework well. But who are 'they,' and why did they carry out a nuclear attack on the United States? To answer these questions we join our Washington correspondent Jeff Kirkland, who is currently at the Pentagon. Jeff, what is the latest word from our military forces?"

"Hello, Pat. The word from the Pentagon is 'intense.' There have been several developments in the last few hours. As we learned early this morning, U.S. Navy P-3 Orion sub-hunting aircraft have been combing the Gulf of Mexico in search of the submarine that launched the missile attack on the U.S. Joining them was the H.M.S. *Birmingham* of the Royal Navy. The *Birmingham* had been traveling in the area recently visiting U.S. ports along the Gulf Coast. The P-3s made contact with the submarine at about four forty-five this morning, moving at high speed and making a lot of noise. The P-3s are armed with anti-submarine torpedoes, but were given the order not to sink the sub."

"By the military high command?"

"Yes. Apparently they are interested in learning everything they can about the submarine before they sink it."

"I suppose, once it's lost it might take months to learn who it belonged to."

"That's right. But there has been a development concerning the identity of the submarine. As the sub-hunter planes have been tracking the vessel they have been gathering a profile of all the particular sounds coming from it. This profile of sounds is called a signature, and it has been compared with signatures of known vessels kept in archives at CIA headquarters in Langley, Virginia. Our sources in the Pentagon say that the type and nationality has been confirmed. The vessel is an old Soviet era, Yankee 2 class ballistic missile submarine."

"A Russian submarine?"

"Exactly."

"Russians," Jason said with a growl.

"But I thought the Russian government denied any involvement in the attack," continued the announcer.

"Yes, and that may be the case. The Russian Navy had replaced the old Yankee class subs in the late nineteen eighties and early nineteen nineties as the newer Typhoon class subs became operational. So while we may know where the vessel was made, we still don't know who's driving it."

"Or who sent it."

"Yes, and this brings me to the very latest wrinkle in this unfolding story. The submarine has just entered Cuban territorial waters and there has been some reluctance from the White House to allow the Navy P-3's to enter Cuban airspace without permission from the Cuban government. However, the *HMS Birmingham* has been tracking the sub as well and her captain has stated that he is determined to pursue it into Havana harbor, if necessary."

"Ha, ha!" Jason laughed. "Those Brits are all right! They don't mind ruffling some feathers! When we were in the Med...."

"Shh!" Kathy said.

The announcer continued. "How long do you think it will take before the issue is resolved?"

"I'm not sure, but it will have to be resolved soon. The *USS Ronald Reagan* carrier battle group is steaming at high speed down the Florida coast as we speak and is expected to join the hunt within the next hour or so."

"Indeed!" said the announcer. "Jeff Kirkland from the Pentagon. Thanks for the update."

"You're welcome."

There was a change in the background tone of the radio broadcast, and then the voice of a different announcer came on the air. He gave his name and the station identification, then said, "For those of you just joining us, we are bringing you live reports from CNN concerning this nuclear attack on America, the first attack on American soil since Nine Eleven. I have some local announcements to bring to you before we get back to our national feed. First, the governor of South Carolina has declared a state of emergency throughout the state and he is asking that citizens limit travel as much as possible. Persons working for essential services, police departments, hospitals, power companies, and the like need the roads to be clear, as well as folks who are still needing to go out to purchase food and medical supplies. So, let's keep travel to a minimum. Our listeners are reminded

45

that a curfew is in effect from sundown until sunup until further notice."

"I guess we'll have to stay on the boat tonight," Jason said.

"Turn it off, will you?" Valerie asked.

Jason switched off the radio as the announcer was talking about blood donations. "Heard enough?"

"No, it's not that. But if we don't cut it off now we'll sit here all day and there's lots to be done."

"Like what?" Kathy asked.

"We've got to get all this stuff put away. We threw everything aboard in a hurry last night and now we're tripping over it."

"You're exactly right," Jason said. "Where do you want to start?"

"Well, I have a good idea where I want things to go, I just need room to work."

"Do you want me and the kids to go topside out of the way?"

"The kids, yes, but you, no. I could use your help."

"Has the rain quit?" Kathy asked.

Jason reached up and opened the companionway door. Outside the sky was still overcast but there was no rain. "Yes, it's stopped."

"Julie," Kathy said, "let's go up on the roof and get our tans started!"

Julie looked around. "Where can I change?"

"You can change in the bathroom," Valerie said, "but wait until we get this stuff squared away."

"Can I go fishing?" Brian asked.

"I was hoping you would," Jason said. "Let me know what's out here."

"I will," Brian said. He stood up and moved toward the companionway. Jason leaned over to let him pass.

"We can go up and have a look around first," Julie said. Kathy nodded.

Valerie gathered the lunch items as Kathy slid out from around the table. "Put this stuff back in the cooler as you go."

Kathy took the items and Jason stood up as she went past him up the companionway steps. Julie stood up to

46

follow, but as she ascended the steps she misplaced her foot
and stumbled. Jason caught her by the forearm.

"Careful, now," he said in a helpful tone.

Julie smiled. "I guess I don't have my sea legs, yet."
Jason released her forearm, but she took his hand to steady
herself. Then she quickly ascended the steps. He looked over
at Valerie who said. "Let's get this stuff put away. Then you
can turn your radio back on."

*

In less than an hour all of the food and supplies were
stowed away. Valerie seemed to have a photographic
memory concerning the volume and shape of every locker,
shelf, cubby, and storage compartment, even finding room in
places Jason had declared full. His tools, along with all boat
parts and supplies, were placed on the upper deck to be
stored in the engine compartment. The kids' suitcases were
neatly arranged on the shelves above the salon benches.

"Now that's what I call secured for sea," Jason said.

"Good. Now I need to lie down. I'm still exhausted from
last night. What about you?"

"I'm going to put that other stuff in the engine
compartment. I can rig up a curtain here, if you like," Jason
said.

"Later. I really need to lie down."

"Okay." Jason leaned forward and kissed her. "I'll be as
quiet as I can."

"I have my earplugs." Valerie stooped into the low
headroom of the master berth. She pushed the two soft-sided
suitcases over to Jason, who placed them one atop the other
across the narrow doorway. He watched her as she settled
herself on the bed. She inserted a pair of earplugs in her ears
and then she took a handful of her long black hair and
covered her eyes with it. Jason smiled to himself and then
ascended the companionway steps.

Up on deck the overcast sky had brightened
considerably. The boat had swung around on the incoming
tide and the stern now faced the narrower end of the creek. A
light onshore breeze was developing. Brian stood on the
swim platform with a fishing rod in his hand, his back

47

against the transom. Jason looked toward the bow where Kathy was pointing out a great heron that stood on the pluff mud at the water's edge. The bird stood frozen as it assessed the newcomers, and then it resumed its slow, deliberate walk, probing the mud every foot or so with its long beak.

"Can we change now?" Kathy asked.

Jason nodded. "Just be quiet, though. Your mom is trying to take a nap." He turned his attention to the items on the deck as one of the girls went into the cabin. He moved the cans of gasoline, the generator, and the water jugs off of the engine hatch and stooped to open the hatch. As he did so, he happened to look up in time to see Julie coming through the companionway. The bikini she wore was one of Kathy's old ones and it did not fit well, hanging loosely on the slender girl's frame. Jason forced his attention back down to the hatch, taking the recessed handle and lifting it from the deck. Hinged forward, the lifted hatch formed a partition to the rest of the upper deck area. He climbed down inside the compartment.

"Need a hand?" Brian asked from over the transom.

"Yes," Jason said. "Would you hand me those items as I ask for them?"

"Sure." Brian set the pole down and climbed into the boat.

Jason could see the teen taking a long look forward. "The gas cans first," he said. "You can slide those water jugs forward for now."

The two stowed the gas, boat parts and tools, and some of the water below next to the engine. Jason frowned at the footprint he had made on the engine but had no rag handy to wipe it off. He looked up at Brian.

"I guess that's it," he said to the teen.

"What about these water jugs?"

"We'll leave those on deck."

"Won't they get hot?"

"Sure. Do you want to wash up with cold water?"

"I see. A natural hot water heater."

"Exactly," said Jason, climbing out onto the deck. Jason closed the hatch and the two lifted the generator back into place against the transom. "Any luck fishing?"

"No, the tide is coming up right now," said Brian. "I

48

might take a swim."

"I think I'll join you."

*

Jason and Brian spent the next two hours swimming in the opaque brown water of the salt marsh creek and readying the inflatable boat for service. Jason found the warm, salty water only marginally refreshing and continued to dive to the bottom where the mud and cooler water felt good. They got out of the water and sat on the swim platform to inflate the raft and rig its motor and battery, talking quietly as they worked.

"Dad, what do you think of Julie?"

"She's all right, I guess. Why?"

"She always seems to be trying too hard to fit in."

"Well, you know she has no family around here. And her own father won't have anything to do with her."

"But we accept her," Brian said. "She doesn't have to try so hard."

"I know. But as we keep showing her acceptance, she will eventually be more at ease. It's hard, sometimes. The pain of this world makes people do strange things to adapt and survive." He finished tightening the motor clamps and then looked up to see Valerie standing behind the transom holding the radio. "Oh, hi. I hope we didn't wake you."

"No, I couldn't get to sleep because it's so hot, so I put on the radio."

"Anything new?"

"Yes. It seems we're invading Cuba."

49

Chapter Seven

"We need help now!"

Jason's eyes grew wide. He hurriedly finished tightening
the motor clamps, and then climbed onto the swim platform.
"Dad, can I take the boat out?"
"Huh? Uh, sure. Just watch out for sharp rocks and the
like. He turned to Valerie. "Turn it up."
She did so and the two listened as Brian cast off the raft.
A correspondent with a slight New England accent was
speaking to an announcer.
"Not as yet. As far as we can tell the operation is
confined to the port of Havana and is strictly concerned with
the submarine that is anchored in the harbor. The Marines
from the *USS Ronald Reagan*, joined by two detachments of
Marines flown to the carrier earlier this morning, have
boarded and taken possession of the submarine. There have
been many officials traveling back and forth between the sub
and the carrier and many of them are still on board as we
speak."
"It's amazing that the *Reagan* battle group could have
covered such a distance in so short a time."
"Oh, absolutely. The military has reacted very quickly to
this crisis."
"Have they discovered the nationality of the submarine
crew?"
"I'm sure the Marines know by now, but we haven't
been told anything official as yet. The scuttlebutt around the

50

ship is that the crew is North Korean."

"North Korean?"

"Yes."

"How reliable is that information?"

"As reliable as scuttlebutt can be, I suppose."

"They're North Korean, for sure," said Jason.

The announcer continued. "What has been the reaction of the Cuban government to this informal invasion of their harbor?"

"So far they have been quiet. There are several Cuban patrol vessels in the harbor, but they're keeping a respectful distance. The Cuban people, however, are another story. The harbor is full of American warships and all around them are small craft filled with curious citizens. I spoke with some people in a small fishing boat before they were waved away, and they seemed very friendly and sympathetic to us regarding the attack."

"Mitch, thank you very much. We'll be getting back to you."

"I'll be standing by."

The announcer continued, "That was Mitch Norwood on board the aircraft carrier *USS Ronald Reagan* in Havana Harbor, Cuba. Meanwhile, across the US, work crews are struggling to cope with the magnitude of the damage caused by last night's unprecedented missile attack. Dr. Vernon Alderman, Deputy Director of FEMA, spoke at a press conference earlier today."

Another voice came over the radio. "Yes. Well, the problem is one of supply. This is a very different scenario from the problems we face from a natural disaster. We are always prepared to repair or replace downed transmission lines, and many miles of power lines can be replaced in a relatively short period of time. But in this scenario many of our power distribution centers have been destroyed. We will have to rebuild these facilities completely from the ground up, and that process could take months."

Another voice in the background asked a question, but it was inaudible.

"We don't know. But in the meantime America is just going to have to change its ways of doing business."

The announcer came back on the air. "But changing its

51

ways of doing business is proving difficult for Americans caught off guard and unprepared in a post-nuclear attack world where all the rules have changed."

Another clip came on the air that had been recorded outdoors. The sound of wind and an occasional vehicle driving by forced a young woman to speak up. Jason could hear a baby fussing next to her.

"Most of the stores are still closed and the few that are open are dealing on a cash only basis. Where am I supposed to get cash? The banks are closed and none of the ATM's are working."

"How long can you get by on what you have?" asked the interviewer.

"Not long. I usually do my grocery shopping tomorrow. We need help now!"

Another voice, a middle-aged man, came over the radio next. "Well, this gas station is being powered by a back-up generator. I guess they're using fuel out of their own tanks. I was supposed to leave for Houston this morning to pick up a load of copper wire, but I've been waiting in line here for nearly two hours. Most of these four-wheelers are getting gasoline, but I can't get my rig past'em to get to the diesel pumps." The voice diminished briefly as it seemed the man was looking around. "I hope I can get in and out of here in the next thirty minutes or so."

A woman's voice came on the air next. She had a Southern accent and Jason could hear her frustration. "I need to get in to work. They already called me to say I need to be there. But the daycare is closed because there is no power. The director said there are liability issues for them to keep kids with no power. Now, what kind of a country have we become where the lawyers tell us what we can and can't do? And what am I supposed to do with my kids? Take them to work with me?"

"Hey, Dad, the motor's not working," Brian called from the raft as it floated up the creek.

Jason looked up from the radio. "I didn't hook it up to the battery, yet. Plug the wires together."

"I did that already but it's not working."

"Is the propeller spinning?"

Brian tilted the motor up out of the water and turned the

throttle on. The propeller spun very slowly.

"Oh, for Pete's sake," Jason said. "The battery must be dead. Break out the oars and row back here. I'll hook it up to the charger."

"Man!" said the teen. He fitted the oars to the oarlocks and began to row, but soon he reached a narrower part of the canal where the current was swifter. He rowed awkwardly and made no headway. Jason watched him and shook his head.

"I've got to go in after him," he said to Valerie. She nodded and sat down on the padded bench. Jason called out to Brian. "Just drive it into that mud bank next to you. I'm coming over to help you."

"I can get it if I can just...." Brian continued the struggle.

"Just stick it into the bank before you go around the bend."

Frustrated, the teen rowed the raft against the mud bank. He removed one of the oars from its oarlock and stuck it down into the mud to hold the boat in place as Jason dove off the swim platform into the creek. Swimming with the current he came up quickly to the boat. With one hand he grabbed the motor mount and took an oarlock with the other. Then he heaved himself up and over the round side of the raft. He moved to the bow and took Brian's position as the teen relinquished the oar and moved to the stern. Then he replaced the oar in the oarlock and he shoved the boat backward into the current. Pointing the raft toward the cruiser, Jason rowed in even, powerful strokes. Soon they were making progress against the bank.

"What you have to do is to make even pulls," said Jason.

"I was trying to do that."

"I know. Speed is not the idea." He demonstrated the rowing as he talked. "Neither is a hard stroke. But long even strokes will do the trick."

Jason pulled steadily and in a few minutes the raft was alongside the swim platform again. Brian tied off the stern and Jason did the same to the bow.

"Pretty good, Dad," said Brian, climbing onto the swim platform.

"Yeah. Not bad for a broken down old man, huh?"

53

Brian snorted and looked out over the creek. "I guess I'm not boating today."

"Here, take this battery." Jason handed it to Brian. "Clip it to the boat's charger." He stood up and noticed that Valerie had put away the radio. "What about the news?"

"I thought we might go for a walk together."

Jason nodded. "All right. Will you hand me my shoes?"

She grabbed Jason's shoes as well as her own, and then climbed down into the inflatable boat.

"Can I come?" Brian asked.

"Sure," Jason said. They cast off and the boat floated swiftly with the current. Jason steered it toward the gray sandy beach, avoiding the barnacle clad rocks and clumps of oyster shells. He nosed the boat up onto the sand and Brian jumped out and grabbed the boat's motor mount while Jason got out and held the boat's forward handle. Valerie stepped away as the guys carried the boat above the high water mark. Jason looked back at the cruiser and confirmed that at low water the windshield barely rose to the level of the marsh grass that topped the pluff mud. The light green grass covered the terrain as far as the eye could see. They stood on a narrow, dry bank that extended along the edge of the creek for about two hundred yards and at the far end a cluster of trees widened into a tiny island. Brian led the way. The firm ground made walking easy except for the stalks of saw grass that irritated their legs.

Soon they emerged from the grass and came to the island. Jason looked toward the cruiser and could barely see it now above the grass.

"This would be a good place to camp," Valerie said.

"Yes," he said, "and we could bring the raft down to this bank."

"I wonder if we'll get tired of all this fishing and hiking and stuff," Brian said.

"I can't imagine I would get tired of it," Jason said.

"You would after awhile," Valerie said.

"Really? You mean I'll miss going to work and sweating my head off and banging up my hands and wrangling with the health insurance companies on the phone and doing my taxes and balancing my checkbook and paying the bills and…shall I go on?"

"No," Valerie said. "I didn't realize you were living in such deplorable conditions."

Jason chuckled. "I admit it's not exactly deplorable, but I sometimes wonder if maybe life has gotten a little over-complicated. That's all. This little outing might be very good for some of us."

Valerie didn't reply.

"Hey," Brian called, "look at this!"

Jason turned around and looked toward where the teen was pointing. About a half of a mile away to the northeast he saw the wreck of a large boat. It leaned over on its side looking weather-beaten but intact. The hull could not be seen above the grass.

"What is it?" Valerie asked.

"It looks like a houseboat, probably broken loose in a hurricane and carried up here by the storm surge," Jason said.

"And the owners just left it there?"

"I don't think they had a choice. There's no way to get a vehicle out to it and you can't really get to it by boat."

"Can we salvage it?" Brian asked.

"I doubt there'd be anything worth salvaging, even if you could get to it."

"We could take the raft."

"Brian," Jason said, "do you see those blank spaces between the grassy areas? Those are creeks. There are at least a dozen of them between here and there."

"But couldn't you just follow the creeks over to it?" Valerie offered.

"You don't understand. Remember when I went out here in the kayaks with those guys from the church to look for the bodies of the two missing boys? Well, we would paddle into a creek, and it would turn back and forth so many times that you couldn't tell which way to go. I would have to stop occasionally and climb up on a bank to see where we were. It was like being in a maze."

"But we could just follow this creek out to the open water there," said Brian, pointing as he spoke, "then cross the open water until we got close enough to follow another creek up to it."

"And then do what? Float it off on the high tide?"

"No. I don't want to float it off, I just want to go look at it." He looked back toward the boat again. "There may be something valuable in it."

Jason began to laugh gently. "Like a treasure chest?"

Valerie bumped his arm and silently mouthed the words, "Don't laugh at him."

Jason nodded. "I'm sorry. You may be right. If it blew out here in a storm and no one's been aboard it, then there might be something to see there, maybe something of value."

"I would just want to look," Brian said.

"I understand." He looked out across the marsh. "We'll plan a trip over there in the next day or so. How would that be?" Brian nodded and Jason patted his shoulder. "But in the meantime, let's explore this patch of land right here. Maybe no one's ever set foot here before."

"I doubt that," Brian said.

They walked around the windward side of the island keeping between the trees and the creek. A steady breeze came off the ocean making the humid air comfortable and in a few minutes they came to the far end where the bank deteriorated into soft mud again. Here they turned around and started back along the leeward side of the island. Brian walked through the trees while Jason and Valerie walked along the water's edge. The trees blocked most of the wind and the air felt heavy and close.

"Ahh! Ouch!" Brian shouted, slapping himself on the neck. Jason looked over at his son and saw him waving his arms wildly and shaking his head. He burst into a run just as Jason felt a small burning sting on his right shoulder.

"What's wrong?" Valerie asked.

"Mosquitoes," Jason said, slapping at his shoulder. "Let's go quickly."

They both broke into a run to join Brian in the open space past the trees. Jason felt the bugs bumping against his face as he ran. Once they were past the trees and into the sea breeze again they trotted over to where Brian stood scratching himself all over. Valerie began combing the mosquitoes out of her hair with her fingers.

"Man! Those little blood suckers are vicious!" Brian said. "I guess there won't be much camping there."

"At least not on the leeward side," Jason said.

56

They arrived back at the cruiser as the sun neared the horizon and the shadows from the bank stretched across the creek. Jason brought the boat to the swim platform and everyone climbed out. Kathy and Julie were on deck listening to the radio.

"Anything new?" Jason asked.

"Yes," Kathy said. "The North Koreans are begging us not to retaliate."

"What?"

"Yeah," Julie said, "they've got people crowding the streets begging America not to destroy them."

"Turn it up."

Chapter Eight

"Twenty-four hours since the world changed."

Kathy did so and Jason could hear a crowd of people talking and yelling loudly. There was no chanting as you might hear at a demonstration, just disorganized calling out and chatter mixed with sounds of weeping and moaning. Individual voices were captured in Korean, and then an English translation was dubbed over it. The translator's voices, a man and a woman's, each spoke with a British accent. Kathy turned the radio up as Korean woman spoke, her voice torn with anguish.

"Please do not shoot your missiles to kill my baby. My son is innocent and has done nothing to hurt anyone. He is only a baby. Please, do not kill my baby."

Next a man's voice was heard, speaking through tears. "Should a whole nation perish for the actions of a few? We did not do it. Come and capture those responsible, but, please, do not kill us all. We have a right to live."

Another man's voice was heard and he seemed to be begging. "We are sorry for what happened to America. It is very bad. But we didn't do it. We didn't even know about it until it was over."

A woman's voice came on next, sharpened by fear. "All we want is to live and work and feed our children. Please, don't kill us for that. We are innocent."

Next an announcer's voice came on the air. "Thousands of citizen's in Pyongyang have turned out to make their

58

pleas before an international array of cameras and microphones. And this scene is being played out in many cities across North Korea."

"Does it seem like this is an event staged by the North Korean government?"

"It's always hard to tell for sure, but my gut feeling is that this demonstration is spontaneous and genuine. I've had people come to me numerous times on their knees, begging and crying with their hands clasped in supplication. They are convinced that they're facing imminent annihilation at the hands of the U.S. It's sad to see, especially from a people already broken by hardship and privation."

"Thank you, Kelly. That was Kelly Lancaster of the BBC coming to you live from Pyongyang, North Korea."

"We're not going to nuke them, are we, Dad?" Brian asked.

Jason shrugged and ran his hand across his scalp. He glanced over at Valerie and saw that she, too, had been affected by the words.

The announcer continued. "From here we take you to Havana, Cuba, where Mitch Norwood has the latest report on the submarine that launched the missile attack on the United States. Mitch...?"

"Yes, hello, I am broadcasting live from the fantail of the *USS Ronald Reagan* anchored in Havana Harbor. I have just come from a briefing given by the Task Force Commander's Office concerning the latest findings from the North Korean crewmembers. We are being told that the attack was launched to commemorate the anniversary of North Korean Independence, or more accurately, the anniversary of the rise to power of the regime of Kim Il Jung. The first missiles were launched to coincide with the dawn of that anniversary in Pyongyang, but an electrical fire had broken out on board, which delayed the launching of the others for about thirty minutes."

"Which explains the delay after the first three hits," said the announcer.

"Absolutely. This Yankee 2 class is a very old submarine, and it's extraordinary that the vessel could complete a voyage halfway across the world. But once repairs were made, the rest of the launches were completed."

"And how did Cuba figure into all this?"

"As we are learning from the crew, Cuba did not originally figure into this plan at all. The plan was to launch the missiles and to flee from the relatively shallow waters of the Gulf of Mexico into the deeper waters of the Caribbean. But the delay caused by the fire denied them thirty critical minutes of escape time. Furthermore, they had not known of the presence of the *HMS Birmingham* in the area, so they fled to the nearest friendly port. They apparently preferred possible capture in port to being sunk at sea."

"And what is the Russian government's reaction to this disclosure? One of their submarines was used in a missile attack on the U.S. How much are they to blame in this?"

"A good question. Some of the sub's officers have revealed that the government of North Korea purchased the sub from the Russian Navy's Pacific fleet back in the mid-nineteen nineties. You may recall that at that time the Russian military establishment had no cash and had begun selling off military hardware to generate money. They weren't even paying their troops in those days. Apparently the North Korean government approached the Russians about purchasing a nuclear powered, ballistic missile-type sub. The Russians were reluctant to sell them such a vessel, but eventually agreed to sell one of their pitifully old Yankee 2 class boats and stipulated that they would provide no missiles with the boat. They even went so far as to remove all of the missile fire control, tracking and targeting equipment from the vessel, and even welded the missile hatches shut. But even with all of those precautions, the North Koreans were still eager to buy."

"I suppose all they had to do was grind the welds off of the doors, stick in their own missiles and fire control equipment, and voila, instant ballistic missile submarine."

"Absolutely. And this accounts for the extensive missile development and testing the North Korean military has been carrying out for the past two decades."

"All they needed was some kind of launch platform to carry the missiles to the launch site. But why the Gulf of Mexico?"

"Another good question. It would seem that at this stage in their program they were only able to produce accurate

60

intermediate range missiles. The Gulf of Mexico was the best location to hit the maximum number of targets, as you can see on this map of the U.S. and the targeted areas."

"How were they able to reach targets so far to the west?"

"The rotation of the earth allows a longer reach when aiming west. The missile doesn't actually fly farther, but its target is moving closer while the missile is in flight. It's not much of a difference but in this case it was enough."

"So what happens next?"

"As I understand it, the next step is to secure the submarine for sea, assign a prize crew, and tow it back to the U.S. A few of the escort ships have already steamed out of the harbor and are standing by offshore."

"Has there been any dialogue with the Cuban government?"

"Not that I'm aware of. There hasn't even been a statement from Havana, either of support or criticism."

"I suppose they realize that America is in no mood for political maneuvering or saber rattling just now."

"Yes, especially in the military."

"Mitch Norwood, from the deck of the *USS Ronald Reagan*, thanks."

"You're welcome."

There was a brief pause, and then a different announcer continued. "In other news, state and local governments across the U.S. are struggling with growing lines of needy citizens who are in no mood to be turned away empty handed."

A woman's voice came on the air. She spoke slowly and with great articulation. "What people need to understand is emergency response and disaster relief assistance simply cannot be set up overnight. This disaster is not even twenty-four hours old. We have no temporary facilities set up, no trucks have arrived with supplies, and we're having a terrible time getting our personnel mobilized. I appreciate the fact that people are frustrated having to stand in line for hours, only to fill out some forms and go home, but that's all we have! There are no bags of groceries to hand out to families just yet, but we're working on it. I've already had two volunteers quit on me who said they were frustrated with peoples' attitudes. We're doing the best we can!"

An interviewer's voice, a man's, broke in. "Is part of the problem that folks were caught unprepared?"

"It would seem that way. Either people are used to living from day to day, or they're out here to get help before they actually need it. But in either case, they need to be patient with our volunteers and staff who, instead of staying home to take care of their families, are here trying to help citizens in need."

The announcer continued. "That was Dr. Janet Wilson, Northeast Regional Director of FEMA. Compounding the problems of state and local governments, particularly in the larger cities, are citizens who are taking the need for supplies into their own hands. This is an excerpt for a report broadcast earlier."

Next came a recording taken outside where sounds of voices and emergency equipment were heard. "There is a curfew in effect from sundown to sunup. Persons caught out after dark will be detained. We have been given orders by the governor to shoot looters on sight. As soon as the National Guard units are mobilized we will have personnel patrolling the streets night and day."

"How long will it take to get the National Guard mobilized?"

Normally, only a few days. I understand that the power outage is causing some delays, but those issues should be resolved soon."

"When are we going to eat?" Brian asked.

Kathy turned the radio down low. "Yeah, I'm hungry."

Jason looked at the radio and sighed, turned to Valerie. "Any ideas?"

"Can you fire up the grill?" Valerie asked.

"Sure."

"Well, there are some chicken breasts with lemon pepper already thawed out. I figure we'll eat the frozen stuff until it runs out, then it's strictly canned food after that."

*

By the time Jason and Brian had the grill rigged, the fire going, and the chicken cooking, the sky over the ocean to the east had grown dark. The dying sea breeze wafted the smoke to the west where the sun had already disappeared behind the land. Jason watched as the scattered clouds above the horizon changed colors from varying shades of orange and pink to gray-blue. Each one cast dark blue rays of shadow into the sky. Valerie came up on deck and stood beside him.

"That smells good. How much longer?"

"Probably another five or ten minutes. How's it coming down below?"

"The girls are cooking vegetables on the alcohol stove. I needed to turn on the cabin lights. I hope that was all right, for the battery, I mean."

"Yes, I just need to switch the batteries over." He turned around to where Brian was fishing from the stern. "Hey, Brian, switch the battery power from A to B, please."

The teen reached down and rotated the switch from "A" to "Both" to "B" and the cabin lights blinked at each interval. Then he went back to fishing.

"Thanks," Jason said. He turned back to the grill.

Valerie watched him in silence for a few moments and then looked up at the darkening sky. "Well, it's been twenty-four hours since the first missile hit."

"Yeah," Jason said, "twenty-four hours since the world changed."

Valerie looked over at him. "How are you doing?"

"Ahh, I was just wondering what Jeremy is up to."

"I'm sure he's all right." She put her hand on his arm.

"Yeah, but...." He broke off.

"But what?"

Jason lowered his voice. "But what if this turns into some wider conflict? We might not be safe from every danger, but at least we're together." He turned the meat over.

"I don't know. I guess it bothers me that he didn't want to come with us."

Valerie patted Jason's arm. "It's natural for him to want to be on his own."

"Not in these times it isn't. It's dangerous. Besides, he's not out on his own. He's with Ruth's family."

"I think you'd feel better if you could talk to him. I know I would."

Jason nodded. "These are done."

Everyone had come up on deck to eat supper in the dim light of a portable electric lantern. Kathy sat in the captain's chair, Julie and Brian sat on the cushioned bench, and Valerie and Jason sat on two folding camp chairs.

"I can't believe how beautiful the stars are out here," Julie said, looking up.

"You can see them better now without all that light haze from the city," Jason said. "I guess that's one benefit from a power outage."

"What's that big cross-looking group of stars right above us?" Julie asked.

"That's Cygnus the Swan. That bright star at the top is Denebola. It is one of the stars that form the Summer Triangle. See the triangle?" Jason said, pointing. "That one there is Vega in the constellation Lyra, and the lower one is Altair in Aquila."

"What are those two you showed me in the telescope," asked Brian, "the colored ones?"

"Alcor and Mizar."

"Where do they get those names?" Julie asked.

"The constellations and some of the stars were named by the Greeks. Most of the rest of them were named by the Arabs."

"Did the Romans name the planets?" Brian asked.

"I'm not sure. I don't think the Romans named much of anything in the sky. They didn't see any practical value in astronomy."

"Is there a practical use for astronomy?" Kathy asked.

"Oh, yes," Jason said, "navigation. The Greeks were excellent sailors. The Romans hired Greek sailors for their ships." He glanced back up at the sky. "The Arabs were excellent sailors, too."

Brian put his plate down on the deck and picked up the portable radio sitting next to him. He switched it on and rotated the tuning dial, but could only hear static or extremely weak signals. "Where's the station that was on before?"

"It should have been tuned right to it," Kathy said.

"Well, it's gone now."

"Maybe they shut down to conserve power," Jason said.

"There's nothing on AM either," Brian said. "What's this SW?"

"That's the Short Wave receiver," Jason said. "It's a form of AM, but the signals can travel all around the world."

"There's, like, seven different channels for the short wave."

"Yes. They're different frequency ranges. Pick one and try it."

Chapter Nine

"They're talking about us."

Brian moved the sliding switch on the radio and turned
the tuning dial. There were little blips of sound with light
static in between.

"Turn the knob slower," Jason said. "You're going right
past the stations."

Brian did so and there came over the radio a voice of a
man speaking in Spanish. He turned past it and got another
Spanish channel. Next came what sounded like a game show
in an oriental language. There was an announcer talking in a
very jovial way with another person and a studio audience
laughing occasionally in the background.

"Is that Chinese?" Valerie asked.

"It sounds like Japanese, I think," Jason said. The
announcer said something with great emphasis and the
audience laughed. Jason could see them in his mind and
found it nice to think that somewhere people were having
fun.

"I'm going to change it, all right?" Brian asked.

"Go ahead," Kathy said.

Brian adjusted the dial and soon came to another station
where an announcer was speaking in French. He spoke very
evenly and it sounded like a news program.

"What's he saying, Kathy?" Jason asked.

Kathy sat very still, listening carefully. "He's talking a
little too fast for me."

"Parlez lentement, s'il vous plait," Brian said, with a grin.

"I know that's right!" Kathy said, and they both gave a high five. "And he's using a lot of terms I've never heard before."

"He keeps saying 'Etats-Unis,'" Brian said.

"What does that mean?" Jason asked.

"United States," Kathy said.

"They're talking about us," Julie said.

"There's the president's name," Kathy said. They all listened carefully, but soon the signal started to fade.

"What's happening?" Brian asked.

"Sometimes the signal will fluctuate because of atmospheric conditions," Jason said. "You can carefully follow it with the tuning knob."

Brian adjusted the radio and the signal came in strong again.

"That's a cheap little radio," Jason said. "The better ones have an automatic fine tune control. Once you get on the signal it locks in and stays there."

Brian tuned the radio and the next channel that came on was an Arabic program. There was an orchestra of Middle Eastern instruments and the music was grand and exotic. A percussion instrument made a sound like hoof beats and Jason visualized a line of camels walking across the desert sand. Soon a woman's voice came in, wailing with great emotion. Jason closed his eyes and let the music carry him off. He could not understand the words to the song, but it seemed to him that the woman was in anguish about a lost love.

"I wish I knew what she was singing about," Valerie said.

"Me, too," Julie said. "It's so beautiful."

"You should hear our Arabic music CDs," Kathy said. "They're awesome."

"You have Arabic music CDs?" Julie asked. "Where did you get them?"

"Millennium Music downtown, mostly. They had a great selection of world music. We bought a traditional one and a modern one."

"What got you started in Arabic music?" Julie asked.

67

"I started collecting music from other countries when I was in the Navy," Jason said. "I saw a lot of neat places, then, but now the music helps me travel in my mind."

They listened in silence for a few moments until the signal started to fade out. Brian adjusted the dial but could not hold onto it so he tuned up until he found another station. This was a South American station and there was a tango piece playing. They listened to it in silence for a few moments, and then Julie spoke.

"Listening to all these different stations makes me imagine what it would be like for a spaceship approaching Earth for the first time. They could tune into the radio stations and hear a sampling of all the cultures of the whole planet."

"The Sounds of Earth," Jason said.

"Exactly," Julie said.

Brian adjusted the dial again and heard Strauss' Blue Danube. An announcer was signing off for the English portion of the broadcast of Radio Austria. Jason noted the time on his watch.

"Radio Austria broadcasts in English?" Kathy asked.

"Many of the stations broadcast in different languages at different times," Jason said. "You can find them yourself and make a list, or you can buy a schedule book, or you can go online and find the times." He leaned forward in his chair, gesturing as he spoke. "A friend of mine used to tune in to the different stations from around the world, and then write to the station. They would send him a postcard or brochure of their station. He had a whole album of different cards from around the world."

"That's cool," Brian said. "How come we don't have things like that anymore?"

"Because now we have the Internet," Kathy said.

"Had the Internet, you mean," Valerie said.

Valerie's words caused an awkward silence until Jason spoke next. "Yeah, there are a lot of older technologies that are pretty cool. Maybe some of them will make a comeback."

"People used to do all kinds of interesting hobbies. They actually made useful things with their time," Valerie said. "Now we just want to be entertained."

68

Brian rotated the dial again. They heard some strange, white noise sound, and then heard some Morse code beeped out very slowly. Jason wished he'd brought his radio handbook with the Morse code key printed inside. Brian lingered there a few moments before moving on. The next station, a preacher reading aloud a passage from the Old Testament in English, came in loud and clear.

"'To whom shall I speak and give warning that they may hear? Behold, their ear is uncircumcised, and they cannot hearken. Behold, the word of the Lord is unto them a reproach; they have no delight in it. Therefore I am full of the fury of the Lord. I am weary of holding it in:' The passage goes on to say, 'For I will stretch out my hand upon the inhabitants of the land, saith the Lord. From the least of them even unto the greatest of them every one is given to covetousness; and from the prophet even unto the priest every one dealeth falsely. They have healed also the hurt of the daughter of my people slightly, saying, Peace, peace; when there is no peace. Were they ashamed when they had committed abomination? Nay, they were not ashamed, neither could they blush: therefore, they shall fall among them that fall: at the time that I visit them they shall be cast down, saith the Lord.'"

Brian glanced around at the others. "Shall I go on?"

"No, hold on," Jason said. "Let's hear what he has to say."

The radio preacher continued, "What Jeremiah is referring to in this sixth chapter is God's coming judgment against the nation of Israel. Throughout the book of Jeremiah we read how the nation had departed from God and His ways. God warned them through his prophets of the coming disaster that they were bringing on themselves, but they refused to listen. Jeremiah even sent a copy of the Word of the Lord to the king, but the king cut it up and threw it in a fire. People didn't want to hear it anymore. But the army of Nebuchadnezzar was on its way. How similar was the state of our hearts in America? We took the Bible out of our schools, scorned prayer to God in our sporting events, and celebrated our wickedness and abominations, even while the missiles of North Korea were on their way."

"Oh, that's great!" Julie said, crossing her arms

69

derisively. "I guess according to him this missile attack is a punishment of God."

"I think he's trying to draw a parallel," Valerie said, "between the attitudes of the people of ancient Israel and modern America."

"Yes, I realize that," Julie said. "God punished them for their evil ways and now he's punishing us the same way. I get it."

"And that bothers you?" Jason asked.

"Doesn't it bother you?" she returned.

Jason could see the girl's eyes full upon him in the pale glow of the lantern. Her face was tense, and she gestured with her hands as she spoke.

"You know," she said, "in every one of those places where those missiles hit there were babies and small children. Are you telling me that God punished them? What evil could a baby possibly do? How could it be destroyed for its sins?"

The boat was quiet for a few moments except for the sounds of the breeze rustling the grass on the bank. Valerie glanced over at Jason, but he kept his eyes on the face of the young woman before him. He could feel the expectant pause of everyone around him. He took a breath and spoke slowly.

"When a nation is following after God, it has the promise of God's protection over it. We live in an evil world. There are people all around us, sold out to do evil and making evil plans against anyone who stands in their way, or has something they want. When a nation or a family or even an individual walks with God, being obedient to Him and putting Him first, then those evil plans are foiled. A person or nation walking with God will never know how many attacks or how much harm was diverted from them. That is the promise of God's protection. But when a nation or family or an individual chooses to go his own way, to be disobedient to God's ways and putting himself first, that person willingly walks out from under God's protection. Then the safety is simply a roll of the dice. A plot against such people might fail, or might succeed. Operating without God means people take their chances."

"And in this case," Valerie said, "with all the things that could have gone wrong with this plan, it happened to have

70

succeeded."

"The craftsmanship of the Soviet Union," Jason continued, "the determination and research of the North Korean missile program, and the abilities of the Korean sailors combined with a little luck to make a success."

"If you think about it that way," Brian said, "then the ones living in disobedience caused the babies to die."

Jason felt a flush of pride in his heart for his son. "That's right, son. Our national defense is not in our satellites or computers. It is not in our military or planes or submarines. It's in God alone. The rest of those things are merely tools. I think that's what that preacher was trying to say."

"I don't know if all Christians believe that way," Valerie said, "but we rely on it."

Julie sat back on the bench. "You rely on the belief that God will find some way to protect those who are obedient to Him?"

Jason nodded. "We were protected from the missile attack, and with this boat He will keep us protected for the rest of the mess that's coming."

"And He'll protect Jeremy, too," Kathy said.

Jason felt a chill go up his spine. He had not been thinking about his other son and when he heard the name an uneasy feeling began to grip him. Where was Jeremy right now? Was he all right? Had he eaten dinner? Was he thinking about them? All these thoughts flooded his mind and there were no answers.

Valerie seemed to read his mind. "Why don't you try calling him again?" she suggested. "We can get this cleaned up."

Jason nodded and stood from the chair. "You can scrub them off in the salt water first," he said. "Then you won't use so much fresh water to clean them."

"We'll get it," Valerie said. "The phone's downstairs on my suitcase."

"Down below," he corrected, trying to force a smile.

Valerie returned a smile and nodded, and then turned to the others. "All right, ladies and gentleman, bring your dishes here. Brian, scoop up a bucket of salt water." She took Jason's plate and cup.

Jason went below and found the phone, then went back

71

up and ascended the tiny steps to the foredeck. He squatted down and turned the phone on, looking up at the stars as he waited for the phone to power up. Without the glow of the city lights he had an impression that they could be hundreds or even thousands of miles away from civilization. The feeling of adventure, normally welcome to him, now only sharpened his agitation about his son. When the phone came on he looked down and saw a message that read "No Service." He shut the phone and opened it again. After another pause the message came on again. The screen showed no service bars and the antennae symbol was flashing. He stood, but it didn't help. In frustration he dialed the number anyway. He hit the call button and the phone seemed to be dialing, but then the wallpaper screen came on again and the "No Service" message returned. He snapped the phone shut sharply and stood, the level of frustration rising quickly within him. He clenched his teeth, drawing the phone back behind him for the throw, but then stopped himself. He let his arm fall down and held the phone before him with both hands.

"Father, I'm sorry," he said. "Please cover Jeremy with your protection. Keep him safe in your hands, Lord." He sighed. "I can endure not knowing if I know he's safe in your care." Jason looked out toward the northwest, in the direction of their home, then turned around and descended the narrow steps to where the others were finishing the dishes. Valerie looked up at him as he approached.

"No luck?" she asked. Jason shook his head. "Why don't you get cleaned up while we finish this?"

"All right," Jason said and went below.

*

The head, basically a small fiberglass closet with one wall that sloped in gradually toward the floor, featured a small sea-toilet attached to the deck and a showerhead on a hose above it. It might have functioned very well as a shower stall, except for the toilet and the low overhead. After placing his shampoo and soap on the toilet lid, he rolled his change of clothes tightly and stuck them on a high shelf with his towel. Then he began the difficult task of

undressing in the tiny compartment. Once his clothes were placed on the high shelf he pointed the showerhead at his chest and began pumping the lever that was attached to the wall. A light spray of cool water came out and with it he wetted his hair and tried to wet as much of his body as he could. Then he stopped pumping and lathered his hair and body. A puff of air came in through the tiny porthole above the toilet and gave him a chill. He closed the window and pumped the lever some more and proceeded to rinse. It took a long time for the fine mist to rinse the shampoo out of his hair, but eventually it was done and he dried off.
Now began the difficult task of putting fresh clothes on without getting them wet against the shower. But he managed it well enough and had just gathered his things when a knock came upon the door.

"Hurry up, Dad!" Kathy said, jovially. "Don't take all night in there!" Then he heard her say to someone else in the salon. "Funny me saying that to him, isn't it?"

Jason opened the door. "Ahh, my child, but you do not understand the difficulties that lie ahead for you!"

"You can't take a long shower here, Kathy," Valerie said. "We have a limited supply of water."

"I know!" Kathy said.

"Don't worry about that," Jason said to Valerie. "Having to pump that handle forces you to take a Navy shower. And," he added, "no hot water guarantees there'll be no Hollywood showers on this boat!"

"No hot water?" Kathy exclaimed. "Are you kidding?"

"No," Jason said. "But at least it's still only September. The cool water actually feels kind of good once you get used to it. So, who's next?"

"I'll go," Brian said.

"I'm next, Foolio," Kathy said. She looked over at Jason. "And I won't be long."

*

The remainder of the evening was spent taking showers and preparing the boat for bedtime. Valerie led the transformation.

"We are not going to let the clutter get out of hand," she

73

said. "Putting everything away every night before bed is the only way to prevent it."

"XO's inspection before Taps," Jason remarked. "I like it."

Jason rigged a small curtain in the doorway to serve as a partition between the master bed and the rest of the cabin as everyone climbed into bed. He yawned deeply and looked up at the window. From this angle he could see the stars twinkling in the blackness. The cruiser bobbled gently and he could hear the pattering of tiny waves against the hull.

"Do you hear that?" he whispered.

"The water?" Valerie asked.

"Yes. That's the kind of thing that makes all the little difficulties worth it."

Valerie said nothing but squeezed his hand gently. He remained looking up at the stars until he fell asleep.

Chapter Ten

"We're in a war."

Jason emerged from the companionway into the early
morning chill, stepping out onto the deck and quietly closing
the door behind him. In his right hand he held his Bible and
with his left he gently turned the captain's chair around so
that it faced aft. Then he knelt down on the deck and bowed
his head.

"Heavenly Father, I thank you for this day and I
surrender it to you. I submit myself and my family, and all
that I have to your authority. In Jesus' name, Amen."

He stood and then sat down on the captain's chair.
Looking out past the stern he studied the view across the salt
marsh. A heavy mist, still and cool, filled the creeks and
much of the grass so that the boat seemed to be floating in a
sea of mist. He took in the stillness, listening for the
occasional swirl of fish in the creek and watching a crane
walking along the grass, nearly invisible in the fog. Then he
turned to his Bible.

He opened it to the Psalms and flipped through the pages
until he saw the opening verses of Psalm Forty-Six. The
words seemed to stand out from the page and he read them
aloud.

"'God is our refuge and our strength, a very present help
in trouble. Therefore will not we fear, though the earth be
removed, and though the mountains be carried into the midst
of the sea; Though the waters thereof roar and be troubled,

75

though the mountains shake with the swelling thereof. Selah.'"

Jason read the rest of the Psalm aloud, and then flipped forward to Psalm Sixty-Three and read it aloud.

"'My soul followeth hard after thee: thy right hand upholdeth me. But those who seek my soul to destroy it, shall go into the lower parts of the earth. They shall fall by the sword: they shall be a portion for foxes. But the king shall rejoice in God; everyone that sweareth by him shall glory; but the mouth of them that speak lies shall be stopped.'"

He closed his eyes and meditated on the words for a few moments, then he turned to Psalm Ninety-One and read it aloud.

"'He that dwelleth in the secret place of the Most High shall abide under the shadow of the Almighty. I will say of the Lord, He is my refuge and my fortress: My God; in Him will I trust.'"

When he had finished reading the passages Jason held the Bible against his chest and closed his eyes. "Oh, Lord, thank you for spending time with me in the morning. Thank you for getting me up early to be with you here in the stillness of the day. I love you very much."

He sat quietly for a few moments looking out over the marsh. Then he turned in his Bible to the books of the Prophets. He skimmed through them randomly, focusing on passages here and there. When he came to the book of Jonah he stopped to read it through and as he neared the end he heard a sound at the companionway. He looked over to see Julie's head sticking out of the door. Her rumpled blonde hair fell to one side of her head and she smiled up at him. He nodded and turned back to his reading. She came on deck and quietly closed the door behind her. Then she faced aft and looked out over the marsh.

"Good morning," she whispered.

"Good morning to you," he returned, looking up from his book to her. She was wearing a large white T-shirt and her arms were folded across her belly to ward off the chill. Every detail of her figure stood out in sharp relief against the thin fabric and he quickly turned back to the text.

"What are you reading?" she asked, stepping over to

him.

"The book of Jonah," he said, without looking up.

"The one where the guy gets swallowed by the whale?"

"Yes."

"It's hard to believe that could happen," she said, looking down at the open pages.

"It actually did happen to a whaler in the eighteen hundreds," Jason said. "But they caught the whale and got him out after twenty four hours. He was fine."

"Really?" she said, with much interest.

She placed her arm on the back of his chair and leaned over for a closer look at the words on the page. Jason could feel her press against his shoulder and a tingling like electricity went through his core. He felt a stirring inside him and he took a deep breath. Then, grasping the book firmly, he held the text up close to her face so she could see. Julie straightened up and drew away from him.

"But the real crux of the story is how God sent Jonah to Nineveh to tell the people to repent of their evil ways or God would destroy the city. They repented and God spared them. Then Jonah got mad because he felt that God had made him look like a liar. God told him that they repented. Why shouldn't he spare them, where there are a hundred and twenty thousand children who don't even know their right hand from their left hand?"

He returned the book to his lap and Julie nodded. Jason continued, "God is more than willing to forgive, if we turn away from our evil ways and turn toward Him."

Julie nodded again, looking out over the marsh thoughtfully. Then suddenly she rubbed her arms and said, "It's kind of chilly up here. I'm going to put something on." She turned around and opened the companionway door. "Do you want some coffee?" she whispered.

"I was going to wait until everyone else got up."

"Good idea," she said, nodding. Then she disappeared below, shutting the door behind her with a distinct click. Jason buried his face in his hands and his skin felt flush to his touch. He took a deep breath and exhaled slowly. "Oh, Father." He took another deep breath, and then withdrew his hands from his face. "Father, I confess my sin before you, because you know everything anyway. Even the deepest places in my heart are known to you." He looked up at the sky. "Father, I confess my sin, Lord, of looking, and of desire. Lord, please forgive me. And please keep me from temptation. Lord, in my weakness, please be my strength." He paused again, taking another deep breath and closing his eyes. "God, I love you so much."

Jason sat quietly, looking out over the salt marsh where the vapor was beginning to burn off with the rising sun. In the cool stillness a flush of happiness filled his heart and he thought he felt the pleasure of God over him.

Soon he heard the latch of the companionway door beside him and he did not look over. "I thought I heard you up here," Valerie said.

He looked over at his wife and a chuckle of relief escaped him. She came up on deck and kissed him. Jason put his arm around her and hugged her to him, feeling her warmth against his skin. She looked at the book in his lap.

"Jonah, huh? I like that one."

Jason nodded. "I like all the prophets."

"I'll get breakfast started as soon as I can roust out the two slug-a-beds. Julie's already up."

"I know."

Valerie looked at him. "Are you all right?"

He looked up at her and smiled. "Yes, I'm all right. God is so good."

"Yes, He is," Valerie said. "All the time."

*

The warm rays of the sun had banished the chill by the time everyone had gotten up for breakfast. The meal, served on deck, consisted of fried Spam and the last of the eggs brought from home. Brian finished first and munched a toaster pastry while he switched the radio on and found the FM station they had listened to the day before. The others ate quietly and listened.

"The attack commenced at nine a.m. local time," said a correspondent.

"Which would be about eight p.m. Eastern Standard Time," said the announcer.

"Correct. There were only a handful of missiles fired and

these were aimed specifically at military targets, mainly air force bases and a few of the larger army posts. The quick flight time of the short ranged missiles caught the North Koreans completely unprepared. Immediately after that the blitz began. The most interesting feature of the attack came in the form of an airborne invasion carried out by large helicopters. There were literally dozens of them, each loaded with between fifty and seventy men. These were used to secure the capital city of Pyongyang. Airborne paratroopers were used to secure strategic towns and industrial sites throughout the country. It has been estimated that there are now over one hundred and fifty thousand troops on the ground in North Korea and many more are arriving by truck as we speak."

"What's the word from Pyongyang?"

There has been no word from there and it is believed that the North Korean government toppled soon after the attack began. The Chinese military is working to establish law and order and are hoping to get affairs of state back to normal as soon as possible. There is talk of a provisional government being set up but we have no details at this time."

"China!" Jason said. "I don't believe it!"

"Why would China invade North Korea?" Valerie asked. Jason shook his head as the announcer continued.

"Any word from Beijing?"

"Not as yet, but I expect we should hear some official statement concerning the invasion sometime later tonight, local time."

"Thank you, Rick. That was Rick Hernandez reporting from our office in Seoul. We'll get back to our report of the Chinese invasion of North Korea as more details come in. In other news, civil authorities in several major cities across the US are struggling to maintain order in the wake of a series of riots that broke out last night. Ralph Jensen has this report."

A sound of blaring sirens was heard along with the noise of shouting and breaking glass. "It was a long night for police and emergency workers as mobs of people went on a rampage through the downtown business district of this large American city. Police and national guard units were quickly overwhelmed and were repeatedly driven back by crowds who seemed to have nothing to lose."

Here another voice broke in. "I've never seen anything like it. We would try to confront them at a certain point on the street, only to find ourselves surrounded and fighting our way to safety. We're in a Catch Twenty-Two. We're told to restore order only, but many of these people are armed. Unless we immediately treat this as a wartime environment in an enemy urban zone, I don't see how we can win."

"You mean shooting them down?"

"I mean doing whatever it takes. We're in a war."

The noise in the background changed as a different part of the tape was started. "Where they're not looting, they're burning. We've tried to establish some kind of secure zone so that our fire department could go in and fight the fires, but there were people taking pot shots at our firefighters. Three of our people were hit and we were forced to withdraw."

The correspondent continued. "The mayhem began to die down in the early morning before dawn and daybreak found city officials scrambling to put out fires and barricade streets in hopes of being ready for a possible repeat of last night's violence."

"Turn it off, will you?" Valerie said.
Brian looked over at Jason, who nodded his agreement, and then switched it off.

"I'm sorry," she said, "I can only hear so much of that."

"I understand," Jason said. He nodded thoughtfully, and then said, "If we can't get a hold of Jeremy today we should plan to go somewhere to see if the land lines are up. Do you still have Ruth's home number?"

"Yes," Valerie said.

"What are we going to do today?" Brian asked.

"I would like to rig up an awning to keep off the sun and the rain," Jason said, "but I have to see how much material I have."

"You can rig the cooler on the swim platform for me," Valerie said.

"Yes, that won't take long."

"Can we go see that boat today?" Brian asked.

"I don't see why not," Jason said.

"What boat?" Julie asked.

"We're going to have a look at a wreck," Brian said, pointing. "You can't see it from here but you can see it from the island."

"What are we supposed to do?" Kathy asked.

"I don't know," Jason said. "What do you want to do?"

"I'd like to take a walk around the island like you guys did."

"Bring some bug spray," Brian said.

"But how are we supposed to get there if you guys have the boat?" Kathy asked.

"We can drop you off on the way," Jason said. "I don't think we'll be gone more than a few hours. Take a lunch."

"What's mom going to do?" asked Kathy.

"I'll guard the boat," Valerie said.

"All alone?"

"I don't mind. It would be nice to have the place to myself for a little while."

Julie looked over at Kathy. "Did you want to go see the wreck, too?"

"I don't think there's enough room for all of us," Brian said.

Julie looked at Brian and pointed. "You couldn't squeeze us all into that raft?"

"Not with one of us rowing," Jason said. "Besides, I'm not sure we can even get aboard the wreck. It might be a tangled mess."

"I have no interest in seeing it anyway," Kathy said. "I want to see the island."

"Yes," Valerie said, "you girls go to the island and let the guys explore the wreck."

"Yeah," Brian said, thumping his chest, "let the men go scope out the wreck."

Jason looked around, puzzled. "Men? How do I constitute a plurality?"

Everyone laughed.

81

Chapter Eleven

"The people's right to keep and bear arms shall not be
infringed."

The sun had passed past noon by the time they returned
to the gray sandy beach where Kathy and Julie were waiting.
Kathy sat on a block of wood staring out at the water with an
annoyed expression. She didn't look up at them as they
approached. Julie stood on the higher part of the bank
looking out over the marsh with the binoculars. She glanced
over at them and waved.

The bow of the raft touched the sand and Brian jumped
out to hold it steady. Kathy rose slowly off of the block with
a sigh and walked over to the raft. She pushed the sea bag
aside with her foot and stepped aboard, sitting down on the
gunwale with a huff.

"How did it go?" Jason asked.

"Fine," Kathy said, "except that I've been ready to go
for an hour."

"I thought you had your iPod," Brian said.

"I did, but the battery died. I would have charged it last
night but I don't know where to plug it in."

"I'll show you," Jason said.

Julie came up to the boat. "Hey, welcome back! How
was the wreck?"

"Awesome!" Brian said. "I can't wait to show you what
I got!"

Julie started to step into the raft, but stopped herself.

"Oh, wait! I almost forgot something." She walked a few yards to where the saw grass grew right up to the water. She reached down into the creek and picked up a cluster of oysters. She placed it on an old cardboard tray and returned to the raft.

"Dinner from the sea," she said, sitting down on the gunwale opposite of Kathy. "It's the right time of year for oysters, isn't it?"

"Yes," Jason said. "September has an "R" in it."

"Good."

"Shove us off, will you Brian?"

Brian did so and hopped aboard and Jason steered for the cruiser.

Valerie stood in the stern watching them as the inflatable boat pulled alongside the swim platform and the party climbed aboard. She took the sea bag from Jason and placed it on the deck.

"Wow! It looks full but it sure doesn't feel full."

"Wait until you see what we got," Jason said.

"Let me show her my stuff," Brian said.

"All right."

Jason opened the sea bag and pulled out a huge piece of folded and rolled up Dacron. It was white and made a crinkling sound as he handled it.

"What is it?" Valerie asked.

"It's a spare jib from the wreck. I'm going to use it to make an awning."

"It was a sail boat?"

"Yes. Half sunk and all rusted out. Most of the sails were on the mast and were ruined. But I found this in a sail locker in the cabin."

"Will it be big enough?"

"It should be." He placed the sail on the deck and then retrieved several coils of thick wire. "These were part of the life lines on the boat. I'll use them to help rig the awning." He placed them on the deck and looked down into the sea bag. "I'll let Brian show you the rest of it." He handed the bag to the teen.

Brian took the sea bag and reached inside. With a big grin he pulled out a bell and shook it to make it ring. "Cool, huh? Dad says we can mount it on our boat." He placed the

83

bell on the deck and reached in to the bag, pulling out a knife and fork. "These will be mine. Dad says they are stainless steel and the knife handle is aluminum so they won't rust." He handed them to Valerie who took them and said, "Very nice."

Next Brian took out the revolver still wrapped in the towel and handed it to Jason.

"Is that the gun?" Valerie asked. Jason nodded.

"Oh, teach me to shoot," Julie said. "I've always wanted to learn to shoot." Jason nodded again, but said nothing.

"And this," continued Brian, "is the crown jewel." He held up a small tea light holder that looked like a small lantern. It had a glass chimney, a shade, and a wire handle.

"Oh, that's cute," Valerie said.

"Yes, and practical," Brian said. "You can put tea lights in it, and hang it up, too."

"Do you have any candles?"

"Yep. There are some in the bag. Maybe we can get some more later."

"Absolutely," Valerie said.

"I brought back some oysters," Julie said, pointing to the swim platform. "Where can I put them?"

"There's a bucket right there," Jason said. "Fill it with water." Julie did so.

Jason looked around at the sky as he wiped the sweat from his brow. "I think it's going to be a hot one today."

"Yes," Valerie said, "the air is so still."

"Anything new on the radio?"

"Where can I plug in my iPod?" Kathy interrupted.

Jason turned to her, an annoyed frown on his face. "Brian, will you show her where to plug in her car charger for her iPod? Since that seems to be the most important thing going at the moment."

Kathy sighed loudly as she turned to follow Brian down below.

"What's her problem?" Valerie asked.

"Oh, I guess the world's not revolving around her like it should," Jason answered. "She feels like we took too long at the wreck."

"Well, too bad," Valerie said. "She needs to grow up."

"Ah, but she's twenty-one, as you will hear."

"I'm twenty-two," Julie said, climbing over the transom.

"Yes," Valerie said, "and of a much sunnier disposition, for sure."

"We're still hoping for Kathy," Jason said, wistfully. Brian came up on deck. "So what are we going to do this afternoon?"

"I was hoping you would catch our dinner while I rigged this awning," Jason said.

"Will do," Brian said.

"I'll help you," Julie said, and the two gathered the fishing equipment and loaded it into the raft.

"To answer your question," Valerie said, "I haven't had the radio on since this morning."

"Well, let's put it on while I work."

*

Jason started construction of the awning while Valerie found a suitable station. Most of the announcements were similar to ones heard previously, but soon she came across a news conference in progress and turned the volume up. A man was speaking flawless English with a Chinese accent.

"The people of China and the people of North Korea have always been friends, which is why we are bringing aid into the country even as I speak."

There was a question from the audience that Jason couldn't make out.

"Yes, that is true. We did assist Kim-Il Sung to power, and have in the past supported his son Kim Jung Il. But that kind of thing was going on all over the world during the so-called 'Cold War.' America, too, had assisted men to power who later were found to be corrupt. Remember Ferdinand Marcos, Manuel Noriega, and even Saddam Hussein? The United States assisted them to power, and then assisted in their removal from power. Now we have done the same."

Another question was heard off stage, but the ambassador broke in angrily.

"Do you think we condone this action? Do you think we would have allowed it to be carried out if we had known about it in advance? America is one of our greatest trading partners! Our largest overseas interests were destroyed that

85

night as well." He cleared his throat to calm himself. "China is willing to assist the American government and the people of the United States in any way it can. Thank you." There was a flurry of inaudible questions and camera shutters as the man left the podium. The announcer's voice came on next.

"That was the Chinese Ambassador to the United States speaking on his country's military intervention and occupation of North Korea. Joining us now is our military analyst General Robert Moser. General, you've heard the remarks of the Chinese Ambassador. What is your take on the official statement as it relates to the facts?"

"Hand me that life line, please," Jason said, standing at the stern next to one of the posts he'd erected.

Valerie handed him the cable, and then studied the rig. "I see," she said. "The posts hold up the cables, and the cables hold up the sail cloth."

"Exactly. The Dacron won't last being out in the sun every day, but we can replace it later using the same rig."

Kathy came up on deck and looked up at the work going on. "This will be nice."

"Yes," Jason said, noting her change in attitude. "It'll keep the sun off."

"Are you sure no one will mind your taking this stuff?'"

"Yes, I'm sure"

"What are they doing?" she said, pointing out to the raft.

"They're collecting our supper," Valerie said.

"Maybe I could join them," Kathy said. "Unless you two need my help here."

Valerie exchanged a glance with Jason, then said, "I think it'd be good if you joined them. But take the sunscreen with you."

"I will," Kathy said. She cupped her hands to her mouth and called out, "Hey, come back for me!" Then she disappeared below.

Valerie looked over at Jason and shrugged. Jason said, "Well don't look at me. I know I can't explain it."

Kathy came up on deck with the sunscreen just as the raft was coming alongside the swim platform. "Do you need any before I go?"

"Not after I get this up," Jason said. "But thanks

anyway."

Kathy nodded and climbed into the raft and the three motored silently away.

"Oh," Jason said, pointing to the radio, "turn that up, please."

Valerie did so and they heard a man was being interviewed in a retail store.

"Well, the military style assault weapons went first. The last of those were sold yesterday afternoon. The shotguns and handguns went next. People seemed to prefer the automatics, but all of the revolvers are gone as well. The lever action rifles went this morning and the last of the bolt-action rifles went this afternoon. Last night we divided the rounds by caliber evenly between the guns that were left so that no one would get a gun and have no ammunition."

"So there are no firearms left in the whole store?" asked the interviewer.

"No useable ones. The only ones left are here for repair or are antiques for which we had no ammunition. The antiques we did have ammo for are gone. Even the black powder arms sold out. I've never seen anything like it."

"Were you able to keep any for yourself?"

The man chuckled. "My collection is still intact. Besides, of course, the ones I sold in the feeding frenzy."

"And all of the transactions were on a cash only basis?"

"That's right. We had no other choice."

"And how were you able to comply with the background investigation requirements?"

"Listen, we have always complied with the law to the fullest extent. But in this situation, the government could not even comply with its own requirements. Their agencies were not available, and the people's right to keep and bear arms shall not be infringed. The laws of this nation do not supersede the Constitution, and when the laws cannot be obeyed or enforced, we are still under that Constitution. We have kept accurate records of every sale, and if this mess is ever straightened out, then we will lawfully submit all records of those sales to the proper authorities."

Jason thought about the shotgun he had tried to purchase and winced inside.

"Well, that's just great," Valerie said, turning the

87

volume down on the radio. "Let's just give everyone a gun and let them shoot it out."

"People have a right to defend themselves," Jason said. "Besides, no one was giving them away. People were paying for them."

"You know what I mean." She pointed to the radio. "I bet that man is a lot richer today than he was two days ago."

"He was selling something people wanted. I bet a lot of those same people had been thinking about buying a gun for a long time, but had just never gotten around to it. I'm glad I already had my guns. I just wish I had one or two more." He smiled as Valerie glanced over at him. "For hunting, I mean."

Valerie shook her head but said nothing. They continued with the awning.

*

They spent the balance of the afternoon erecting the awning, then fishing from the swim platform. Brian used the cast net to catch shrimp and small fish for bait for everyone. The afternoon sea breeze came in with the heat of the day and made the air comfortable, especially under the awning. As the first lengthening shadows of evening approached Jason and Brian cleaned and filleted the best of the fish. The rest were released unharmed. They ate grilled fish that night, seasoned with lemon pepper and served with canned vegetables. They had just begun eating and were listening to a short wave radio report from Radio Aruba about stranded American tourists when Julie suddenly let out an exclamation.

"My oysters!" She put her plate down on the deck and leaned over the transom to where a bucket hung from a string below the surface of the creek. She hoisted the bucket up, poured out most of the water, and then placed the bucket on the deck. Using a flat screwdriver Julie set to prying the oysters loose from the cluster. When that was done she took one in her hand and placed the screwdriver on the deck.

"Hand me my knife, will you?" she said to Kathy. She took the knife and said, "Now, watch. These aren't actual oyster knives so you have to be careful not to stab yourself.

I'll show you how to do it."

"Do you mean you eat them raw?" Brian asked.

"Absolutely!" Julie said. "That's the best way."

"Aren't you supposed to boil them?" Kathy asked.

"Some people smoke them," Valerie said.

"I tried to smoke one once," Jason said, "but I couldn't get it lit."

"Oh, ha, ha," Kathy said.

"Now, watch," said Julie as she demonstrated how to pry the shell apart carefully and cut the shellfish from the top half. Then she broke the top half away and tossed it into the creek. She handed the bottom half of the shell with the oyster still in it to Kathy, and then repeated the process until everyone had one. Then, still squatting on the deck, her knees bracketing the bucket, she explained the final step. "Now, take your knife and cut the little meaty thing that holds the oyster to the shell, and then pinch the oyster between your thumb and the blade. It seems a little awkward at first, but soon you'll be shucking them like a pro."

"I don't think I can do this," Kathy said with a nauseous frown.

"I don't think I can do this, either," Brian said.

"Oh, sure you can," Jason said. "We should eat from the sea whenever we can."

"It really is good" Julie said, "kind of salty." She picked up the oyster and dropped it into her mouth. "And it's satisfying."

"Come on everyone," Jason said. "Try at least one." He picked up his oyster and dropped it into his mouth. It was smooth and salty and slimy and he swallowed it quickly before it could gag him. He looked around at the others. Kathy sat holding the shell in front of her. Valerie had eaten hers and was dropping the shell over the side. Brian was beginning to wretch.

"Brian, you're not supposed to chew it!" Julie said, smiling.

Brian stood up suddenly and, turning around, spit the oyster into the water. He spit a few more times and threw the shell in after it. Then he sat down and took a drink.

"It's okay," Valerie said, "but I think I'll stick with the fish."

89

"Me, too," Kathy said.

"You haven't even tried it," Julie said.

"I can't." Kathy handed the oyster back to her friend.

"Well, it looks like it's just me and you," Julie said to Jason. She leaned forward and stretched herself out toward him, holding the shellfish in her hand.

Jason took the oyster from her fingers and watched as she quickly shucked another. It was a large one and as she picked it up several inches of the gooey mass hung down below her hand. She raised the knife high and tilted her head back. As she lowered her hand the oyster touched her tongue and slid into her mouth. She dropped the rest of it in and swallowed, tossing the shell nonchalantly over her shoulder.

Jason ate his oyster and threw the shell over the side. Julie quickly handed him another and shucked another for herself. Jason was about to eat it when he noticed the eyes of the rest of his family on him. Valerie was watching him closely. He ate the oyster quickly and threw the shell away, craning his neck to see the ripples it made in the water.

"One more," Julie said.

"Go ahead," Jason said. He continued to watch the ripples, faint now in the darkening creek, then he turned back to see Julie lifting the oyster from the shell. He looked down at his plate of fish, and picked up his fork.

"Mmm," Julie said. "That was good." She stood up and emptied the bucket of its remaining water into the creek.

"Yes, it was," Jason said. "Thanks."

Julie sat back down and took up her plate again. "You're welcome."

"And thank you guys for the fish," he said.

Brian and Kathy nodded their heads and everyone continued the meal in silence. The radio had lost its signal and no one noticed.

Chapter Twelve

"Exciting times for people of the Muslim World"

After dinner Jason and Valerie did the dishes while the kids took turns washing up and preparing for bed. Since none of them had gone swimming they each opted to take a "bird bath" by washing off from head to foot with the baby wipes instead of taking another cool water shower. Once the dishes were put away Jason and Valerie sat on the cushioned bench under the awning as Jason tried to call Jeremy once again on the cell phone. He tried the number twice despite the "no service" indication, and then calmly closed the phone again.

"Still no good," Valerie said.

Jason shook his head. "I think we should go into town somewhere and see if any of the land lines are up. We could try the IOP marina. Maybe someone has an ice machine running. We're getting low."

"I noticed." Valerie looked up toward the awning. "This is so nice to keep off the sun, but the only draw back is that you can't see the stars."

"I can roll it back," Jason said. "I tied it off at the windshield so that we can roll it back whenever we want."

"That's okay."

Jason looked around at the deck. "I suppose I'll need to tie those water bottles to the bow hand rail. That will allow them to warm up in the sun and will free up some more space down here."

"That'll be good. Now we only need to find a place for that generator."

"Uh-huh. But I'm afraid that'll be a little more difficult."

Just then Brian came down from the foredeck carrying the short wave radio. "Hey, Dad, listen to this. What do you think he's saying?"

"Turn it up."

Brian did so and Jason could hear a man speaking in Arabic. He was speaking slowly and clearly and would repeat the word "ibn" after a group of several words.

"I believe 'ibn' means 'son of'," Jason said.

"He's reciting his genealogy?" Valerie asked.

"That's my guess."

The man's voice continued. "Ali Zainul Abideen, Ali ibn Hussein, Hussein al Shaheed, Hussein ibn Ali, Hussein ibn Fatimah, Ali Amir al-Mo'mineen, Ali ibn Abu Talib, Fatimah at Zahraa, Fatimah ibn Muhammad." The man's voice stopped, but all around him cheer arose. It sounded as if the man had been speaking in a stadium and the cheering continued long after he had spoken. Many of the people started chanting something in Arabic, and soon the whole assembly was chanting the same words.

An announcer broke in, repeating the words that the crowds were chanting. "Muhammad al-Mahdi, Ahul al-Bayt!" He then continued speaking in Arabic and it was apparent he was explaining the significance of the event and the words.

"I wish we could understand what was going on," Valerie said.

"See if there is another channel covering it," Jason said. Brian adjusted the radio dial and soon came to another channel covering the same event. The chanting of the crowd could still be heard in the background, but this time with an interview between a woman who spoke English with a British accent and a man speaking English with a Middle Eastern accent. The man was speaking as Brian tuned in.

"Thus he has established his lineage through his father to Hussein ibn Ali, of the Ahul al-Bayt. But most remarkable is his lineage through his mother to Hassan al Askari, also known as Hassan ibn Ali. Thus, through both parents he has established his bloodline to the Fourteen Infallibles, which includes the Ahul al-Bayt, and the Prophet Mohammad himself, Peace be Upon Him."

"Dr. Al-Mukhtar, the phrase 'Ahul al-Bayt' is one that is unfamiliar to most Westerners. Would you explain it for our listeners?"

"Certainly. The Ahul al-Bayt refers to the household of the Prophet. According to the Hadith, the Prophet Muhammad spread his cloak over his daughter Fatimah, her husband Ali, and their two sons Hassan and Hussein. He declared them to be his family and prayed to Allah that He would always keep them pure. This established the line of the Twelve Imams which continues to this day."

"Well, other than his lineage, what do we know about Muhammad Abul Qasim?"

"We know that his father was a Colonel on the Saudi Armed Forces and Muhammad Abul Qasim served as a lieutenant in the Persian Gulf War. According to his own writings, the sight of Muslims fighting alongside Western infidels and gloating over their defeated Muslim brothers disturbed him. He felt that the Islamic world could never be unified as long as Muslims continued fighting each other. He wrote that all Muslims must put aside nationalistic and cultural identities if they are ever to stand together against the infidels and see the world united under the banner of Islam. After the war he left the military and enrolled in a series of Islamic schools, seeking to enlarge his knowledge of Allah and the Quran. In nineteen ninety-six he became a mullah."

"Is it significant that he is presenting himself to the world on the anniversary of the September Eleventh attacks on the U.S.?"

"Yes, it is very significant. Significant, too, is the fact that he first appears here in Medina. There are many in the Muslim world who see the United States as an evil antagonist to the cause of Islam. They see the striking down of the power of America as a sign from Allah that the time has come for the advent of the Al-Mahdi and for the submission of all peoples to the will of Allah."

"These are very exciting times for people of the Muslim World," said the announcer.

"These are very exciting times for people of the entire

93

world," said the man.

"Dr. AI-Mukhtar, thank you for joining us today."

"It has been my pleasure."

"Well, isn't that special," Valerie said.

Jason nodded grimly.

"I don't understand," Brian said. "Who is this guy they are talking about?"

"He is like an Islamic messiah," Jason said. "Others have come along in history claiming to be him, and one group believes that he has been alive for twelve hundred years. But I guess that now that this disaster has happened to us, someone figures he can make it stick." Jason raised his hand to his face and rubbed his forehead slowly. "God only knows what this will mean for us as a nation now that we're standing around waiting for the lights to come back on."

Brian switched the radio off. "But the Bible says that if anyone says, 'Here is Christ' or 'There is Christ' that we should not believe him."

Jason dropped his hand from his face and smiled up at his son. He glanced over at Valerie who was nodding. "That's right, Brian," he said. "When Jesus comes back every one will see him at the same time, and they'll all know exactly who he is."

"And remember," Valerie said, "no matter what we see or hear, God is still in charge. He is still on His throne. He will guide and protect those who love Him, and He will put down all rebellions against His will."

Jason nodded. "Amen to that."

*

Jason lay still in the master berth for a few minutes listening to the sounds of the boat. Valerie lay quietly beside him and he could tell that she had not fallen asleep yet. He glanced up to see that the partition between the master berth and the salon was fully shut, and then he reached over and took Valerie by the hand. She squeezed his hand gently. He moved his foot over until it touched her foot. She responded by rubbing her foot lightly against his. Thus encouraged, he rolled over on his side to face her.

With his body pressed against hers he leaned over and

94

kissed her on the mouth. She returned the kiss, but broke away.

"Don't get yourself worked up," she whispered.

"Why not?" he whispered back. He placed the palm of his hand onto her belly and began to caress large, lazy circles across it.

"Because the kids are only three feet away through that curtain, that's why not."

"Ahh, they're all of six feet away." Jason's caressing circles began to sweep lower down on Valerie's belly.

She took his hand firmly and returned it to his side. "I mean it. Not now," she whispered firmly.

Jason sighed deeply and rolled onto his back again. Valerie took his hand and gave it a slight squeeze. "Maybe we can go on a walk together sometime, just you and me," she said gently.

"I'll hold you to it."

Valerie squeezed his hand again, and then she leaned over to him. "Goodnight," she whispered. She kissed Jason and then rolled over to face the opposite wall.

Jason told her goodnight and patted her shoulder. Then he reached over to the top of his suitcase and grabbed the short-wave radio and earphones. He inserted the earphones and switched it on. The power indicator LED cast a soft red glow against the walls of the sleeping compartment. He adjusted the tuning dial and heard the familiar noises of the radio universe, sharper now through the headphones. He heard the mysterious buzzing sounds and the signals in Morse code. Some of the signals were fast and obviously electronically generated while others were slow and hand-keyed. He listened to the eerie tones that changed in pitch as he tuned past them, wailing their protest or agony. He tuned past the foreign radio programs, hoping for some new information about the purported Al-Mahdi, but could seem to find nothing on him. Then he came across a familiar voice and he fine-tuned the signal. It was the preacher they had heard the previous day, and Jason kept his finger on the tuning dial to keep the signal clear.

"Having a river flowing under the walls of your city is a marvelous technological advantage," said the preacher. "It provides a wonderful source of water during a siege, as well as a hub of commerce for the accumulation of wealth. But if someone can remove the water from the riverbed, you suddenly have a highway running right through your impregnable defenses and into the heart of your city. Do you see the parallel? Our electrical power and computer technology gave us an astounding advantage over our rivals and enemies. Our military forces and espionage activities, as well as our navigation, communication, banking and commerce, all profited by the technology. It gave us a sense of invincibility. We couldn't be touched, or so we thought." He paused. "I have often wondered how it was that the Babylonians didn't know what the Medes and Persians were up to. Here they had a massive army upstream of them, carrying out one of the largest engineering projects of the Ancient World, and they had no idea what was going on. But in light of recent events I think I understand now. Like us, they were so secure in their sense of invincibility that they saw no need to be intently looking for threats. Or maybe they figured it was someone else's job. I'm sure there were at least a few soldiers diligently standing guard along the massive walls and watchtowers. Some of them may even have reported the falling water level in the Euphrates River. But the Bible tells us there was a drunken celebration that had been going on for three days. No one heard the cry of alarm, the Median and Persian soldiers rushed in under the walls, and the city fell. The power of Babylon was broken forever.

"In the same way, we Americans were so concerned about our own comfort, or gain, that we failed to see the vulnerability in the technological wall we had built around ourselves. In speaking of the End Times, the Apostle Paul wrote in First Thessalonians 5:3, 'For when they shall say, peace and safety, then sudden destruction cometh upon them, as travail upon a woman with child; and they shall not escape.' Another passage from the Book of..."

Just then Valerie turned over and looked at him and the radio. She wore an expression of annoyance as she sighed deeply and turned back to face the wall. Jason didn't need to ask if the radio was keeping her up. The red glow seemed brighter now that his eyes had adjusted to the dark, and he wondered if she could hear the sounds from the earphones in the quiet compartment. He switched the radio off and removed the earphones, and then replaced them on the suitcase. He lay back again and looked up at the window. The awning obscured the stars, and he was sorry he had left it in place. He closed his eyes and listened to the sound of the water against the hull until he fell asleep.

*

Early the next morning Jason emerged on deck with his Bible and his iPod. He shut the companionway door softly behind him and walked over to the transom. Looking out over the marsh he saw the air clear of mist. A light breeze blew from the mainland and high above him long wisps of cirrus clouds stretched out of the western sky. The stern of the boat faced in the direction of Charleston, and he scanned the horizon closely for any sign of other boats in the area. Then he stepped over the transom and into the raft. Placing his Bible and iPod into the sea bag, he stood up and tied a long rope to the stern cleat. He tied the other end to the bow of the raft and allowed it to gently drift away from the cruiser. As the last of the coils fell from his hand he dropped the rope into the water and sat down in the bow of the raft, his back toward the cruiser.

He looked around him and saw fiddler crabs moving around on the soft mud of the creek bank. They jostled one another testily as they prodded the water's edge for food. Next to the raft a large fish swirled the water and was gone. Downstream of him, toward the opening of the creek to the main channel, he could hear the slapping of a mullet as it jumped clear of the water to evade some predator below. Jason took out his Bible and began to read.

He read out of the Gospel according to Mark and then he closed his eyes in prayer. After a little while he took out his iPod and listened to some Praise and Worship music from Belfast, Ireland, singing softly along when he knew the words. When that album was done he switched to the classical genre and turned on a Frederic Chopin CD.

As he listened to the melodic strains he thought about one of the first dates he and Valerie had shared. He had taken her to hear the Charleston Symphony Orchestra on the

97

opening night of its Romantic Season and the music was grand and wonderful. They played Dvorak's "Carnival Overture," Rachmaninov's "Piano Concerto #2" (one of Jason's particular favorites), and Tchaikovsky's "5th Symphony." The music was bold and delicate and sharp and dreamy and meticulously executed. The emotional power of it had filled his heart, intoxicating him, and more than once he had to wipe a tear from his eye. Valerie had held his hand and before the date was over, a date between friends only, Jason began to realize that he could fall in love with her. Before a month was out he had fallen deeply in love with her, and six months later they were married.

As Jason thought about that now, and with the music of Chopin flowing through his heart, he began to feel a comfortable glow within himself. *We need to go hear the Charleston Symphony Orchestra again,* he thought. *We haven't been in some time.* But as soon as the thought had come into his mind a cold chill had followed it. What if there is no more Charleston Symphony Orchestra? What if there were no more symphony orchestras playing in the US ever again? He thought about that reality, and his heart went cold within him. Surely the orchestra would not be meeting now for rehearsals or performances, but what if it never met again? CDs were nice but they couldn't compare to live performances. But what if they were no more?

The news began to settle on him in much the same way as if he'd been told a loved one had died. A new element of the magnitude of what was destroyed two nights ago descended upon him, and the thought filled him with a sense of painful loss. What if they never played again? What if it's really over? He felt his throat tighten as a tear streamed down his face.

He was listening to the dramatic part of "Etude #11" when he felt a tugging at the rope tied to the bow of the raft. He pulled one earphone out and turned around to see Valerie standing in the transom pulling on the line that held the raft. The others were breakfasting on deck under the awning behind her.

Valerie called out to him. "Hey, Michael, row your boat ashore and get something to eat."

Jason waved and nodded. He put his Bible in his sea bag

and pulled himself up to the cruiser. He tied the boat off and stepped up on to the swim platform.

"What are you listening to?" Valerie asked.

Jason took an earphone off and held it against her ear. "Chopin. This piece always makes me think of two people who are in love, and then have a bad fight, but then when it's over they are still very much in love."

"Ahh," Valerie said. "This must be the in-love part."

"Yes," Jason said.

"Well, I wanted you to get some breakfast before it got cold. The girls made it."

"Thanks." He switched off the iPod and stepped into the boat.

*

At eight a.m. Jason started the engine while Brian pulled up the anchor.

"Try to rinse off as much of the mud as you can," Jason called.

"I'm trying," Brian said, bobbing the line up and down, "but the mud is all the way up past the chain."

"I know."

Jason could hear the repeated splash of the anchor in the water, then Brian hauled it aboard and stowed it away in the locker. Jason eased the motor into reverse, guiding the boat backward until it emerged into the main creek. Then as Brian stepped through the split windshield and onto the deck, Jason spun the wheel around and headed for the Intracoastal Waterway.

They passed through the larger creek as it veered to the right and soon came to the channel that led to the ICW. Jason steered left and after a few minutes they came to the Intracoastal Waterway itself. Ahead of them, between Dewees Island on the left and Isle of Palms and Pine Island on the right, Jason could see the blue water of the Atlantic and the white of the breakers on the bar. He steered right onto the ICW and looked around. There were no other boats in sight. Brian sat on the cushioned bench across from him, twisted around to gaze at the ocean. Valerie sat next to him looking at a magazine. The girls were sitting in the camp chairs near the stern and Kathy appeared to be playing a game on her cell phone. Julie was staring out at the boat's wake.

Soon the opening to Morgan Creek and the Isle of Palms Marina came into view. He saw many boats tied up along the outer dock, but few people. In one smaller boat an older man, a younger man, and a boy were preparing to go fishing. On another dock a man and two women were carrying boxes out to a sailboat tied up at the end of the pier. Jason selected a slip along the outer dock near the ramp and steered the boat toward it.

"Brian," he said. "Get ready with the bowline, will you?"

"I'll get the stern line," Valerie said.

"Thanks."

Jason eased up to the dock and the two tied the boat to the cleats. Jason shut down the engine and removed the key, and then he turned to speak to the others. "I'm going to lock the companionway so get whatever you need now."

"Where are we going?" Kathy asked.

Jason pointed to the three-story building that stood next to the marina. "I'm going to check with the Harbormaster's office to see if any of the phone lines are up. And I want to see if they have any ice."

"I need my purse," Julie said.

"But I'm not ready to go into any office or store. I haven't even brushed my hair yet." She was still holding the cell phone in her hand and Jason could see the video game on the screen.

"You've got five minutes to get ready."

Chapter Thirteen

"Adaptability is the key to survival"

Ten minutes later Jason locked the door to the cabin and climbed onto the dock. They all walked to the marina offices and Jason could see a sign for the Harbormaster on an upper floor. The lower floors featured a restaurant and a boating supply store. Everything appeared to be closed.

Jason headed for the steps and said, "I'll be right back."

"I'll go with you," Valerie said.

"I'll wait here," Kathy said. Julie and Brian cupped their hands against the store window and peered inside at the fishing gear.

Jason and Valerie ascended the steps to the Harbormaster's office, but found the door locked. They turned to head back to the steps as a young man came bounding up after them. He wore shorts and a collared shirt and had a white ball cap on his head.

"Can I help you?" said the young man.

"Yes," Jason said. "What time does the office open?"

"Whenever. We're on an 'as needed' basis currently. That's why I came up. Is there something I can do for you?"

"Can you tell me if the phone lines are up?"

The young man grimaced. "Not that I know of. There're some people saying that lines are coming on and off sporadically, but I haven't caught them back on myself."

"Could we try?" Jason said. "We're trying to get hold of my son in town."

The young man nodded compassionately. "Sure." He unlocked the door and led them inside. He placed a desk phone on the counter where Jason could use it then backed away.

Jason lifted the handset and placed it against his ear but heard no dial tone. He pushed the button on the receiver a few times and dialed a few numbers but the phone remained dead. He replaced the handset and turned to the young man. "Thanks for letting us try."

"Not a problem, sir. I was hoping it would work for me, too. I haven't been able to contact my parents since all this began. They're in Atlanta."

Jason shook his head sympathetically. "Do you know of anyone selling ice?"

"We don't have any here, but there's a convenience store about a block up the road that has had some. There's a truck coming in from time to time with it. He's got some other things, too, as I understand."

"Is there any charge for me tying up the boat? We're just going to pick up supplies and head back out."

The young man shook his head and motioned with his hand. "No, sir."

"Well, thank you. And good luck to you."

"No problem, sir. And good luck to you, too."

Jason and Valerie headed back down the steps. The kids were sitting on a bench.

"Did you get hold of Jeremy?" Brian asked.

Jason shook his head. "No, the phone lines are still down."

"What now?" Kathy asked.

"There's a convenience store nearby. I thought we might see what they have."

"Are they open?" Kathy asked.

"They're supposed to be. Let's find out."

The kids rose from the bench in unison and the group headed away from the building. Jason led them through the nearly empty parking lot to the main road. The two-lane road had been recently paved and it led them past a small boatyard and the many fine homes that lined the creek. The neighborhood seemed quiet, but a few of the houses had extra cars parked out front, some with out-of-state plates. At

102

one home a family was unloading suitcases from a European SUV and taking them inside. No one took any notice of Jason and his family.

Soon they came to the convenience store that seemed to be the center of activity for this end of the island. A few cars were there, but most of the traffic came and went on foot. As they neared the door, Jason noticed a man leaning on an empty newspaper machine watching them as they strode up. His salt and pepper hair and a graying beard put him in his late forties and he watched the girls with keen interest. When he noticed Jason watching him, he casually looked away.

A folded piece of cardboard held the front door open and they stepped inside and looked around. The open door did little to relieve the stuffy and uncomfortable air inside. It had been a clean, upscale sort of convenience store and the people perusing the nearly bare shelves didn't appear to notice the dirty floor that scratched underfoot. Jason walked over to the cash register where the clerk was speaking to a well-dressed elderly couple. He spoke with a Philadelphia accent.

"No earlier than five o'clock," the clerk said, "and possibly later. A line usually starts at about four. Get here early."

The elderly couple nodded their thanks and moved away from the counter to talk.

"What comes in at five?" Jason asked.

"Ice truck. And as I was just saying, get here early."

"How much will you have?"

"They've been bringing a partial refrigerator truck load. Yesterday's was only half full and some people were getting testy. We send for a cop when it comes in."

"How much does it run?"

"I am told to charge a hundred dollars for a ten pound bag. Limit two per household."

"A hundred dollars for a ten pound bag?"

The man made a gesture as if to say, "I'm sorry, but I don't set the prices."

Jason shook his head. "I guess the prices are set by what they think the community will bear."

The man repeated the gesture. "We're also accepting gold."

103

"Gold?" asked Jason. "You mean like gold coins?"

"Coins, jewelry, whatever. Just bring what you have and we'll tell you how much ice you can get for it."

"I never knew ice could be so expensive."

"The driver is paying an arm and a leg just to fill the truck halfway. Most places aren't getting any ice at all."

"Thank you." Jason turned around as Brian stepped up to him.

"Man," Brian said, "all they got is souvenirs and South Carolina T-shirts."

"What are you looking for?" the clerk asked.

"Tea light candles."

"I keep things like that here behind the counter." The man pulled up a small bag of tea lights and set them on the counter. "How many do you need?"

"How much are they?" Brian asked.

"Twenty dollars a bundle. But I'll sell you two bundles for thirty-five."

"You've got to be joking," Jason said. "A bag like that normally costs a dollar."

"Yes, sir, but the demand has increased enormously. Do you need bleach?"

"Bleach?" Brian said.

"For water purification."

"We already have some," Jason said, flatly.

Brian opened his wallet. "Dad, can you help me with the lights?"

"Yes, what've you got?"

They pooled their money and bought two bags of the tea lights.

"Thank you, sir. And remember to get here by four to get a bag of ice."

"Thanks." He turned to Brian. "Where's your mother?"

"She's over there looking at 'girl things.'"

Jason glanced around the store. "Show me those T-shirts."

They walked over to the rack of t-shirts and souvenirs. He looked absently through the merchandise and noticed that the shirts and tourist trinkets were the only items still at their regular high prices. He was studying a shirt when an old man with an Australian accent sidled up to him.

104

"You won't find what you'll need there, mate."

"What do I need?" Jason asked.

"You need protection," the man said. "Protection from what's coming."

"Do you mean like a gun?"

"No." The man scratched his white beard as he watched Brian move over to the candy aisle. "There ain't a gun made that'll protect you from what's in the air. You've already been breathing it."

Jason gave no reply but waited for the man to continue.

"Allow me to introduce myself. Ed Kelly's the name."

"Jason Ribault." Jason shook his hand.

"I'm talking about the radioactive fallout, mate." He waited for a response from Jason, but when none came he shook his head. "That's the problem. No one knows anything about civil defense any more. In the old days we knew the dangers. We also knew we could survive. Now no one believes there is a nuclear threat. Then we get a limited nuclear strike that knocks the lights out and we stand around like sheep waiting to be poisoned by the fallout." He gestured with his hands as he spoke. "We're on the East Coast. The prevailing winds are from the west. We've been lucky after that first strike, but the people in eastern North Carolina have been breathing that radioactive dust for days. They've reported cases of radiation sickness as far away as Raleigh, and that's a hundred miles from Charlotte."

A prickly feeling spread across Jason's scalp. "What are the symptoms of radiation sickness?"

"When it's bad, they say it feels like being sunburned all the way to your bones. But we haven't gotten any doses like that. We might be breathing a little of it now, but some of us have protection."

"You don't look protected to me."

"Aw, but I am." He tapped his throat right up under his jaw. "Potassium iodide, that's the ticket."

"I don't understand."

"The radioactive dust, once it's inhaled it travels through the bloodstream and settles in the pituitary gland. That's how all the cancers start. The potassium iodine settles there first and keeps the radioactive particles out. But you've got to start taking the tablets as soon as the first nuke hits."

105

"Are you selling it?"

"No, mate. I've only got enough for me. I got mine online a way before all this started. But I hear there's a man in North Charleston selling it. On Azalea Street, I believe. Got a whole stock. You'd better get it while you still can. Better build a bomb shelter, too. These attacks aren't over yet."

"No?"

"Not by a long sight. Haven't you heard? There are still over one hundred suitcase sized nukes unaccounted for after the fall of the Soviet Union. No one knows where any of them are. How many might be on U.S. soil right now? How many are on their way here? Maybe all of them, if that nut case in Saudi Arabia has his way. Of course, he'd like to save a few for Israel. We ain't heard the last of him, you mark me."

"Why are you telling me this?"

"Cause you seem like a nice man. I'd like to see the nice people survive all this, instead of birds like that one over there."

Jason looked over to where Ed was pointing and saw a man in an expensive looking short set with a collared shirt and leather sandals arguing vehemently with the clerk about the price of bottled water while his trophy wife and daughter looked at the rack of post cards.

"Adaptability is the key to survival," Ed said. "Those who cannot adapt will go the way of the dinosaur."

"What did you call those tablets?"

"Potassium iodide. Hey, and if you're going, don't forget to take a driver's license and an electric bill or something in your name. That posse guarding the bridge won't let you back on the island unless you can show some proof of residency."

"Thanks, Ed." Jason held out his hand.

"You're welcome, mate. And good luck to you."

"Good luck to you, as well. And God bless you." Jason turned and noticed Valerie coming up behind him. "Find anything?" he asked her.

Valerie shook her head. "There's nothing here."

Kathy walked over followed by Brian. "They're out of chocolate."

106

"I found a book on salt water fishing," Brian said.

"Where's Julie?" Jason asked.

"She said she'd wait for us outside. It's too hot in here."

"I agree, let's go. But first I want you to meet," Jason turned to face Ed, but the man had moved away to another part of the store. He turned back and said, "Let's go."

Brian paid for the book, which cost only five dollars, and they stepped outside. The air felt cooler outside by comparison and Jason squinted his eyes in the bright sunlight. There seemed to be as many people coming into the store as leaving it, although there was little to buy. Jason wondered if they were drawn to the activity of people coming and going, or was there some lingering desire to haunt a place where food and supplies had once been plentiful. As he reflected on this, he looked around and saw Julie talking to the man at the newspaper machine. He now sat atop the machine and she stood next to him. They laughed as they talked, but the laughing died down as Jason and the others approached.

"This is the family I am staying with," Julie said, introducing them by name.

Jason noticed that the man's eyes lingered long on Kathy and Valerie as Julie said their names. But he stuck his hand out and smiled broadly as Jason's name was said.

"Billy Johnson," the man said. "Good to meet you."

Jason shook the man's hand cordially and nodded.

"Two guys and three girls," Billy said. He spoke with a thick Southern accent. "That sounds like a good ratio." His remark fell flat, so he quickly took the conversation in another direction. "Julie says you all are staying in a boat back in one of the salt marsh creeks. Up by Copahee Sound, I take it."

Jason shot a glance at Julie. Her eyes met his and her expression grew puzzled. He looked back at the man. "We move around a lot."

Billy glanced at Julie, then back to Jason. "I'm sorry. I don't mean to intrude on your business. I was just thinking that it was a fine idea. You can get away from all this craziness and even do some hunting on those islands. There's wild pigs on some of 'em, I hear. And deer, too." He waited for a response from Jason, but none came. "Do you

107

do any hunting?"

"Some."

Billy nodded thoughtfully. "Yeah. It would be pretty easy hunting on those islands. Probably could even take game with a bow." He waited again, but again no response came. "Unless of course other people in your group scared 'em off. How many boats are back there with you?"

"Hard to say. There are boats coming and going all the time," Jason said.

"Ahh," Billy said, nodding thoughtfully again.

"Well," Jason said. "I guess we need to be heading back. Nice talking to you."

"I'll help you cast off," Billy said. He made as if to hop off of the newspaper machine. "I've got nothing better going on."

Jason held up his hand. "We've got it, friend. But thanks, anyway."

Billy's face became puzzled. "I don't mind helping."

Jason's hand was still held up. "I'd really rather you stayed here."

Billy's face darkened, but he nodded politely. "All right, then. Have a nice day."

"You, too." Jason dropped his hand and turned to face his family. "Let's go."

They all turned and headed across the parking lot toward the road.

"Talk to you later, Julie," Billy called out. Julie turned around and waved happily.

A flash of anger rose up in Jason and for the first time he seriously considered putting Julie out of the boat. Putting her ashore here would be convenient, he thought, but I guess it wouldn't be fair to her. The proper way would be to get her back to her car at the house. He was trying to figure out a way when he felt a tug on his arm.

"What are you thinking about?" Valerie asked.

Jason took a deep breath. "I was thinking about how easy it was for some people to give away our situation to a complete stranger."

Julie looked over at them with a surprised look. She opened her mouth to speak, but then said nothing, keeping her eyes toward pavement as they walked.

108

"I suppose you didn't tell him what weapons we have aboard, or what calibers they were?"

"I didn't know what weapons we had aboard," Julie said, her eyes still down.

"I didn't think so," Jason said. He turned his face to Valerie. "That's why he was talking about hunting. He was trying to draw out information."

"He seemed all right to me," Julie said.

"Of course he did. He was very friendly," Jason said, his anger softening. "But you have to listen to what people are actually saying or asking, not how they're saying or asking it." He looked back toward the store before it passed out of sight and saw Billy still looking after them. He had come off of the newspaper machine but was still standing next to it. Then a line of bushes blocked the view and Jason looked back toward the marina.

"Like when he was asking how many boats are in our group?" Valerie asked.

"Exactly. It's not just thugs in a ghetto who will try to take advantage of this mess we're in. Anyone with evil intentions will make their move now."

"I'm sorry," Julie said, quietly. "I wasn't thinking about it like that."

"It's all right," Jason said. "But you know now. It would be nice if we never had to think like that, but we do."

"The Bible says we are to be wise as serpents but harmless as doves," Valerie said.

"Exactly," Jason said, returning his hand to his side. "People might be completely innocent, but you never know."

"Like when we were on long trips," Brian said. "If you got to talking with someone you never told them where we were heading."

"Right."

"I remember that," Kathy said. "I remember how you would call us when you were working late. You used to never tell us when you'd be home on the answering machine. You'd just say 'I'll be home soon.'"

"Yes," Jason said. "You never know who is listening. It's not paranoia, it's just being careful."

"What are we going to do?" Valerie said, gesturing toward the store.

109

"I guess we'll go back to the same spot for now," Jason said. "It's as difficult to find as any other place. Besides, he won't be able to follow us without a boat."

They walked in silence for a short while until the marina came into view. Brian opened his book and flipped through it as they walked. They walked out onto the dock and boarded the cruiser in silence. As they readied the boat to leave Jason could feel a somberness descend over everyone. They were leaving the excitement and activity of the people on the shore and returning to the quiet desolation of the salt marsh. Jason wanted to say something to brighten the mood, but nothing came to him. They cast off the lines and the dull throb of the motor increased as Jason put the boat into gear and moved out into the Intracoastal Waterway once again.

Chapter Fourteen

"It all depends on the power situation."

Noon found the cruiser at its former anchorage, swinging lazily from its drooping anchor line as Jason and Valerie prepared for lunch.

"It's too bad we couldn't get any ice while we were there," Valerie said, taking several items out of the cooler. "This stuff on top is already starting to get warm."

"Is there any ice in there at all?" Jason asked.

"Just a little sloshing around in the bottom. The stuff down there is still cold but another hot day will finish it."

"Well," said Jason, "we'll just have to eat cold meats and cheese for the next few meals." He took the items from her and placed them in a row on the transom, then he helped Valerie over the transom and onto the deck. "Okay, everyone, lunch is served. Sandwiches and cold cuts are the fare. Have as many as you want, double thick."

"I feel like having peanut butter and jelly," Kathy said.

"Well, feel like having ham and cheese instead. The peanut butter will last longer without refrigeration."

They all sat down at the various places on the deck furniture and began passing the ingredients to one another. Once everyone had started eating Jason motioned to Brian at the captain's chair. "Brian, hand me the radio, please."

Brian did so and Jason placed the sandwich on his lap. Using both hands he switched on the radio and turned the dial. "That old-timer in the store said some things that got

111

me thinking."

"Like what?" Julie asked.

"Like...." But just then Jason found an interesting announcement and turned it up. A woman with a British accent was speaking. "Listen."

"...another night of violence as self-appointed militia units sought to restore order in a predominantly upper middle-class neighborhood. Things appeared quiet until several Molotov cocktails were lobbed from an ambush. The fighting erupted again with shots breaking out on both sides and when it died down twenty-eight were dead and an unknown number were wounded. Victor Rotherham files this report."

The voice of a man came over the radio. The spot sounded like it had been recorded outside and Jason could hear the sound of a large diesel engine idling nearby. The man spoke with a British accent.

"Last night's fighting centered mainly in the city's business district as armed militia units, commissioned to protect commercial interests, were overwhelmed by large numbers of rioters. Area Commander Pomeroy faced a daunting task."

The sound of the broadcast changed and another man's voice was heard. He had a voice like an American drill sergeant and an occasional shot could be heard in the distance.

"A group of local businessmen had requested that we provide armed patrols through this area. At approximately twenty three hundred hours a gang throwing rocks and bottles attacked one of our units. Our patrol unit fired some shots in the air to disperse the crowd and then called for back up. But as the back-up units were arriving, the crowd reassembled and began attacking storefronts further up the street. Our men advanced to disperse the crowd and were attacked with small arms fire and homemade firebombs. Several of our men were hit and one was killed. They took cover and returned fire, and then began a staged assault up the street. Reinforcements were called but before they could arrive our people were surrounded from the side streets and the buildings. They fought their way into a building and the fighting was continued room to room. The reinforcements

112

arrived and the crowd was dispersed."

Victor Rotherham continued his report. "Order was restored for the moment, but with twenty eight dead and at least forty more wounded, this became the bloodiest clash since the lights went out across America only four days ago."

The sound of the broadcast changed again and this time Jason heard a woman's voice crying words of agony. Around her, other people were sobbing or shouting.

"My baby! They killed my baby boy! Oh, Lord Jesus, he was only fourteen years old! They killed my baby boy!"

"What happened to your son?" Victor Rotherham asked.

"Those killers shot him down! He was out looking for food for us, for his baby sister, and those militia people killed him! Who are they anyway? What right do they have to be policemen around here? Why do we have armed gangs patrolling our streets and the government doesn't do anything about it? My sweet baby boy is dead!"

Victor Rotherham continued. "It is horrifying to see what America, once the mightiest nation in the world, has come to in so short a time."

"Victor," the announcer said, "tell us about the two sides involved."

"Well, as for the militia groups, they are armed citizens who have organized into military style units. Many of them have had military or police training and they claim to represent the law-abiding citizens. As one militiaman told me, he had been sworn into the US Army to protect and defend the Constitution of the United States against all enemies, foreign and domestic, and he believed he was still under that oath. In some cities they have worked in conjunction with law enforcement officials, even to the point of being deputized. But in other cities where law and order have broken down entirely, they operate alone, with neither authority from nor accountability to any elected officials. And there, say the critics, is where the problem lies. Unlike police officers, who are accountable to the courts, these militia units are accountable to no one."

"I sense a similarity to the Vigilance Committees of San Francisco in the eighteen hundreds."

"There are similarities, yes, but there are grave

differences. In San Francisco in the eighteen hundreds the majority of the people stood with the Vigilantes in their efforts to stem the rising tide of crime in that city. The elected officials were ineffective or corrupt. But in modern America the people themselves are divided. In that sense, it is becoming more like a civil war here. While some are working to restore law and order, others see the current system as corrupt and bias and in need of an overthrow. And that, I believe, is the spirit that is driving the so-called rioters and looters. They, like everyone else, are frightened by the present crisis, but unlike everyone else, they don't believe they'll be helped by their government and must take matters into their own hands."

"But what of the charges of looting and mayhem that are being leveled at them?" the announcer asked.

"Well, that is the other side of the question. They claim to be out looking for food and medicine, like this mother's fourteen-year-old boy, but are breaking into all kinds of establishments. This same boy was shot in an electronics store, so there's plenty of blame on both sides."

"How are these two groups being supplied?"

"As for the militia units, the vast majority of them are gun owners and are bringing their own weapons and ammunition with them, which can be a logistical nightmare for the police departments that have taken them in. How they expect to be re-supplied for the long run is still a mystery. The rioters have some firearms but mainly rely on superior numbers and makeshift weapons. They prefer to flee rather than fight in most cases, and these elements may prove superior in the long run."

"Are you saying that you don't expect the militia units to survive for long?"

"It all depends on the power situation. The militia strategy of creating checkpoints and controlling certain areas will work well if the lights come back on soon and the established governments are back to work in a timely manner. But the longer this crisis drags out, the worse it will be for them. On the other hand, the rioters have their own long-term problems ahead, for while they may be united in spirit, they are largely disorganized and at present have nothing to evolve into if the established government falls.

114

Once that happens, they may begin to prey on each other."

"Victor Rotherham, thank you very much."

"Thank you, Linda."

"That was Victor Rotherham reporting from the United States. In other world news, the President of Pakistan was attacked today as he traveled on a three-day tour of military installations in that country and it is unclear at this time if the President has survived the attack. If successful, this will be the third assassination of a moderate Muslim leader by Islamic Extremists in as many days."

"Oh my word," Valerie said. Jason shook his head.

"Israel today," the announcer continued, "concluded its second day of heightened military alert status in the wake of renewed rocket attacks by Syria and Iran. The Persian Leader has threatened to use chemical weapons against the Jewish state if the Israeli leaders will not agree to step down and allow a Palestinian-led Muslim government to form in the Holy Land. Meanwhile, Israeli families are spending more hours in their gas resistant rooms, reminiscent of the days of the Persian Gulf War in nineteen ninety-one when Iraqi leader Saddam Hussein made similar threats."

Jason's eyes met Valerie's and he shook his head again. He remembered the images on the news of Israeli families huddled together in closets that had been sealed with duct tape and six mil plastic. He remembered frightened faces peering up at the camera through gas mask face plates while Scud missiles exploded in the skies over head.

"And from Medina, Saudi Arabia, Islamic leader Muhammad Abul Qasim, widely known as the al-Mahdi, spoke out with great vehemence against the government of the United States for what he calls its 'failure to protect its own people against very real external and internal threats.' He went on to criticize the US government for its 'failure to provide sustenance and the other necessities of life' to its citizens. He called the US's lack of decisive action 'shameful' and claimed that people under such leadership had a 'divine and holy right and obligation' to overthrow such leadership. The United Nations Premier, who was on hand at today's rally, echoed the words of the al-Mahdi, and pledged support for freedom fighters in the United States, though he was unclear as to what form that support would

115

take."

Jason shook his head again.

"The al-Mahdi did cite names of prominent US leaders whom he claimed were 'worthy of trust and support'." The announcer read off a list of names, most of which were at least partly Middle Eastern.

"Turn it off, please," Valerie said.

Jason looked up at her and hesitated. "What's wrong?"

"Nothing's wrong. I just don't want to hear any more."

"Well, I would like to know what's going on."

"Okay." Valerie began to gather up what remained of her lunch.

"What are you doing?"

"I'm going to finish my lunch in the cabin."

"No, wait." Jason switched off the radio and placed it on the deck. "Just stay here, I can catch up later."

Valerie nodded and resumed her meal. After a few moments she said, "I'm sorry. I can only hear so much before my stomach starts twisting itself into knots."

"I understand," Jason said. "It's all right."

They ate in silence for a little while, then Julie asked, "What did that guy mean by 'Freedom Fighters?'"

Jason shrugged.

"They're probably talking about those militia dudes," Brian said.

"I don't think so," Kathy said.

"Do you mean they're talking about the guys fighting the militia?" Julie asked.

Kathy nodded. "That's what it sounds like to me."

"But how can they be considered 'freedom fighters?' They're just going around wrecking and looting things."

"It's all politically driven," Jason said.

Valerie, now finished with her meal, stood up abruptly with a sigh. "I'm going to take a nap." She balled up the paper towel she held and walked briskly toward the companionway.

"I'm sorry, Mom," Kathy said.

"It's all right," Valerie said, as she disappeared below. "I just don't want to hear any more right now."

Everyone sat quietly for a few moments, then Brian said, "Do you mind if I use the cast net? I'd like to go fishing."

116

"Not at all," Jason said. "Let's get this stuff cleaned up first. I'll ride with you."

"I'll clean this up," Kathy said. "You all go. I think I'll take a nap also."

"All right, thanks," Jason said. "I'd like to bring the radio and go for a walk."

"I'll go fishing with you, Brian," Julie said.

Chapter Fifteen

"Entire households are being systematically wiped out."

Ten minutes later Jason pushed the bow of the inflatable boat away from the swim platform and Brian steered the boat toward the gray sand beach. Jason looked back to the cruiser and saw that Kathy had already gone below. He turned himself and looked toward the beach.

"The tide sure is low," Brian said.

"Yes, it is," Jason said.

"It might not be good for fishing, but I'd like to try anyway with live shrimp."

"That's a good plan," Jason said, "but if you only get a bucket full of shrimp, that's a win, too." He looked back at Brian and the teen grinned.

"Oh, yes. I love shrimp," Julie said.

"We do, too," Jason said.

Brian nudged the bow of the raft against the sand and Jason stepped out onto the beach. Still holding the radio, he started to push the boat off into the creek, but Julie stepped out suddenly.

"Hey, where're you going?" Brian said.

"Just a quick minute," Julie said. She stood directly in front of Jason, her face grave as she looked deeply into his eyes.

"I'm sorry I told that man those things back at the store. I never thought I might be endangering everyone. I really didn't."

118

Her eyes seemed as though they were about to tear up. Jason shook his head gently and said, "It's all right. You didn't know."

"I wouldn't want to do anything to hurt any of you," Julie said, her last words becoming choked with a sob. She stepped forward suddenly and, putting her arms around his neck, hugged him tightly.

Jason had not expected a hug, but even as it began to register in his mind as such, he knew that this was more than just a friendly church hug, or a hug between family members. Julie's arms held his neck tightly, her face buried under his chin. In addition, he could feel the young woman's entire body pressed against him. A shock like electricity went through him and again he felt a deep stirring inside. He waited a polite moment for her to draw away, but she did not. His heart began to pound and he fought off an urge to slip his hands around her waist. Instead, he reached up and grabbed her arms firmly, but not roughly. Then he gently pried her grasp from him and guided her hands down to her sides. He released her and said, "It's all right."

Her face was still very sad, but no tears had formed in her eyes. She nodded and turned to board the boat.

"Have a nice walk," Brian said. He didn't appear to have noticed the incident.

"Good luck fishing," said Jason.

Brian nodded. Julie sat in the boat and Jason pushed it off the bank. Brian backed the boat out on to the creek and then headed upstream. Jason could see Julie watching him, but he turned away and walked on to the higher ground of the bank.

Jason continued his short ascent to the top of the bank. At the top he stopped to survey the entire view of the salt marsh. He could see no other boat except for the raft and as he looked in its direction Julie waved. Jason turned away and began walking down the far side of the bank. Another tiny beach of gray sand lined this narrower creek and crabs skittered away into the saw grass as he approached.

Jason stepped up to the water's edge and squatted. He stared out over the water for a few minutes before he spoke.

"What is it, Lord?" asked Jason. "Please, help me to understand." He stared down into the murky water. "Is it that she doesn't know what she's doing, and she's just a product of this world, or more specifically, a product of our perverse culture gone mad? I'd like to believe that. I'd like to believe that she could be shown the right way. People today have not been taught proper values or morals. All they know is the junk they get from the TV and radio. But I suspect that it may be something deeper. Maybe she knows exactly what she's doing. But to what end?"

Jason took a deep breath and let it out slowly. "Father, I wish it didn't affect me so. And I confess it does. Please forgive me, but it does. I think I can stand against it, even ignore it, and then something like this happens and it takes me completely by surprise." He sighed again. "Father, I love you so much. And I love Valerie so much, and I don't want to do anything to harm either of those relationships." He slapped his knee with his open palm. "And, Lord, I know, I know that if I went through with something like this, within seconds afterward I would hate myself, and hate her, and I would know that my integrity would have been crushed. I will have crushed it! And at that moment in time there will be nothing I can do about it. It will have been too late." He lowered his head and rocked forward until he was on his knees in the shallow water.

"Father, please strengthen me against it. Please be my strength. You promised you would provide a way out. Please, help me to see it."

He kneeled quietly for a few minutes, deep in thought. Then he whispered. "I should tell Valerie. She is my protection in things like this. If she knows about it, too, then it's not a secret I have to bear alone. But the time must be right. I must present it the right way. Maybe Valerie can talk to her." He nodded. "I've got to be firm with Julie. The next time it happens I need to set her straight in no uncertain terms. But, I'll talk to Valerie first, hopefully. I don't care what awkwardness it may cause. I didn't start this."

Jason took a deep breath. Then he raised his head again and the sight that met him startled him. There, across the narrow creek stood a great heron. Its head rose nearly four feet high and its orange-yellow eyes blinked nervously. It had come through the grass on the opposite bank and apparently hadn't noticed Jason until he raised his head.

Jason stared in wonder. The bird was beautiful, and he had never been able to view one so closely without binoculars. It stood blinking for a few moments, until a sound in the grass behind the bird caused it to turn its head slightly. Then it spread its wings and took to the air, rising over the small creek at an oblique angle to Jason. The heron beat its long wings heavily and for an instant blotted out the sun.

Jason watched in awe until it wheeled around and landed farther down the creek. He let out a short laugh. "Thank you, Father. Thank you for that wonderful sight." He chuckled again to himself. "It's a beautiful bird. You are such a marvelous artist, Lord. Thank you for sharing that with me."

He stood up and looked around again. As he reflected on the surroundings he heard a faint, low buzzing sound in the distance. It was coming from the south, and as he listened it began to sound more like an outboard motor. He walked backward up the bank until he could see above the surrounding grass. He stared in the direction of the sound but could see nothing until a flash of red caught his eye. It was the short, flat sunshade of a center console fishing boat. The glimpse had gone again, but the boat seemed to be moving slowly up the Intracoastal Waterway. He regretted leaving his binoculars on the cruiser, but as he watched the boat passed briefly into the open again between two shelves of grass. He could not see details from this distance, but in the glimpse he saw three men apparently on a fishing trip. One of the men stood in the bow looking out with a pair of binoculars. He continued watching for the boat, but it made its way up the Waterway without coming into view again.

He walked back down to the water's edge and headed upstream along the bank of the small creek. He came to a piece of block timber that was about the size of a small cooler. It sat right at the high water mark and had the remains of a rusty bolt sticking out of one side. He walked over to the block and sat down, the wood settling a little deeper in the marl under him. He held the radio before him and switched it on.

"Seventeen people were killed in the blast and more than fifty were wounded," a reporter said.

Another man's voice came on the air, recorded outside.

121

The sounds of emergency vehicles could be heard in the background.

"He drove right up to the front entrance and stopped. Since so many people are out of work we've had a lot of volunteers helping out. The truck was a bread delivery vehicle so everyone came up to help unload. Our coordinator stepped up to the driver...."

Here the man's voice faltered. He choked back a sob, and then he took a deep breath and continued. "I'm sorry. The coordinator was a long time friend. Anyway, she stepped up to give directions to the driver, and that's when the bomb went off. I was around the back of the building working with some other folks to give out food baskets when we heard the blast. Big sheets of metal peeled off of the building and flew over our heads. One piece fell onto the line of people waiting and cut an elderly lady's arm real bad." The man's voice began to choke up again. "I just can't believe anyone would do this. We were giving out food, for crying out loud!"

The reporter continued, "Although this is the third attack of this kind against a church in the last twenty-four hours, this has been by far the deadliest. But the collective injury may be greater still."

A woman's voice came on the air, speaking with good enunciation and strong passion. "This is not just about one church. A whole community has been wronged. We had members of our congregation volunteering their time and labor to earn food to be distributed here at the church. Needy people, many more than normal, were being helped every day. But now our supplier has stopped the program, and I don't blame him. They see us as a target. I was speaking to another pastor across town whose congregation was running a similar program, and now their program is grinding to a halt. No one is showing up to get the food! But that's the real strength of terrorism. Kill one group of people and everyone else is afraid."

"Reverend, what do you say to the criticism that claims churches are attracting people to their doors but are not taking enough steps to adequately protect them?"

"We are doing what we can to help people. We had no way to predict an attack of this nature. If we had shot the man to protect ourselves, those same people would've found some reason to criticize that, too." The pastor paused for a moment. "Even the Lord Jesus couldn't make those kinds of people happy."

The reporter continued. "And so, with community churches being targeted, and citizens fearful, this avenue of relief may dwindle, or die out altogether. Back to you."

"In other news...." continued the announcer.

"Where was it?" Jason asked, shaking the radio. "Where were the other churches that were attacked?" He focused his attention on the radio once more.

"...files this report," the announcer said.

"Imagine you are a doctor or a medical student in a Middle Eastern country and you have an opportunity to practice or go to medical school in the United States or Canada. Days before you go you are visited in your home by some men from the local mosque. One of them may be a Mullah. In a friendly and business-like manner they inform you that while you are practicing in America you will create a database for people you come in contact with who are pastors or rabbis, or other prominent religious leaders. You will collect this information in detail, including family members' names and addresses, and you will periodically send this information back to the local mosque where it will be organized and compiled with information gathered from other mosques. You refuse, for ethical reasons of course, and are told that if you don't comply your family members at home will be killed. As ghastly as that scenario is to contemplate, it is exactly what has been going on in the lives of many immigrants from the Middle East during the last twenty years or so. Under threat of death they have been gathering information on not only religious leaders, but on anyone else who might be regarded as an enemy of Islam."

"Is the information gathered now being used in this latest series of murders of church leaders across the country?"

"Absolutely. The perpetrators are using the chaos going on now in the U.S. to carry out these attacks under the guise of random violence. And no connection was made until Dr. Rashid came forth with this startling revelation."

"Did you say family members were likewise being

123

killed?"

"Yes. Entire households are being systematically wiped out. And, of course, they are at a higher risk than most people because their job, indeed their life's work, is to put themselves at the disposal of the needs of others."

"And what about legitimate American citizens who may be from a Middle Eastern country or of Middle Eastern decent? Has there been a backlash against them?"

"Yes, and that, too, is a tragedy. It seems that none of them are above suspicion, and that is a dangerous place to be in these lawless, violent times."

"Tell us about the pastor who was murdered with his family this morning."

The reporter told of the pastor and his ministry. He had led a large congregation and had written many books. He was nationally known and was well regarded, even by those who disagreed with him. Jason had heard him speak at a rally once, and had even read two of his books. He knew that the pastor had loved the Lord truly and deeply and, as the reporter spoke about him and his life's work, Jason's heart sank. He listened as the tears welled up in his eyes, and then he switched the radio off and placed it in his lap.

"Oh, Father," said Jason. He buried his face in his hands and wept.

Chapter Sixteen

"There's a boat coming!"

An hour later Jason walked over the bank of the small
island where the trees stood. After he had composed himself
he had continued his walk in the direction Brian and Julie
had gone. Now, coming over the island he could see them
anchored in the creek, sifting through their catch in the
bottom of the raft. He watched as they collected the shrimp
in a bucket filled with creek water and tossed the other items
over the side. When they had finished they stood and while
Brian gathered up the net for another cast, Julie pulled the
boat forward by the anchor line. Jason walked over toward
them. Brian was about to throw the net again when he
looked up and saw his father.

"Oh, hey, Dad. Did you have a nice walk?"

"Yes, so far."

"Anything new on the radio?" Julie asked.

Jason shook his head.

"Do you want us to give you a ride back?" Brian asked.

"No, that's all right. I think I'd be in your way."

"Not really," Brian said. "We've barely caught a thing. I
was going to do one more cast and then maybe try up by the
boat. I don't think there's anything here."

"Maybe it's the wrong time of year," Jason offered.

"Maybe."

"We did get some little fish," Julie said. "And some
crabs, and a few shells."

"And a bottle," Brian said.

"Wow," Jason said.

Jason watched as Brian cast the net and retrieve it. He and Julie sifted through the catch again, then they stood up Julie pulled up the anchor and Brian motored over to the bank where Jason stood. He pushed the rounded bow of the raft through the grass to get as close as he could to the mud bank. Jason stepped out onto an old plank that lay on the bank and then took a long, half-jumping step into the raft. Julie took his arm briefly to help steady him.

"Thanks," Jason said. He sat on the gunwale opposite of Julie and Brian backed out into the creek. Julie slid the bucket over so Jason could see. He looked inside and could see several shrimp of various sizes gathered in the bottom.

"It's not very much," Julie said, "but it might make good bait for later."

"I'll change the water to keep it fresh," Brian said.

Jason nodded. "How is the battery doing?"

"It's getting a little sluggish. I'll put the solar charger on it when we get back."

"Or you can switch it out with the other one. You can plug this one into the boat."

Brian nodded.

Soon they came up to the cruiser and tied up to the swim platform where Valerie stood against the transom. Julie and Jason climbed out of the raft while Brian unclipped the battery and handed it up to Jason.

"Did you have a good walk?" Valerie asked.

"Yes. Did you have a good nap?"

"I did."

"That's good. Now I think I want one." He kicked off his shoes and started for the companionway.

"Anything new on the radio?"

"You don't want to know," Jason said as he disappeared below.

*

"Jason! Wake up," Valerie said, shaking him by the shoulder.

Jason had been in a deep sleep. He rubbed his eyes and

126

sat up. "What's wrong?"

"There's a boat coming!"

Valerie backed out of the small space as Jason flung off his blanket and crawled into the salon. Brian was sitting at the table with a nervous look on his face. Valerie backed up against the door of the head to give him room.

"Where are the girls?" he asked.

"Up front," Valerie said.

"We were fishing from the bow when we heard the motor coming."

Jason nodded as he ascended the steps. The light in the sky told him that the afternoon had been far spent. Astern of the cruiser Jason saw another boat turning around. The tide was coming in and the stern faced up stream. The boat, a red striped center console boat with a flat red sunshade, had driven past the cruiser and was now coming about. There were three men in the boat including Billy Johnson from the convenience store. Billy waved, but the other two, a sullen Hispanic man and a rough looking white man, just stared at Jason. They had the bow of their boat pointing toward the cruiser now and were motoring slowly toward it.

Jason turned and spoke into the companionway. "Brian, get my gun."

"Jason?" Valerie said.

"Hurry."

Brian scrambled for the master berth, then handed up the single action twenty-two-caliber revolver. Jason hesitated before taking the gun.

"It's all I saw," Brian said.

"Find the other one," Jason said. "It's in the case. Stand here in the doorway with it. And don't shoot me in the back." Then he turned around to face the stern again, shifting the revolver behind his back as he did so.

The boat had come up to the swim platform by now and Billy and the Hispanic were about to climb onto it.

"Dad?" Kathy said from the foredeck.

Jason ignored the query. "That's far enough."

"Well, hey, friend," Billy said, smiling broadly. The other two wore grave expressions. "Thought we might check in and see how y'all were doing." He continued to climb onto the swim platform.

"We're doing fine," Jason said, "and we're not receiving visitors today."

Billy stood erect on the platform and the Hispanic man tied the boat to the stern cleat. "Well, that's a mite unfriendly. We just stopped by to say 'Hi.'" He began to swing a leg over the transom.

Jason brought the gun around into full view and cocked the hammer, the four clicks clearly audible over the other boat's idling motor. "I said we're not receiving visitors today. Get back in your boat and cast off. And you at the wheel," he said to the third man, "keep your hands where I can see them."

Billy still rested his leg on the transom, but came no farther. "I don't understand all the hostility, friend," Billy said. His expression darkened. "You've got no reason to pull a gun on us." He looked closely at the revolver. "That looks like a twenty-two."

"It's a twenty-two magnum," Jason said, hoping that the magnum cylinder and rounds were still in the gun. "And I can hit you in the eye from here," he added. "Now, get back in your boat and cast off."

Billy hesitated, then the congeniality slowly returned to his face. "All right. Have it your way friend." He withdrew his leg from the transom and then paused. "Is there any thing y'all would like us to pick up for you while we're in town?"

Jason, still pointing the gun at Billy, shook his head. "Won't do any good."

"How's that?"

"Because the next time I see you out here I start shooting. And this is the least I got. Understand?"

Billy's face clouded over again. He stared at Jason for a long time, and then nodded his head slowly. But it seemed that he nodded not so much to Jason, but to himself. Then he motioned for the other man to cast off and the two climbed back into their boat. The driver let the incoming tidal current push the boat away from the cruiser, and then he put the motor into forward gear and steered past the cruiser toward the main channel.

"Have a nice evening, ladies," Billy said as the boat went by. All three men were staring at the two young women on the cruiser's foredeck. The boat turned left onto the larger creek and was soon out of sight.

Jason uncocked the gun with his thumb and let his hand fall to his side. He looked toward the companionway where Brian held the thirty-eight-caliber revolver in his right hand. He and Valerie wore anxious expressions, as did the two on the foredeck. Jason nodded briefly, and then spoke in an even tone.

"Brian, bring me that gun. I want you to dump the water out of that five-gallon bucket, dump the shrimp too, and put the bucket in the raft. Then I want you to go to the bank and fill the bucket with as much marl as it will hold. Julie, go with him."

Brian stepped forward and handed Jason the gun, and then moved to the swim platform. Julie joined him. Jason looked up at Kathy.

"Kathy, can you still see the boat?"

Kathy turned around and straightened up to look. "Yes. It's over there now, still moving away." She pointed as she spoke.

"Good. What I want you to do is keep your eyes on that boat until you can't see it anymore. And then watch for it until it comes again."

"Is he coming back?" Kathy asked.

"I don't know yet."

"What are we going to do?" Valerie asked.

"We're going to shift anchorage. Help me get this awning down."

They began taking down the awning as the raft motored over to the nearest muddy bank. Jason noted the raft's speed and felt satisfied to know that Brian had installed the spare battery on his own while Jason had slept. As he and Valerie rolled up the fabric Jason looked up to see Kathy watching the raft.

"Kathy, keep watching that boat. Stand up if you have to."

Without a word the young woman stood up and turned her gaze to the south. She held up her hand to shield her eyes from the sun.

"Here," Jason said. He grabbed his binoculars and handed them up to her. "You've got the most important job right now. You're our radar. I've got to know as soon as they are in sight."

Kathy nodded and, taking the binoculars, began to watch diligently.

Brian and Julie were starting back to the boat. Jason helped fold the fabric one time and then said to Valerie, "Stow that below, would you?" She nodded and Jason stepped over to the side of the boat. The two were coated up to their wrists in gray-black mud. The bucket sat between them full to the top with marl.

"What now?" Brian asked.

"Paint the hull with it. We've got to cover up this white."

"Paint?"

Jason leaned over the gunwale. "Here, hand me some." Julie scooped out a big dollop and placed it in his hands. He divided the goo and began to smear it on the freeboard of the hull. "It doesn't have to be perfect, it just needs to dull the white and break up the outline. Think of the saw grass as you do it."

The two nodded and began to smear the mud onto the hull. Jason straightened up and looked up at the sky. They had another hour or so of daylight, maybe two. He looked down at the creek and could see it was nearly high tide. Things might work out perfect, as long as Billy and his friends gave them just a little more time.

Valerie came up through the companionway. "Does the frame come down?"

"Yes." Jason moved toward the stern to wash his hands off. As he lifted his leg over the transom he accidentally kicked his bare foot against the generator. "Ouch!"

"Oh, honey," Valerie said. "We should get rid of that. We don't even use it."

Jason continued his climb over the transom "It'll come in handy one day." He bent down to wash his hands on the creek. "We'll take this frame down and then help them cover up this white." Jason looked up and was glad to see Kathy still searching the horizon with the binoculars. He nodded his satisfaction.

*

130

The sun was touching the horizon by the time Julie and Brian were back aboard. Billy and his friends had not returned, but Kathy kept up her vigil on the bow, moving only enough to allow Jason to mud paint the foredeck. They had coated everything, even the windshields. And now, having washed the last of the mud off themselves Jason went to the captain's chair and studied the horizon.

"All right. Good job. Brian and Julie, as soon as you are done I want you to take everything out of the raft and deflate it. It won't do any good to have darkened the boat and have that inflatable stand out like a light bulb. And anyone who wants to be topside must be wearing dark clothes."

"I'll need to change," Kathy said.

"Let your mom change, and then she'll come up to relieve you," Jason said. "And by the way, get anything you may want later right now. I'll be switching the breakers off once we get started so that no one accidentally flips on a light switch."

"Where are we going?" Valerie whispered.

"I figure we'll move a little farther up the coast and put an island or two between us and Isle of Palms. I'll need to look at one of my charts."

"Maybe they didn't mean any harm."

"Shoot," Jason said, "did you see how they scrambled aboard? They'd have come on, too, if I didn't have the gun. People on friendly visits don't do like that." He paused. "Even if I was wrong about them, it's no loss."

He looked out at the horizon again. The sun dropped completely out of sight and slowly dragged its beams with it. The blue-gray clouds over the cities of Charleston and Mount Pleasant were rapidly shedding their pink and orange undersides. The cruiser, lying sideways across the creek at the slack water of high tide, had just begun its swing toward the sea again. He looked back to see Julie and Brian rolling the air out of the raft. He switched on the engine.

"I'm going to put another shirt on over this, a Navy Blue one," Valerie said.

"Good idea. Brian, just stick it down in the corner and we'll lay a dark towel over it." Jason adjusted the weight of the two guns in his pockets, then looked out over the horizon again.

Chapter Seventeen

"Father, please, help us."

It took thirty more minutes for darkness to overtake the land completely. Everyone changed clothes, covering their face and arms as much as possible. Jason would have preferred to have them wear the mud, as he had done, but he was grateful to have young eyes on deck, so he let them cover themselves as they saw fit. Keeping the engine at idle, he kept the stern of the cruiser toward the current. The banks were extremely hard to see now, only slightly less black than the infinite blackness of the water. By contrast the hull seemed to stand out like the moon, but he knew the mud paint would make it hard to see.

As he waited for Brian to haul the anchor aboard, Jason looked up at the stars. He had never seen the stars so bright over the city and wondered why it took a power outage to enjoy them. The quiet rattle of the anchor chain refocused his thoughts.

Looking forward into the gloom Jason could barely see Brian's limbs moving as he put the anchor away. The anchor and chain went quiet and Jason heard the muffled thump of the locker lid. Then he saw the teen, silhouetted against the stars, stand up and make his way to the cockpit.

"I decided to put the mud on after all," the teen said.

"I can tell," Jason said. "I could barely see you up forward."

"Good." Brian lifted his arm and pointed off to the left

of the cruiser. "We're getting kind of close to that port bank."

Jason looked over but couldn't tell. "Thanks. Stay up there to watch, will you?" He turned to Valerie on the cushioned bench. "Here we go."

A gentle, metallic clunk came from the stern as the engine slipped into gear. Jason steered the boat away from the bank, then he brought the controller back to neutral and let the big boat drift out with the tide. All was silent except for the deep throb of the engine at idle and the light offshore breeze rustling the grass.

"Dad, boat," Brian said.

Jason looked up and saw the teen's black figure pointing away toward the south. He looked in that direction but could see nothing. "Which way is headed?"

"I'm not sure. I..." Brian hesitated. "'I can see his red running light and his white stern light. He seems to be coming up the Intracoastal Waterway. He's moving fast."

"Good work," Jason said. "Let me know if he turns toward us."

"How will I know if he's...?" Brian stopped himself short. "I can see the green light now, too."

"Damn," Jason cursed. "I'm sorry, Lord. Father, please, help us." He put the boat into forward gear again.

As the cruiser emerged from the mouth of the creek Jason turned to the right, farther up the main creek instead of out toward the main channel. He increased the motor's speed, but only a little. "Where is he?"

"I think," Brian said, "I think he's stopping."

Jason increased the engine RPM's a little more. Ahead the creek seemed to be veering to the left. He could see a little easier now with the banks farther apart and the brighter stars reflecting off the water. Ahead and next to the left bank, an island had formed where a high bank had split away from the main bank. Jason steered to come in behind the island. He knew it wasn't much, but it might be enough.

"I think he's moving again," Brian said. "Yeah, I can only see the red and white lights now."

"He's coming up the creek," Jason said.

"I love you, Jason," Valerie said.

Jason looked over but could not make out her form

against the mud-darkened interior of the boat. "I love you, too." He reached over to pat her at arm but couldn't find it. "It's going to be all right." He put his hand back on the wheel and put his right hand on the controller. By now the sound of the approaching boat could clearly be heard coming up the creek.

"Brian, eyes ahead, now, I want to come in upstream of this island. Watch for snags."

"All right," Brian whispered. "He's right there."

Jason stole a glance behind them. Not one hundred yards off the stern he could see the other boat slowing down as it approached the creek that had been the cruiser's anchorage. Its engine slowed to idle and Jason could hear a distinct *click-click* of a weapon across the water. The white stern light swung around and then both lights disappeared behind the creek bank.

"How's it look, Brian?"

"We're a couple of boat lengths past the island," Brian said. "I can't know how deep it is."

Jason steered left toward the creek bank, easing off the throttle as he did so. He turned the boat's bow upstream again and heard Kathy's voice from the transom, surprisingly calm.

"Here they come again."

Jason turned his head to look and saw the other boat backing out of the small creek. The white light seemed unnaturally bright against the darkness and the red bow light blazed angrily. Jason cut the engine and let the boat drift. He had no idea how close he was to the bank. The cruiser seemed to be holding its breath.

In the other boat angry voices could be heard over the idling outboard motor. "I was there the whole time, wasn't I? I'm telling you they didn't come that way."

There was an angry growl and then another voice that Jason couldn't make out.

"It's too narrow for a boat that size," said the first voice that Jason now recognized to be Billy's. "They had to have gone upstream on this here creek."

"Girls, get below now. Get into our stateroom. Brian, come down here."

As the ladies scrambled through the companionway,

Jason whispered, "Pray."

"We will," Julie whispered.

Brian climbed down into the cockpit. Jason heard a jumble of voices from the other boat, then its engine cut off. The creek became completely quiet, save for the light rustling of the breeze in the grass and the gentle lapping of the water against the hull.

Jason leaned toward the companionway and gave a "shh" to the ladies below. Then he pushed the door to without latching it. By now the other boat had drifted a little farther down the creek so that he could only see the lights of it sporadically through the bushes on the tiny island.

"Give me the light," said a voice on the boat. Soon after a beam of white light broke out and began to feel its way along the opposite bank from the cruiser. Farther and farther up it reached along the curve of the bank until the island interrupted it. The broken beam of light swept over the cruiser, its stern facing the other boat, and Jason caught his breath. But the light continued along the near side of the bank and winked out as it returned from where it came.

"You must've painted the stern extra thick," Jason whispered.

"I can't believe they didn't see us."

"One time in the Navy we painted our whole ship black for the same reason."

"They're probably gone by now," Billy said, "but I'm telling you they're up this here creek. I know it."

"Give me that chart," snapped the other voice, and Jason could see the white light directed downwards into the cockpit.

Just then Jason felt a change in the motion of the cruiser. It was a dampening movement and Jason's heart stopped.

"What was that?" Brian whispered.

"The stern drive just went into the mud."

"Can you raise it?"

"Not without making noise." He looked back and forth between the island and the bank. "And I don't know which way we'll swing."

The motor on the other boat roared into life and Jason could make out the white stern light swing around until the red and green running lights were visible again. He reached

135

down with his left hand and took the twenty-two revolver from his pocket. He bumped the butt of the gun against Brian's chest and felt the teen's hands close around it.

"Take this," Jason whispered. "It's got the twenty-two magnums in it. I checked it myself."

Brian took the gun and Jason took out his thirty-eight. "Don't do anything until I tell you. But when I tell you, shoot for that spotlight. Shoot at it until it goes out. Then get down behind the generator."

"All right."

"Remember you have to cock it every time you fire."

"I know how."

"Are you nervous?"

"No," Brian said, nervously.

"It's going to be all right. These pigs have come to do us harm," Jason said through clenched teeth. He knew that anger could be a potent force to drive out fear. He hoped to instill it in his son. "We have a right to defend ourselves. We have a right to kill them."

Jason looked over at the other boat. It was proceeding up the far side of the creek where the scour of the tidal currents would have made a deeper channel. The spotlight was still directed down into the cockpit as the men studied their chart.

"Once you knock that light out, I come up firing. I need to preserve my night vision to shoot accurately."

As they watched the boat, Jason began to notice a change in the attitude of the cruiser. The foot of the stern drive had created a pivot point, and the gentle push of the breeze was slowly pointing the bow toward the bank. Once it pivoted so far, the tidal current took over and brought the bow farther along. The combined effect kept the stern facing the intruder. A warm glow filled Jason's heart as he realized that the cruiser was presenting the narrowest outline possible.

As the boat slowly motored past, only a mere thirty yards or so from the cruiser, the spotlight broke out again. But this time it pointed farther up the creek, past where the cruiser lay fixed to the bottom. Jason breathed a sigh of relief as he watched the boat moving farther away. He stared at it until it passed around another bend to the right.

"All right. We've got to get off this bank before the tide

136

leaves us stranded here." Jason turned to face the wheel and switched the motor on. "Thank you, Father." Then he turned to Brian. "Tell the girls that they've passed us, but we are going to get out of here before they come back. Then you come back up."

Brian held the revolver out for Jason to take.

"Stick it in your pocket for now," Jason said, doing the same with the thirty-eight. Brian stepped below. Jason put the boat in reverse and increased the throttle. The boat strained, but did not break loose. He pressed the button that adjusted the stern drive and raised it incrementally. If the propeller came clear of the water before the stern drive broke free of the mud then they would be stuck there for another six hours. He raised the stern drive some more and estimated that it must be nearly forty-five degrees to the vertical position. There could only be a few inches of water under the keel. He increased the RPM's again and felt the boat break free. He backed into the deeper water just as Brian came up again.

"Get on the foredeck. Tell me if you see them."

As Brian climbed on to the foredeck Jason lowered the stern drive and put the boat into forward gear. Even at low RPM's the boat moved swiftly with the current.

"I see the green and the white stern light so they're still moving up the creek."

"Excellent," Jason said. "We're going for the ICW so watch ahead a little for me, too. But let me know if they turn around."

"I will."

Jason increased the engine's speed and steered into the main channel. In five minutes they were traveling the wide Intracoastal Waterway heading northeast, away from the city and all they knew.

Chapter Eighteen

"This is an alliance like the world has never seen."

Jason looked up from the chart he was studying to check his watch. Three forty-five a.m. found the cruiser completely quiet and gently swinging at its anchor, the horizon calm in all directions. The chart had been laid out on the dashboard under the windshield and he stood in front of the closed companionway to read it. His left hand held a penlight, his fingers closed around the bulb so that only the smallest amount of light would shine out between his fingers. For additional caution, a large dark beach towel was spread over the windshield. He looked up every few minutes to scan the horizon, but all remained quiet. The breeze had died down and the only movements that could be heard or seen were the occasional swirling of a fish and the silent procession of stars gliding slowly into the west.

They had anchored off a small island known as Marys Island. It lay to the immediate North of Dewees Island where several channels met to form two large intersections and three small islands, Marys Island being the southern most. The four channels each joined the Intracoastal Waterway.

Jason had decided to stop here because he was leery about finding a new anchorage in the dark in unfamiliar waters. This spot allowed him to see a long way down the ICW while remaining hidden from any traffic from the city. And there were many escape routes. He studied the chart with great indecision. Billy and his crew had thrown a whole new complication into his short and long term plans, vague as the long term plans were. He needed to find a place farther away from the city, less accessible to boat traffic, yet not too far from the supplies that would surely be needed in the future. It was a tall order, and the kids' desire to be nearer to a beach made it taller still. The obvious answer was to head up to Bulls Bay, but where to anchor in that large area of open water, salt marsh, wooded islands, and endless miles of creeks was difficult to pinpoint. He sighed aloud and switched off the penlight.

He took one good look around with the binoculars, and then sat in the captain's chair. Reaching over to the cushioned bench, he grabbed a blanket and threw it over him. Jason sat quietly and reflected on the previous evening's events. The excitement had died down and the corresponding depression rose to take its place. They had seen no more of the other boat and decided to wait until morning to continue. In retrospect he wished that Valerie had elected to spend the early morning watch with him, but they had agreed upon a watch schedule shortly after anchoring and he had gone right to bed. Brian and Kathy had taken the first watch, too keyed up to sleep, and Julie volunteered to take the mid-watch, but Valerie had been reluctant until Jason told her that he would take the morning watch at three a.m. He said that he would get the boat underway at dawn while they all slept in. Besides, he thought that paired up they would be less likely to fall asleep while on watch.

He had reminded them that in the Navy during wartime, the penalty for falling asleep on watch was death. This was, he had reasoned, because if the watch stander was asleep and the enemy came everyone could die. And with that admonition still ringing in their ears, he went off to his bunk for a fitful night of tossing and turning.

He had been marginally awake when Valerie had come to bed sometime later. She had crawled into the low compartment and taken her place in the bunk beside him, but before she settled down to sleep she kissed him on the mouth. It was a long, tender kiss and it had stirred him out of his twilight slumber. He had returned the kiss and had wondered if it would go further, but Valerie simply told him

139

she loved him and bade him goodnight. He returned the sentiment, but the kiss had not helped him to fall asleep.

But eventually he had fallen asleep and did not rouse when she had gone on deck for her watch. When it was his turn she had gently shaken him awake, and then made room for him to come out.

The routine reminded him of his days in the Navy, without the kisses, of course. Instead, one got a jolt in the ribs when it was time to relieve the watch. But, the coffee would have been better, as the Navy ships kept fresh coffee in the pots twenty-four hours a day. For his watch this morning he had stirred some instant coffee into a cup of lukewarm water and had gulped it down without cream or sugar. Gritty and bitter, it had served more as a restorative for mental alertness than as an enjoyable beverage.

He thought about the in port watches he had stood while stationed aboard the *USS Bowen* at the old Charleston Naval Base. His favorite in port watch was Main Deck Rover Watch. Although the M-14 rifle was heavy to carry around, the freedom to roam around the ship was worth the extra weight. He strove to keep a good watch for terrorists, but in the process he would comb the water and sky for animals or birds, as well. He used the mounted binoculars, the "Big Eyes" to look at the stars and planets.

Once Jason had been on the Main Deck Rover Watch when the ship was tied to a pier in Guantanamo Bay, Cuba. A friend who was fishing had hooked a barracuda from the forecastle and Jason had leant him a long boat hook to bring it aboard. Another friend joined and two of them, not Jason who was on watch, managed to bring the four-foot long fish onto the pier. The officer of the deck met them at the quarterdeck and told them to "get that fish off of the ship." Jason could still see the barracuda snapping its jaws defiantly at the officer.

The memory pleased Jason. Then he thought about the hours on watch he had spent reading parts of his green Gideon's Bible that had been given to him in boot camp. "My soul shall be satisfied as with marrow and fatness; and my mouth shall praise thee with joyful lips: When I remember Thee upon my bed, and meditate on Thee in the night watches," he said aloud, quoting Psalm 63. "Thank

140

you, Father, for those memories. It was good being a young man in the service in those days. Or does it always look better in retrospect?"

He thought about how lucky he had been as a young man, and then he thought of Jeremy and his heart darkened. What was his son doing this very night? Was he well? Jason longed to speak to him, to know he was all right.

"Father, please cover Jeremy with your protection, as you've protected us. Please help him to remember we love him." Then Jason was struck with a thought. What if he came out to find them? He wouldn't be able to, the cruiser being hidden. "Father, please help us to get in contact with him. Somehow, Lord, I've got to know how he is." Jason reflected on his words, then said, "Thank you for protecting him and guiding him, Lord."

Jason sat quietly for a few minutes, and then he stood again and swept the horizon with the binoculars. Seeing nothing, he set them down and picked up the radio from the cushioned bench. He switched it on and sat back down in the captain's chair, tuning it to the station where he had before heard the preacher. The station seemed to be broadcasting twenty-four hours a day. As Jason listened he heard two men speaking as in an interview.

"Well, maybe it isn't obvious to most people in the world, but it should be obvious to anyone familiar with the Book of Revelation. The appearance of this person, whom the Muslims are calling 'Isa,' is lining up perfectly with Bible Prophecy."

"And Isa is the name Muslims use for Jesus."

"Exactly. Now to the Muslims, this person lines up perfectly with their Koranic prophecies. These prophecies state that Jesus will return to the earth in bodily form and join with the Muslim Messiah, the one we know as Al-Mahdi, to fight with and destroy Dajjal, which is the devil. Their prophecies state that he will arise in Damascus, which was fulfilled yesterday. It also states that Isa will perform great miracles and signs to convince people of who he is, and as we saw in broadcasts throughout the day, this is occurring as well. And mark my words, sometime in the next few days, as he rises in stature, people will ask him to lead the Great Caliphate in its Jihad against the Devil and

141

everyone who stands against Islam."

"But I thought that role was being fulfilled by the Al-Mahdi."

"It is, and will be. But, as Islamic prophecy predicts, Isa will decline the leadership role, saying that he only wants to serve the cause of Islam. And, he will give his full support to the leadership of the Mahdi."

"How can we expect this to be received in the West?"

"Well, never underestimate the power of signs and wonders on the carnal mind. People who don't know Christ personally will be easily fooled. They will see the signs and wonders and miracles as proof of the Isa's divinity."

"But even devils can perform signs and wonders."

"Exactly. That's why true believers look to scripture for their answers. Jesus promised that the Holy Spirit would guide us into all truth, but most people nowadays aren't looking to scripture for truth. They hear a speech by some religious leader and take it as fact, and many will be led astray that way."

"Earlier you said that this Mahdi was the son of perdition whom Paul spoke of. Could you please elaborate?"

"Yes. In Second Thessalonians chapter two, versus three and four, the Apostle Paul says 'Let no man deceive you by any means: for that day shall not come, except there come a falling away first, and that man of sin be revealed, the son of perdition; Who opposeth and exalteth himself above all that is called God, or that is worshipped; so that he as God sitteth in the temple of God, shewing himself that he is God.' We have seen the falling away from the faith, not only in our culture, but across the world. This is important because fewer and fewer people know the truth and are able to expose the lies of the devil and his Antichrist."

"Which is this Isa?"

"No. Remember that according to Koranic prophesy, Isa is Christ returned and the Mahdi is their Islamic Messiah. But we need to compare these events to the Bible, and particularly the Book of Revelation. In that Holy Book, the Antichrist is a political and military leader. It is the false prophet who is the religious leader who performs miracles and convinces the world to follow the Anti-Christ."

"And the false prophet is this Isa."

142

"Exactly. He will hold sway over millions, even some professing to be Christians. He will convince them by his words and conduct and miracles to put their trust in the Antichrist."

"But true followers of Christ know better. For even Jesus Christ himself said in Matthew chapter twenty-four, verses twenty-three and twenty-four, 'Then if any man shall say unto you, Lo, here is Christ, or there, believe it not. For there shall arise false Christs, and false prophets, and shall shew great signs and wonders; insomuch that, if it were possible, they shall deceive the very elect.'"

"Exactly. Verse twenty-seven says, 'For as the lightning cometh out of the east, and shineth even unto the west; so shall also the coming of the Son of man be.'"

"I love that verse."

"Me, too. The 'humble servant' portrait of Christ has been done already. The Lord Jesus came that way the first time to start His Church. But when He comes again, He will come on the clouds, in Glory, riding a white horse, wearing a vesture dipped in blood."

"Amen. Revelation chapter nineteen says He is coming in Glory to judge and to make war. He will put down the rebellion on the earth and establish His throne, a kingdom which shall last a thousand years."

"Hallelujah! I get so excited by those passages."

"Me, too. We're close now. Please, come, Lord Jesus."

"Yes. Come, Lord Jesus."

"Yes," Jason said, "please come quickly, Lord Jesus."

"And now we are going to take a little break with some sacred music. When we return, we'll continue our talk about the Al-Mahdi and his confederation of nations he is drawing together. Who are the nations and what are the implications of this? We'll be back in a short while."

Jason set the radio down and stood up to take another sweep of the horizon. To the southwest all was still dark and he could see the stars right down to the land. A line of high cirrus clouds was moving in, their wispy fingers winking out the stars, or relighting them, like ghostly hands playing some slow, celestial adagio. Jason watched the steadily unfolding scene for a few moments, seeing if the music from the radio played in time to the heavenly display. It didn't, so he

143

continued his sweep. To the east, the first gray light of predawn began to brighten the sky and he was glad to see it. Although he wasn't sleepy, he felt weary, and he knew that even a little bit of comfortable rest would send him into a delicious slumber. The coming of the daylight would shake it off, but for now, he sighed and continued his sweep of the horizon.

Once satisfied that all was clear, he placed the binoculars down on the cushioned bench and took up the radio again. The music was going on longer than he could have wished. It was an old hymn, being interpreted by a large orchestra. The arrangement was grand and melodic and was full of much musical ornamentation but Jason found it boring. He figured it might be a while yet before the program continued so he put his finger on the tuning dial and began to scan slowly. He soon came to a weak news station.

"Three people were killed today and nearly a dozen were severely injured as police cracked down on this second day of violent protests across Paris. The uprising began Monday following the arrest of Imam Abdul al-Sabbah at one of the largest mosques in the country. As has been the policy of French Authorities throughout the last decade, al-Sabbah was held for deportation and the mosque was closed following a series of statements made by the Imam that the government classified as inflammatory and seditious."

A man's voice speaking to a crowd in Arabic came on with an English interpretation. "The Lights Out Attack in America," the voice said "was a judgment of Allah against The Great Satan, as was the Nine-Eleven attack. Judgment now waits at France's door. France must bow to Islam and the will of Allah."

The correspondent continued, "Since the Nine-Eleven attacks were carried out by Islamic terrorists, and The Lights Out attack was an act of war, the government deemed that the Imam's statements were a call to violence, one which officials could not ignore. The Imam was seized, the mosque was boarded up, and police officers were posted to keep people away. The protests began soon afterward as the faithful began gathering in the streets surrounding the mosque. Al-Sabbah had not even boarded the plane before the clashes broke out, and some here believe that the Imam

144

himself was directing them. As additional police were called in to disperse the crowd, rocks and Molotov cocktails were thrown at them, and before the end of the day rubber bullets and tear gas were used in an effort to quell the violence. The riots triggered demonstrations at several other mosques in Paris, as well as in Lyons, Marseilles and Toulouse. In Lyons, rubber bullets and water cannons were used against the demonstrators, but the violence continues to spread. France's Interior Minister is urging the nation's Imams to call their followers to peace and a restoration of order. This came as military reservists are being called up for active duty throughout the country."

Jason had to adjust the dial to stay with the fading signal.

"In other news, workers in Riyadh are continuing to clear away debris and rubble from the site where a violent explosion destroyed the Saudi Royal Family Palace, presumably killing everyone inside. The Saudi Interior Minister announced today that the rescue mission has been officially downgraded to a recovery mission and the Saudi government has yet to release an official death toll of those lost in the blast. Of particular concern is the question of how many members of The Royal Family were inside the palace at the time of the explosion. Three members of the Saudi Royal Family were abroad at the time, although two have been assassinated in the last seven hours. The third, last seen in Italy, has presumably gone into hiding."

Jason played with the dial as the signal weakened, but eventually it was lost in the background static. Once it was gone he turned back to the preacher. The signal was still audible, but was noticeably weaker. The music was gone now and the two speakers had resumed their conversation.

"The fact that he has given his blessing to this sham government being set up in Mecca is proof of his intentions. He doesn't care about what has happened to the Saudi Royal Family."

"It does seem that he's in a hurry. He's urging alliances between governments that are in open rebellion to existing established authorities, in violation of those nations' constitutions."

"Exactly. And how many of those rebellious provisional governments are staffed by Al-Qaeda or other Wahhabi

145

members? I know that two prominent Al-Qaeda members are being set up as ministers in this new Medina government."

"And that's a crucial point. But of this alliance, what nations are involved and what are the roles each is expected to play?"

"Well, the centerpiece of this Alliance is the Arabian Peninsula, which includes the nation of Saudi Arabia."

"What are they calling it now?"

"The Islamic Republic of Arabia, which has absorbed all of the smaller kingdoms, emirates, and countries on the entire peninsula."

"Those emirs and kings allowed themselves to be absorbed into this new nation?"

"That's what I am told. And that's not really as far-fetched as it sounds to the Western mind. In the great Caliphates of the past, a Pasha would rule the Islamic World from one location and the local potentates would stay in power where they were, provided they gave their allegiance to the Pasha. It is a well-ordered hierarchical government, and everyone knows his place and is happy in it. Where one falls in the structure is manifest as the Will of Allah. And this Mahdi is far more powerful than any Pasha or even Caliphate of the past."

"Such an alliance puts half of the world's oil reserves under one flag."

"Yes, and that is on the Arabian Peninsula alone. Most of the other nations that are being wooed to join are oil producers. Iran, Iraq, Indonesia and Nigeria were among the first to join. And they are politically strategic nations, giving Al-Mahdi sway over a variety of people groups. Other nations that are not big oil producers, but who have great commercial connections and strong standing armies include Egypt, Pakistan, Syria, Algeria, Morocco, Sudan, and Libya. This is an alliance like the world has never seen."

"You said earlier that seven of these nations have been chosen to form a Pan-Islamic Security Council. How is that significant?"

"It's significant because the book of Revelation tells us that the Beast will have seven heads and ten horns. Seven nations will lead the alliance and ten others will provide

146

military and logistical support. If you count the number of Islamic nations signing with this Alliance, you will see the number is seventeen, excluding the ones already absorbed by the IRA."

"Is there any truth to the rumors that the Al-Mahdi is preparing a peace treaty with Israel?"

"I have seen no evidence of that as of yet, but it wouldn't surprise me. He is probably waiting until his alliance is completed where he can be in a stronger position to negotiate. The Nation of Palestine will be a chip and the real prize will be Jerusalem."

"I can't see the Israelis agreeing to that."

"We shall see. Remember, if this alliance looks frightening from a distance, imagine how it must look when it surrounds you."

"Mmm," the announcer grunted. "We've heard about other nations, non-Islamic nations, trying to get in with this alliance, Venezuela for instance. How do you see that playing out?"

"I'm sure their participation would be welcomed, but I can't see them being received as full members of the alliance. Instead, they would probably be relegated to some satellite role. Like many Christian groups in the Middle East in the past, they would be allowed to participate economically, but at the cost of a heavy tribute. By joining they would be essentially buying protection."

"It seems Venezuela would be quite a prize for the Mahdi."

"Yes. It would give him even greater control over oil production. And that's a large bargaining chip."

"Doctor, I'm so glad you could join us."

"It's been my pleasure."

"Now we'll be taking a short break, and when we return, we'll examine the unprecedented trip by the Isa to the Christian leaders of Rome, Athens, Moscow, and London. Back in a moment."

The music started again and Jason stood up to look around. The sky was getting lighter and to the east the sun began to break over the edge of the horizon. Jason started the engine and let it idle, then quietly pulled up the anchor and stored it away in its locker. He went back to the captain's

147

chair and put the boat into gear. Looking out to the southeast between the islands he saw an oily smooth sea. Far offshore a breeze chopped the surface into small ripples that reflected the sunlight like shifting fragments of broken glass. The ocean was beautiful, and Jason's heart yearned to be upon it. He took a long look, and then turned the wheel and headed inland once more.

Chapter Nineteen

"I think there's a road somewhere on this island."

It was after eight a.m. when Valerie came up on deck. Her hair was rumpled from sleep and as she rubbed her eyes she looked like a young girl. He smiled to see her. She closed the door behind her and stepped over to him, embracing him tightly. She kissed him, a quick peck on the lips out of concern for morning breath, and then held him tightly again. It made him happy to feel her close to him.

"How are you doing?" she asked him.

"I'm all right now that the sun is up."

"So, where are we?" she asked, looking out ahead of the boat.

"Somewhere behind Bulls Island. We'll follow this creek out to where it joins a small bay not far from the ocean."

"Really? How far?"

"Only about a couple of hundred yards, I think. Not far."

"Maybe we can go for a walk on the beach later," she said, caressing his back.

"I'd like that," he said.

"I was proud of you last night," she said.

He shrugged. "I felt pretty inadequate."

"You were wonderful."

He nodded but said nothing. She embraced him again.

"Remember that time," he began, "when we ran off to Beaufort for the weekend?"

"Yes, I do," Valerie said. "I think the lady at the front desk of the hotel thought we were running away to have an affair."

"We were," Jason said with a smile. "We were running away from the kids."

"I'd like to go back there again," Valerie said.

"Me, too," Jason said, not wanting to consider the impossibility of it.

He heard the click of the companionway latch and looked to see Julie coming up on deck.

"Oh, hi," she said. "I hope I'm not interrupting anything."

"No," Valerie said, still holding Jason, "you're all right."

Julie stepped past them on her way to the transom and looked out over the creek. "Wow, what a pretty morning."

"It is pretty," Jason said.

Valerie looked up at Jason. "I want to make you something nice for breakfast."

"Like what?"

"I'm not sure, yet, but I'll look around and find something good."

"All right, then. Thanks."

"I'll help you, Valerie," Julie said.

Breakfast was as good as anyone could have made it. Kathy got up to help Valerie, and Brian took a trick at the wheel so Jason could eat. Valerie had tried to make homemade pancakes, but did not have all of the necessary ingredients. Milk was substituted with powdered milk and water and eggs were substituted the same way to make a type of scrambled egg dish, complete with salt and pepper. But, unfortunately, there was no substitute for baking powder, so the pancakes were flat and more resembled crepes. Fried Spam slices served as a side dish.
Valerie was disappointed. "Had I known that I didn't bring baking powder I wouldn't have tried it."

"These are good," Kathy said.

Being up most of the night had given Jason a powerful appetite and he appreciated the effort. He sliced the Spam long ways and laid a piece in a crepe. Then he rolled it up and held it to his mouth like a cigar. "You should try them this way. It's good."

"You need a light?" Brian said, with a grin.

"Yes, please," Jason said, biting the end off of the pancake roll.

"I don't like Spam," Kathy said.

"You need to eat everything that's put before you," Valerie said, pointing to her daughter's plate. "You'll become iron-deficient again."

Jason finished his breakfast and looked out ahead where the creek was joining with a larger creek. "Brian," he said, stepping forward to where the chart still lay on the dashboard, "go right at this channel."

Brian nodded.

Valerie stepped up next to him and studied the chart. "Have you decided where we will be going?"

Jason shifted the chart over so she could see. "There was another place I saw earlier this morning. Where was it? Oh, that's right. See this small bay here, next to Bulls Bay? It's got a couple of different escape routes. I think that's important."

"Is there a beach nearby?"

"Not in this small bay." He ran his finger along the chart as he spoke. "But either we can take the raft along the coast to this little indent here, which is where the beach starts, or we could go ashore right here and walk to the beach area. There are some old roads and trails marked on the chart."

"Why not just anchor next to the indent?"

Jason unfolded the chart some more. "Because if we anchored there we would be immediately visible to any one who entered Bulls Bay from any direction. I would rather be hidden as much as possible."

"I see."

They followed the large creek behind the southern end of Bulls Island, and the successively smaller creeks that drained and filled the salt marshes, until they came to the narrowest of the streams that would connect to the system of creeks behind the northern end of the island. Over this vast gray brown expanse stretched a seemingly endless carpet of saw grass broken only by small groups of trees here and there. The narrowest of the creeks was more than enough for the cruiser, even at low tide, and they emerged into the small bay at a little after eleven a.m. As they passed the southern

151

end of the small island that sat in the middle of the small bay, Kathy sat up and pointed to the south.

"Hey, there's a dock back there," she said. Everyone turned around to look. Jason picked up the binoculars but saw neither boat nor person.

"Does anyone live on that island?" Valerie asked.

"I didn't think so," Jason said.

"No one lives on it," Brian answered. "The dock is there for the ferry boat that takes tourists out."

"How do you know this?" Jason asked.

"I went on a field trip out there for school."

"I would have liked to have gone with you on that trip."

"They wouldn't let you have the day off, remember?"

Jason nodded. "Well, maybe I can see it today. What's over there?"

"There are some old buildings that were built by a man in the nineteen twenties. And some fresh water ponds loaded with alligators."

"Hmm," Jason said, still studying the view with the binoculars.

"Did you want to go back to look at the dock?" Brian asked.

"No. Go on up to where the mouth of this bay meets Bulls Bay, where that open water is ahead," Jason said, pointing. "I'd like to anchor there."

"Look how clear the water is!" Julie said.

Jason looked down at the water and thought that he could see the bottom through the rippling green water. It was an unusual sight in the Charleston area, and it made him wish he'd brought his mask and snorkel and fins. With three large rivers emptying into it the harbor of Charleston was always too muddy for good underwater visibility.

"I want to go swimming," Kathy said.

"Me, too," Valerie said.

Jason directed his eyes back up toward the unbroken line of trees on Bulls Island. Where the trees extended out to the salt marsh the ground seemed swampy, but farther inland the ground seemed to rise and he wondered if it dried out as well.

"Brian," he said, "what are the woods like on that island?"

"I don't know. Like any woods, I guess."

"Like the woods next to our house?"

"No, not as wet."

"That's excellent."

"But it's marshy around those ponds."

"Naturally. What other kinds of animals are out there?"

"They told us lots of migratory birds, deer, rabbits, and the like. They said there had been red wolves, too, but not in a long time."

"That sounds great." He turned to Valerie. "This may be a good spot for us to stay awhile. We can eat well here, too."

"The deer?" she said.

"Sure, why not?"

"Well, you don't have a rifle or a shotgun."

"I have the twenty-two magnum. Your dad's friend kills deer with a twenty-two magnum."

"Yes, but he shoots them through the bathroom window."

"The bathroom window?" Julie asked.

"Yes," Kathy said. "Where he lives they come right up to the house."

"Well," Jason said, looking back out over the island, "we'll see."

"We're getting kind of close to the entrance, Dad," Brain said. "Where do you want to drop anchor?"

Jason looked around, and then pointed to a small cove where a stand of trees reached out to about fifty yards from the water of the small bay. The marsh here seemed drier, and there was a small crescent-shaped indent where a short, white sandy beach had formed. He turned to Valerie.

"There's your beach."

Valerie studied the coast where several such beaches had formed. "That's all the beach there is?"

Jason pointed as he spoke. "No. The beach starts out in the larger bay and runs continuously around to the far side of the island, where we were this morning. But this will be good for the moment." He winked at her and climbed up to the foredeck. He went to the bow as Brian eased back on the throttle. The water was clear and Jason watched closely for rocks or any other underwater obstruction, but there was only white sand. A small bit of chop was blowing in from

153

the larger bay and occasionally a wave would hit the hull just right, sending a hissing spray over the bow. Jason could taste the salt on his lips and the warm sunlight on his skin and it made him smile.

As the cruiser neared the beach Jason gave a signal for Brian to round up into the wind. The water here was sheltered from the wind and chop and he told Brian to put the boat in neutral. Then he let the anchor go and watched it settle on the bottom.

Jason could see the anchor and chain lying on the sand, seeming to move away from the boat. As the rope, polished from much use, passed through his fingers, he held it once and watched the tension cause the anchor flukes to dig into the sand. Then he released the line again, satisfied that the anchor would hold well. The convenience of anchoring in clear water pleased him. He let out the proper amount of line, cleated it, and then returned to the cockpit.

"You can kill the engine now," he said to Brian. "Well done."

"I want to go swimming," Kathy repeated.

"I want to go in the woods," Brian said.

"I want to do those things, too," Jason said, "but after last night I think we should have some new rules. I thought about it a lot this morning."

"What new rules?" Kathy asked.

"Well, for starters, we all need to be alert. Everyone is responsible for keeping an eye out during the day. And I think we should keep with the watches at night." Everyone groaned at this. "At least for a few days, to make sure we're not being followed. Next, we need to make sure no one goes off alone. We should always have two wherever we go or whatever we decide to do."

"We've always done that," Kathy said.

"I, just yesterday, went for a walk alone," Jason said. "Next, any group that goes out of sight of the boat needs to have a gun. You all know how to shoot the revolvers, except you, Julie."

"I want to learn," Julie said.

"I'm sure you'll have the chance, but from now on, we keep the pistols close."

"So, I guess there is no way to get off this crowded boat

154

and spend some time by myself," Kathy said.

"Not now, honey," Jason said. "I'm sorry, but it has to be that way, at least for a little while."

"Once we see that everything is all right," Valerie said, "then maybe we can have some time to ourselves." She looked over at Jason to see if he agreed.

"Sure," Jason said, "but in the meantime you could get away from the boat a short way. But for now I recommend staying within shouting distance."

"So what are we going to do right now?" Kathy asked.

"What do you want to do?"

"I want to go swimming."

Jason gestured with his hand toward the water. "Carry on."

"I want to go in the woods," Brian said.

"I would like to have a look around the island," Jason said. He looked at Valerie. "Want to come?"

Valerie looked out at the water. "I would really like to go swimming."

"All right, I'll leave the thirty-eight with you. You both know how to shoot it." He took the revolver out of his pocket and handed it to her. "It's loaded. Keep it handy but try not to let it get wet with the spray. I need to clean them both out and oil them."

Valerie took the weapon gingerly and placed it on a towel on the cushioned bench.

"What about you, Julie?" Kathy asked. "You want to go swimming?"

"Later, definitely, when it gets hot. But for now I would like to see some of the island."

"Well, let's get ready," Jason said. "If you will put us on the beach, Valerie, then you can keep the boat. We won't need it." Valerie nodded. He turned to Brian. "I'm going to get the twenty-two long rifle cylinder and some extra bullets."

"Can I shoot squirrels if we see any?" asked the teen.

"Sure. Your mother can show you how to clean them."

"Oh, yippee," Valerie said.

*

155

Twenty minutes later Jason, Brian, and Julie ascended the muddy bank above the white beach at the cove of Bulls Island. Jason turned around to watch Valerie motor up to the swim platform and tie off, then he turned back around to face the island.

Brian and Julie had already started ahead. The ground felt firm here but Jason knew that it could get softer at high tide. The saw grass continued before them to the nearest tree line, surrounding the clusters of sable palms closely, but farther in the grass thinned out completely. The trees there were surrounded by brush and grew more thickly at the start of the high ground.

Ahead near the first line of trees Jason could see Brian swatting at the mosquitoes. The teen looked back at Jason, and Jason signaled for him to keep going. Despite the mosquitoes the going was easier through the outer trees.

Soon they were on to the higher ground and pushing through the heavy brush. The low branches scraped against their legs and arms and the mosquitoes still had not let up.

"I don't remember it being this thick," Brian said, shoving aside branches with his bare hands.

"Sometimes it's thick around the edge of the woods but more open once we get in deep," said Jason. "If it doesn't thin out we'll go back and find another place."

"Don't we have a machete?"

"It's still in the garage. I didn't think to bring it on the boat with us."

They continued and after a few minutes the brush thinned out, making the way easier. Only occasionally did they have to skirt around thick briars or creepers.

The trees were arranged into consecutive lines, like huge fingers that stretched out from the central part of the island to the northeast end. Between the thick lines of trees lay either salt marsh, as near the anchorage, or grassy shaded meadows on the higher ground. The lines had been formed over the centuries as the topography of the bay and islands shifted. Tidal currents and the occasional storm had formed the bays, and the oyster beds had taken root in them. The beds trapped and held silt, which became a haven for the saw grass. The grass solidified the silt into salt marsh, which, in turn, allowed the trees to grow. The trees moved out farther

156

to claim the marsh, bringing the brush with them and forming the high ground. And the ocean tidal currents and the occasional storm chewed away whatever it could in an ever evolving, ever renewing seascape.

As they cut across one of the high ground clearings Jason looked toward each end for signs of wildlife. There were plenty of squirrels and birds, but he could see nothing larger. Ahead of them, the slender trail of a deer path threaded into the next finger of woods. Jason pointed it out to Brian. "Let's see where that trail follows."

"Where does it lead?" Julie asked.

"I'm not sure, yet," Jason said. "I think there's a road somewhere on this island."

"There are several dirt roads," Brian said. "I think we're coming up on one now."

A few moments later they emerged onto a narrow dirt road. To the left it seemed to go straight for a long way, and Jason could see where the trees opened out at the far end. To the right the road curved to the left and cut out any view in that direction.

"Which way?" Brian asked.

Jason pointed to the right. "That way is back toward the dock, is that correct?"

"Yes," Brian said, "and the old buildings."

"I'd like to see that later." Jason looked down the road to the left. "But let's go this way first, and we can get a good look around in the open. I'd like to see how bad the boat sticks out."

"Sounds good," Julie said.

Before they started down the road, Jason stopped and took out a pocketknife and scraped the bark from a pine tree near where they had left the woods. Then he went into the trees and marked another one that showed the direction they had come. Satisfied, he rejoined the other two on the road. "Better than bread crumbs," he said. "Let's go."

Chapter Twenty

"Justice and prosperity under the Islamic banner."

They moved swiftly along the road and after a mile or so they emerged from the trees to an area overlooking another marsh. The road ran along a causeway that separated the marsh into two parts. To the left was salt marsh that extended only a few dozen yards to where it met the broad expanse of Bulls Bay. To the right several dozen yards of marsh lead to a fresh water pond where several turtles were clustered together on a log. Ahead the pond joined with the causeway where a large alligator lay across the road warming in the noonday sun.

"How are we going to get past?" asked Julie.

"We'll make a little noise and he'll move."

"They're afraid of us?"

"Sure. It's in the Bible," Jason said. "In Genesis, after the fall, God said He would fill all the animals with a dread of us."

Jason stepped forward and gave out a loud, "Hey!" The alligator opened his eyes slowly, one eye fixed on Jason, but he did not move.

"Hey!" Jason shouted again, this time waving his arms as he stepped forward. The great reptile watched him for a few moments longer, then turned and retreated for the safety of the pond. It dove down, but then surfaced again out away from the bank. It turned sideways to them, only its eyes and nostrils clear of the water, and watched Jason intently.

158

"Look at all of them!" Julie said, pointing out over the pond.

Jason looked out and could see dozens of eye and nostril combinations in assorted sizes, low in the water and easy to miss.

"Is it safe to go any further?" Julie asked.

"Yes," Jason said. "We'll just stay to the center of the road. I really want to take in the view of the small bay from out here. Come on." Jason loosened the revolver in his pocket and walked on.

The trees on the saltwater side extended out a little farther than on the freshwater side and just past them the bay came right up to the road forming a small, protected cove. On the far side of the cove began a beach that separated the salt marsh from the bay and it continued up the coast until it passed out of sight around the northeast point of the island.

"This would've been a nice place to anchor," Brian said.

"Yes, but we would be instantly visible to anyone coming out on the bay from any of those creeks over there," Jason said, pointing back toward the mainland. "We're not totally invisible where we are, but at least we're hidden from much of the larger bay."

They walked forward until Jason could see back in the direction of the cruiser. He took out his binoculars and studied the anchorage area. "Look. You can't see the boat from here. It's on the other side of that point."

The other two looked as Jason did a scan of the entire Bulls Bay. He searched slowly along the whole panorama, then lowered the binoculars. "Looks like we're all alone. What say we head back and have some lunch? I'm getting hungry."

"I'm not really hungry," Brian said. "And I was kind of hoping to maybe bag a few squirrels for dinner."

"You'll have to get quite a few," Jason said. "There's not much meat on them."

"I know, but I'd still like to try. One of those clearings we saw looked promising."

"All right. We'll head back that way. Here," Jason said, handing Brian the revolver. "Put the long rifle cylinder in it before you hunt. Save the mags for the big stuff."

Brian nodded and took the revolver and extra cylinder

159

and stuck the plastic box of bullets in his pocket. Then the three of them started back down the road into the woods. After a few minutes they came to the trail and, turning onto it, soon came to the clearing. Jason pointed to a place near the edge of the trees and whispered.

"I guess I'll find a place to sit down and rest."

"Why don't you just go back to the boat? I'll be all right here."

"No. We don't want to leave anyone out here alone."

"I'll stay with him," Julie said. "He can teach me how to shoot as well."

"Are you sure?"

"Yeah," Brian said, "we'll be fine. Besides, I know how you old guys get cranky if you don't eat. Ha-ha!"

Jason chuckled and shook his head. "Okay, I'll head back. I've got stuff to do on the boat anyway. Be careful and don't stay out too long." He nodded to Julie. "And be sure you teach her the Rules of Gun Safety before you let her shoot."

"Safety first," Julie said.

"Exactly," Jason said. "Have fun and good luck."

Jason headed back to the boat as Julie and Brian found a concealed place in the brush to still-hunt.

*

Thirty minutes later Jason was back aboard the cruiser. He had found Kathy and Valerie sunning themselves on the small patch of beach and after the usual consolations to Valerie about leaving Brian in the woods with a gun he took the inflatable boat out to the cruiser.

He topped off the boat's fuel tank with five of the portable tanks in the engine compartment and then did the same with the water jugs. Then he moved the generator back to its place against the transom and picked up the short wave radio. He searched for a clear signal and soon found one in French with an English translation.

"The Mahdi met with leaders of nine European nations in Cairo, Egypt today to discuss his proposal for ending the unrest that has plagued the European continent for the last forty-eight hours. In addition to halting the current violence that has rocked every capital city in Europe, he made guarantees that he could prevent any further outbreaks. As a sign of good faith, the Mahdi gave orders that the rioters in Marseille should disperse and go home. Within an hour the streets of that city were quiet, broken glass in the streets, overturned cars, and the occasional burned-out storefront being the only evidence there had been any trouble at all. With his bargaining power thus assured, the Mahdi began to list his demands. These included the immediate expulsion of all Jews from the nations attending, and a withdrawal of all political, military, and economic support of the State of Israel. Despite the controversial nature of the demands, three of the nations have already agreed to them, and the other six are still waiting for official approval from their own governments."

Jason shook his head. His stomach growled so he picked up the radio and brought it below, setting it on the salon table as he made a sandwich.

"In other news," continued the announcer, "the Isa concluded his visit with the College of Cardinals in Rome today and left a favorable impression with the Vatican's governing body."

Another voice came on the air, an older man speaking in Italian. A younger man's voice gave the translation. "We were surprised when he spoke to us. His wisdom and grace certainly had appeal, but there was a spiritual magnetism about him that we could not deny. We have always expected our Lord Jesus Christ to come again in power and glory, but as for this man, who can deny his reasoning, his gracefulness, and his absolute love for people? He even performed a miracle in St. Peter's Basilica. What are we to make of him? This is the question that is dividing us, and many are searching the scriptures for answers before we can have any hope of an official ruling. But there is one thing we can agree on, he has a magnetic sway over everyone."

The announcer continued. "The Isa met with the Pope in a closed door session, but details of that meeting have not been disclosed at this time."

Jason shook his head. Then he took the sandwich, along with a can of fruit and the radio and ascended the steps to the cockpit area. He sat on one of the folding chairs in the stern

161

and placed the radio on the top of the transom next to the towels drying in the sun. He took a sip of the juice in the can and began to eat while he listened to the next report.

"In the United States today, Imams across the country began appealing to Americans, particularly in the inner cities, to embrace Islam. As one Imam put it, 'Americans need to join with the holy wave of Islamic righteousness, or be drowned under it.' Speaking from makeshift mosques and handing out free food, the Imams promised a new day of justice and prosperity under the Islamic banner."

Jason heard a rhythmic splashing approach the boat and then felt someone climbing on to the swim platform. He looked up to see Kathy standing behind the transom, dripping wet.

"Why didn't you yell? I would have come to get you," Jason said.

"I wanted to swim," Kathy said, taking a towel and tossing it up around her shoulders. As the towel came up and around, the end of it brushed against the radio's antennae, toppling it over into the water next to the boat.

Jason heard the soft slash and froze. His eyes met Kathy's as she paused, her face puzzled for a moment. Then he saw her look down over the side and gasp. Jason stood up and looked down into the water. On the sandy bottom lay the radio, face up; it's shiny, metallic antennae seeming to waver beneath the ripples.

"Oh, Dad, I'm sorry. I didn't mean to hit it."

Jason sighed. "It's not your fault. I shouldn't have put it up there."

"What are we going to do?"

"I guess we are going to do without it."

"Do you want me to go in after it? I know I can get to it."

Jason studied the wavering image of the radio. He could remove the battery and flush it in fresh water to remove the salt, but he doubted if the digital components would survive. He frowned and said, "No."

"Are you sure?"

"Yes, it's ruined. Don't bother with it."

"I'm sorry, Dad."

He looked at her and shook his head, "Don't worry

about it. It wasn't your fault." He rubbed his face with his hand. "I was dumb to put it there."

"What are we going to do about the news?"

"I don't know. Maybe we'll...." His sentence broke off and he waved his hand for emphasis, but no words came. "We'll find something."

"I'm sorry."

Jason put his hand around her shoulder and hugged her across the transom. "It's all right, really. I'll just ask God if I can have another one. Maybe I'll get one with automatic fine control."

Kathy nodded but said nothing. Jason kissed her on the side of her head and released her.

"I guess I'd better go change." Kathy climbed across the transom and disappeared below.

Jason sat down to finish his lunch. He studied the small bay and then looked up at the sky. The sun felt warm and the afternoon sea breeze had not developed yet.

"Hey," Valerie called from the beach.

Jason looked toward the shore and saw Valerie waving to him. Beyond he could see Julie coming through the outer strand of trees alone. She walked quickly.

"Come get me, will you?" Valerie said.

Jason nodded and waved, then climbed over the transom and into the raft. He motored over to the beach, bringing the nose of the raft on to the sand just as Julie stepped onto the beach from the marsh.

"Wait up!" Julie said.

"Where's Brian?" Jason asked.

"He's still back in the woods. He stumbled over a root and turned his ankle."

"How bad?" Valerie asked.

"Not bad. It's not even swollen. He just wanted you to come have a look at it before he tried to walk all the way back."

"I don't have my shoes," Valerie said.

"He asked for you," Julie said to Jason. "We moved to a different place, but I'll take you there."

"All right." Jason rose from the boat and stepped onto the sand. "I'll go have a look at him."

Valerie nodded and stepped into the raft. Jason pushed it

off from the shore, and then he and Julie started off toward the trees.

Chapter Twenty-One

"But God is faithful."

The pluff mud, much softer now with the high tide, made the going slower. It tired Jason by the time he reached the second tree line, but they plunged into the woods of the high ground without hesitation.

They emerged from the trees into the first clearing and Jason stopped to look down the meadow for Brian. Seeing no one, he pushed ahead but soon realized that Julie had fallen behind. "Which way?" he said.

Julie, out of breath, pointed to the trees beyond the clearing. Jason turned to look in that direction and heard Julie stumble to the ground. He looked back and saw her on her hands and knees, a large root at her feet. She looked up at him and sighed as he stepped over to her and held out his hand.

"You all right?" he asked her. "I don't want to have to carry both of you back," he said with a smile.

She took his hand, but then sat back on her haunches. She kissed the palm once, then twice, and a look of yearning supplication came over her face.

Jason looked down into her eyes and felt a fluttering sensation in his heart, and at that moment he recognized the origin of the feelings that had been rising from his heart like a geyser. The sensations, coupled with the burning desire, and the images, the images, the images, all came at him in a flood. A seeming infinity of pages from scores of magazines, endless passages from stacks of books, scenes from videos uncountable, all these passed through his mind, and with them came the feverish desire to see more. His face went flush, his heart pounded, and his breathing ceased altogether as he looked into the yearning eyes of this beautiful young woman kneeling in submission before him.

But he had mastered this. He had repented of it, renounced it, been anointed as a seal against it. In every way he had been healed of the addiction, yet the same driving spirit that was behind all of those images was standing before him now, alluring him, enticing him, and controlling his mind. It was narcotic.

Taking his other hand in hers, Julie slowly pulled herself to her feet. Then, still holding his hands, she snaked her arms around him, embracing him across the small of his back. She pressed herself to him, her body against his, her face snuggling against his neck and Jason nearly swooned. She released his hands and embraced him tightly around his lower back.

In that moment, just before the last thread of will power was about to break, a scripture came to mind. "But God is faithful, who will not suffer you to be tempted above that ye are able; but will with the temptation also make a way to escape, that ye may be able to bear it." Jason hesitated, wavering back away from the cliff.

Julie seemed to sense the hesitation and drew her face away from the nape of his neck. She looked into his eyes, her face so close to his that his eyes could not focus. Then she leaned forward and placed her mouth on his in a slow, lingering kiss. Jason felt a deep stirring, his mind began to swoon, and he inched toward the cliff again.

In that moment, a different image flashed into his mind. A boat, at night, floating backward down a tidal creek, its motor's foot pivoting in the sand, keeping the invisible stern facing a passing enemy bent on bloodshed and violence.

All is lost, he thought, and a new flood of feelings began to rise up on him. Anger, loss, pain, all mixed into a form of anguish that threatened to tear his soul apart. He pulled his face away from hers and tried to take a step backward, but still she clung.

"No," he mouthed, uttering the word but with no sound.

166

He shook his head.

"We both want this," Julie said, softly.

"No," he whispered, again trying to step back from her. But Julie, still holding him tightly, leaned in again and began to kiss the nape of his neck.

Through clenched teeth, Jason growled, "I said no!" He grabbed her shoulders and tried to pry her from him, but she held on tightly. Finally, mustering all of his strength, Jason shoved her back. Her foot tripped over a root and she crumpled awkwardly to the ground.

The anguish that now flooded Jason's heart and mind exploded through him, driving out all lust and desire and unrighteousness before it. In tears he shouted down at the girl, "I rebuke you, devil, in Jesus' Name! In His Holy Name I command you to leave us alone! Be gone from us, and return no more, in Jesus' Name!"

Julie looked up at him and Jason watched her face transform from shock and amazement, to humiliation, shame, and finally to profound grief. As her eyes welled with tears, she lowered her head and covering her face with her hand, began to weep bitterly.

Jason stood looking at her for a few moments, unsure of what to do next. Her crying became groaning sobs as some great wellspring of pain, long-suppressed, was broken up and released. She never once looked up at him. Her hand remained over her down turned face and her body shuddered with deep sobbing of loss, pain, and remorse. As Jason watched her, his heart began to melt. No longer was she the temptress, alluring him to his own destruction, but a young woman, not unlike his own daughter, broken and beaten down, trying to remain unfractured in an abusive and uncaring world. He began to weep for her, the emotional wrangling of the last few minutes splintering any shred of self-composure. He knelt beside her and put his hand on her shoulder. She continued to cry bitterly, and he let her cry.

After what seemed like several minutes, Julie gathered herself enough to speak. "I'm sorry," she whispered between sobs. "I'm so sorry."

Jason, too, began to gather himself. He took a few deep breaths and patted her shoulder. "It's all right now."

But Julie shook her head slowly and began a new round

167

of sobbing. He patted her shoulder in a fatherly way as he searched for words that would comfort her. Unsure of what to say, he silently prayed. And then an idea occurred to him to start with the basics. He drew a breath to speak.

"Julie, God loves you so much," he began. "He's pursued you all of your life, and He wants so much to be a part of your world. You're His daughter, and He is so proud of who you are. God doesn't love anyone more than he loves you."

"How could He love me?" Julie said, still covering her face with her hands.

"He can love you because He's known you from the beginning. He knows all the good things about you. He knows the hurts, the disappointments, and the struggles. Every tear you've cried He's cried with you. If you let Him into your heart, he will forgive you of all of the sins of the past. You will start a new life with His hope, His guidance, and His grace.

"You don't know the things I have done."

"It doesn't matter. Jesus, who never did anything wrong, and was holy before God, took the punishment for your sins, and mine. He shed His blood to wash away all of your sins, so that you can stand before God the Father, clean, holy, and just as if you had never sinned. Then the Holy Spirit of God will come in to share His life with you. It's truly the best way to live, and the only way to die."

Jason paused a moment, then said, "We weren't meant to live in this fallen world. We were meant to live in Eden, in a life of wholeness, with God at the center."

Jason paused again, allowing her to consider his words. After a few moments, he asked softly, "Will you accept Jesus Christ as your Lord and Savior, letting Him forgive you of all sin?"

Julie let her hand fall away, but kept her eyes focused on the ground. She shrugged her shoulders.

A thought came to Jason, warming his heart. "I wish you could hear his laughter of delight over you."

Julie gave no reaction.

Just then the report of a gunshot came at them through the trees. To Jason it sounded like the light pop of a twenty-two long rifle cartridge and not the sharp crack of the twenty-two magnum round. It did not sound very far off. Jason felt that it was too soon to break the moment, but the silence lingered on and became awkward.

"I guess Brian got his squirrel," Jason said, patting her shoulder again. "I guess we should check on him." He stood up and held out his hand to her. She took it and rose to her feet, wiping the tears from her eyes with her hands.

"I take it he's that way," Jason said, pointing.

Julie nodded, still not looking up at him. "He's all right," she whispered. "His ankle, I mean. It's all right."

Jason took a step toward her and put one arm around her shoulders, hugging her to him. "I love you, Julie. You've always been like another daughter to us. I always want it to be that way."

She nodded, still keeping her eyes to the ground, but said nothing.

Jason kissed her on the side of her head, and then released her. "Let's go find that boy." They started across the clearing together.

As they walked through the grass Jason felt a singing lightness in his heart that he could barely contain, as if he were basking in God's pleasure over him again. He knew that he had broken through a barrier within himself, and thereby kept his family's safety intact, and he wanted to celebrate. But it would be a celebration between him and God alone, and that would be enough. He stole a glance heavenward and smiled.

At the far side of the clearing Julie led Jason into the trees. A few snipe flew up and away from them, but otherwise he saw little wildlife beside the occasional spider web stretched between the trees. They were making a lot of noise, and rightly so to prevent being shot by his over-enthusiastic son. For insurance, he whistled loudly. It was a sharp, high-pitched whistle like one might do at a sporting event.

Julie looked back at him, puzzled.

"I want to make sure he knows we're coming," Jason said.

After a few minutes they emerged into the next clearing. Julie stopped for a moment to look around. The meadow was empty of wildlife.

169

"Where do you think he is?" Jason asked.

Julie pointed across the clearing, a little farther down. "Do you see that fallen log and the stump next to that tree? That's where we were."

"He's probably hiding and trying to scare us."

They stepped forward out into the open meadow. As they crossed the uneven ground Jason looked at the trees ahead. He felt a puzzling sense of unease that he could not define. He searched the trees ahead but saw nothing. Julie stopped and pointed to a dead squirrel on the ground not very far from the log. There was fresh blood on the squirrel's coat.

"That must be his," Jason said, and they started toward it.

They were within a few paces of the animal when a voice boomed out from the trees. It was a loud, deep voice and it was not Brian's.

"Stop right there! Put your hands up!"

They both stopped in their tracks. Julie looked at Jason with fear in her eyes. Jason looked toward the trees to see if he could determine where the voice had come from. Suddenly there was a deafening blast from the trees nearest them. Jason felt the slap of the concussion on his face, throwing him into a temporary confusion. Behind him he could hear the spray of shotgun pellets hitting the trees.

"I said put your hands up, now!" shouted the voice. It was accompanied by a metallic *click-click* of a weapon cycling a fresh round.

Jason's hands shot up, and Julie's did the same.

"Now, turn around and get on your knees, right now!" They both did so and immediately there came a crashing noise from the tree line. A moment later Jason saw out of the corner of his eye a man descending on Julie, pushing her forward on to the ground. In the same moment he felt something strike his back between his shoulder blades driving his face down onto the grass. A knee held him to the ground while his arms were quickly jerked around behind his back. He felt his wrists being tied together with a piece of rope.

Jason tried hard to suppress the panic that welled up within him. His mind raced as he thought about Brian. Was he nearby? Could he see what was happening to them right

170

now? Jason hoped the teen would have the presence of mind to remain quiet. Someone needed to go back and warn Valerie and Kathy. He tried to turn his head to see Julie, but a root next to his face prevented him.

The knee that had been pressing into his back lifted off of him after the knot around his wrists was jerked tight.

"All right," said the man's voice to the second man. "I'll get'em on their feet. You go fetch the boy."

Jason's heart went cold. The second man spoke. His, deep voice sounded younger and he stuttered severely.

"We-w-we've got to give them the t-t-test."

"Man, I ain't fooling with that. We're taking them to the pond."

"N-n-no. We've g-g-got to give the-the-them the test."

"I told you I ain't fooling with that. Now go get the boy."

Jason felt a hand lifting him from under his arm. He staggered to his feet and turning, saw the same being done for Julie. Helping her was a young black man. He was tall, over six feet, and well muscled. His face was strikingly handsome and he wore old jeans, a T-shirt and work boots. He struggled to form his words. "M-m-momma said we've g-g-got...."

"Mama ain't here. Now git the boy and let's go."

Jason looked at the man holding him by the arm. He was an older black man, probably mid to late forties, and about as tall as Jason. He was of a stockier build than Jason, but nothing like the other man. In his waistband was Jason's twenty-two-caliber single action revolver.

The younger man stood shaking his head, and then he faced Julie. "H-h-has je-je-je...." he stammered. He grimaced and then tried again. "Has je-je-je, je-je-je...."

"Aw, come on, man!"

The younger man looked at the older one and said, "W-we've...."

"Yeah, I got it," the older man said. "Let me ask them or we'll be here all night, confound your hide." With a tug on Jason's arm the man turned to face him. His eyelids were half closed and his eyes seemed intelligent and annoyed.

"Has Jesus Christ come in the flesh?" Jason's face must have registered some surprise for the man tugged his arm

171

and said, "Don't think about it, just answer."

A sense of peace flowed over Jason's mind. "Yes. Jesus Christ has come in the flesh. He came in the flesh on this earth and His spirit has come in to my flesh and lives in my heart. He's my Lord and Savior."

"S-s-see?"

The man holding Jason's face darkened as he turned to the other. "See what? It's a fifty-fifty answer."

"Th-t-h-they...."

"Man, damn that. I'll tell you what, just to please you, we'll take them back to the house and hold them there. We'll let Mama talk to them, but if Mama don't buy it...." Here he turned to look at Jason. His eyes were still half closed but a devilish grin came over his face that reminded Jason of some mischievous voodoo witch doctor. "Then you get to tell it to the alligators."

Jason nodded. The man turned to the younger man and said, "Now go get the boy. Leave her there. She ain't going anywhere, are you, darling?"

The younger man hesitated, then released Julie and moved in to the woods. Jason took the opportunity to look around. Julie was watching him, a frightened look on her face. The man holding his arm let Jason go and walked over toward the trees where he had placed his pump shotgun. He stooped over to grab it and when he straightened up he faced Jason, his right hand adjusting the revolver in his waistband. He noticed Jason staring at the gun.

"This yours?" the man said, patting the gun. "It's nice. Thanks." He stepped over to Jason. "Of course, I prefer my handguns nickel plated, but, as a gift, this will do fine."

Jason was about to reply, but stopped when he saw Brian coming out of the trees with the young man behind him. The young man held a double-barreled shotgun pointing toward the ground instead of at Brian's back and Jason felt some relief at this. As they came toward him Jason saw an expression of fear and shame on Brian's face.

"They took your gun, Dad," he said. "I'm sorry."

"It's all right. Are you okay?"

Brian nodded.

"All right, then," the older man said, "Let's move out. We're going to follow these trees up the clearing until we

172

reach a path, then we'll hang a left. Forward march."

Chapter Twenty-Two

"Folks need to stick together in times like this."

They all began walking over the uneven ground. The younger man walked ahead with Julie and Brian close behind, and then after a small gap came Jason and the older man. Jason noted that he held the gun pointed at them, but his finger was out of the trigger guard.

"M-m-my name is Twony," the younger man to Julie said. "D-d-don't be afraid."

"Don't waste your energy talking, Twony," the older man said. "We've got a long way to go."

Twony shook his head but said no more, and the group continued in silence. The clearing grew increasingly narrow and the ground became more uneven as the tree roots met in the middle. As the walkers began to spread out, Brian slowed until Jason caught up to him. He gestured with his head to get Jason's attention and then whispered.

"What about Mom and Kathy?"

"I don't know yet. We'll have to see how these people are. But I don't want to mention them prematurely." Jason stole a glance behind him and saw the older man staring fixedly at him. Jason nodded his head and then faced forward again. He gave a subtle shake of the head to Brian, and they resumed their march in silence.

The clearing continued to narrow until it became a trail. Jason's shoes, having been wet earlier, were now rubbing blisters on his feet. He knew the other two must be tired, and

174

he hoped they wouldn't have much farther to go.

Soon they emerged onto a narrow dirt road and turned left. The road, little more than two wheel ruts with grass in the middle, made for easier walking than the trail. Jason looked back to study the place for some kind of reference, but was prodded forward by the muzzle of the older man's shotgun. He continued forward.

Judging by the light of the sky Jason could tell that the afternoon waned and he tried to calculate the time. He knew that Valerie would begin to worry, and he dreaded the thought of her sounding the air horn to beckon them to return to the boat. For the moment he had absolutely no plan for what may be ahead, but he knew that he must keep the cruiser a secret for now.

Up ahead, Twony's hand came up as a signal for all to stop. He looked back to the older man and pointed ahead. Jason looked down the road and saw a deer farther ahead. It was a doe and it was feeding along the edge of the road. Its backside was facing them.

"Forget it, Twony," the older man said. "We'll get it later. We need to get these knuckleheads back to camp first."

Twony nodded and Jason could see the disappointment in his face. But he started forward again and everyone else followed. The deer looked up at them suddenly and then darted into the woods.

Eventually, the rutted dirt road joined another one, still dirt but wider and hard packed. Jason surmised that it was the same road they had traveled earlier, only farther to the southwest. They turned right and followed the new road for what seemed like a mile until it opened onto a large grassy clearing. Here the road split, dividing to form two sides of the clearing. To the left it continued through the woods to the ocean and to the right it followed the edge of a fenced compound and then continued along the woods until it disappeared to the right.

Beyond a stand of trees at the center of the clearing rested a large, old house that seemed to be the center of some activity. Surrounding it at irregular intervals stood several makeshift shacks and tents. There were places prepared for campfires before each one, complete with a small bundle of firewood. Basins for water sat next to the doorways of the simple dwellings with cardboard or wooden boxes containing non-perishable food. A few of the places had coolers.

Jason could see people, twenty or so black folks, each engaged in some chore. Some women gathered clothes from a clothesline while others tended a chicken coop. He saw some boys at an old fashioned well pump filling the basins with water. Others delivered firewood to each of the small dwellings. In one area an older man and some young children sorted through shrimp at a table. A cast net hung from a tree branch nearby. A few looked over but most were too engaged in their work to notice them.

They were led to a picnic area as one might find in a park, with wooden tables and public restrooms. They sat down at one of the tables under a large tree and Jason kicked off his shoes. They sat for a short while waiting. The shadows around the clearing grew longer and Jason began to worry about Valerie again. He hoped she would be patient.

"Can I get some water?" Brian asked.

"Yes, please," Julie said. "I haven't had anything to drink since this morning."

"Yeah, Twony, get us all some water," the older man said. He sat on the bench wearing the same grin he had given Jason earlier.

But Twony didn't grin. Instead his face showed his keen annoyance as he turned toward the older man. He sighed deeply as he leaned over the man. "Robert, I've h-h-had just...."

"I'm only joking, man," Robert said, still grinning but now holding his hands up before him in a conciliatory gesture. "Would you please get us some water while I watch these hoodlums?"

But Twony stood there, his eyes narrowed, leaning over Robert, his right hand balled into a fist. Jason thought the younger man might hit the older one and he knew it would be a stunning blow.

"Please?" Robert said, his grin fading.

Twony held his posture a little longer and then straightened up. He gave another sigh and looked away from Robert, cocking his head to the right as he did so. "Mmm-mm-mm," he grunted with much emphasis before moving

176

away toward the old house.

The grin came back to Robert's face, but Jason looked away. Robert's antics did not impress him and he realized he would enjoy seeing Twony knock Robert off the bench. He looked around at the perimeter of trees and knew that they were closer to the ocean than they had been at the boat anchorage. Here in the open clearing Jason could feel the afternoon sea breeze and he was grateful for it. Out of the direct sunlight with a breeze made the temperature quite comfortable.

They all rested quietly until Twony returned with a pitcher of water. He offered it to Julie first, holding it up to her mouth and tilting it so she could drink. When she had finished Twony offered it to Brian. Robert made as if to speak, but a grim look from Twony made him hold his peace. The pitcher was passed to Jason's mouth, and he drank the water deeply. The water tasted bad, almost brackish, and Jason deduced that it must be from the well he had seen, but it was cool and wet and he was grateful for it. When he could drink no more he raised his head and the pitcher was taken away.

"Thank you," Jason said.

Twony nodded kindly and handed the pitcher to Robert. The man looked inside and grimaced as if to complain that there wasn't enough left, then he raised it to his face and took a few swallows. When he was finished he poured what was left of it on the ground.

Twony had reached out to take the pitcher, but then froze. His expression darkened, surprising Robert when he turned back to face him.

"What?" the older man said. "I thought you were finished. I thought everyone was finished."

Twony snatched the pitcher from Robert. "I-I-I'm getting tired of your grief."

Robert stood up and held out his hand for the pitcher. "Let me get you some more. I'll go fetch a second round for everyone."

Before Twony could answer they noticed a man, rotund and sweating profusely, coming up the road. He came running around a curve from the direction of the dock and the mainland and had a short rifle slung on one shoulder.

When he came within earshot he called out.

"Robert, Twony! Come on out to the boats. Hurry!"

"What's wrong?" Robert called.

"There's a boat anchored up by the far end of the island." He noticed Jason and the other two and stopped running. He looked at Jason and pointed to the north. "Is that your boat up there?"

"Yes, it is."

"What happened to it?"

Jason started in alarm. He stood up. "What do you mean, what happened to it?"

"Well, it looks like King Kong evacuated his bowels on it."

Jason was puzzled for a moment, and then began to laugh. "No, that's mud. We were trying to keep it hidden at night." He laughed again and the other man laughed, too, He had a warm and friendly face and appeared to be in his late thirties.

"Well, we'd better go down there right away. They're unloading one of the boats to go investigate it."

"Yes, please let me go down and talk to them. I uh," Jason paused, unsure of how much information to reveal, but as he looked into the warm, brown eyes he felt a sense of trust. "I still have family on that boat."

"Let's go, then." The man waited as Julie and Brian stood up and Jason slipped his shoes back on. Then they all walked briskly down the road to the dock.

The road curved to the right into the woods, but soon emerged from the trees onto the salt marsh. It ran along the trees on the right and to the left the vista of the small bay stretched out beyond the gray mud of the marsh. Ahead the road curved left onto a causeway that led out to a cluster of docks where several men were unloading boxes and jugs from one of the boats. Some of them stopped briefly to look over at Jason's party. A small group of women and children came across the causeway, walking very slowly and carrying boxes or bundles. An older woman carrying two grocery bags led the way. Very small and frail looking, she wore thick glasses and a simple, white cotton dress. The two groups met at the end of the causeway and stopped.

The rotund man spoke first. "Mama, this man says the

178

boat's his."

The old woman looked at Jason and Twony took the grocery bags from her. "Is that true?" she said.

"Yes, ma'am. We didn't know anyone was on the island."

"Why did you come out here?"

"We figured we'd try to get away from the madness going on in the city. I thought we'd be safe out here."

"And now you got your hands tied behind your back and guns pointed at you."

"Yes, ma'am."

"You're not from around here, are you?"

"No, ma'am."

Mama nodded slowly. "I could tell by your accent." Then she turned her attention to Twony. "Antoine, did you give them the test?"

"Yes'm. Th-th-they passed, too."

"Then why are they still tied up?"

All eyes turned to Robert, who seemed to be taken by surprise by the sudden attention. "I wanted to be sure before I went to cutting them loose."

"Robert," Mama said (she pronounced his name 'roar-bet'), "if you had more faith in God then you would be sure." She faced Jason again. "Do you love the Lord?"

"Yes, ma'am, I do, very much. He's my Lord and Savior."

"Robert," she said, "cut these folks loose."

Robert lowered the gun and let it rest in the crook of his arm. Then he drew a small knife out of his pocket and cut the fastenings that held their wrists.

"Thank you," Jason said, rubbing his wrists.

"What's your name?"

"Jason Ribault. This is Julie and my son Brian."

"I am Wilhelmina Carney." She reached out and shook Jason's hand. "But most folks call me Mama Carney, or just Mama."

"It's good to meet you."

"Mark," Mama said to the rotund man, "tell the others to hold off a minute."

Mark stepped back and whistled and gestured with his hand. The men in the boat stopped and took a break.

179

"Mr. Ribault," said Mama to Jason, "please feel free to bring your boat up to the dock. You're welcome to stay with us."

"Thank you, Ms. Carney, but I don't want to impose."

"It's no imposition. Folks need to stick together in times like this."

"Well, thank you very much. I really appreciate it. And if there is anything we can do to contribute to the effort, please let me know. We'd be glad to help."

"You wouldn't happen to have a spare generator, would you?" Mark asked, his face smiling expectantly.

Jason looked at him and smiled broadly, reflecting on the irony.

Mark held his hands up before him in a disarming fashion. "Not that I'm trying to be pushy or anything."

"We've been looking for a generator for three days," Robert said.

Jason laughed. "I happen to have one on board you can have."

"Mr. Ribault," Mama said, "we don't want to take anything that would be an inconvenience to you."

"No, ma'am," Jason said. "It would be a pleasure to give it to you. We've carried it around for three days and haven't used it once. I'd love to get the deck space back."

"Man, we sure could use it," Mark said.

"It's yours. It's even full of gas. I don't remember why I brought it."

"Well, now we know," Mark said, smiling. "Thanks, brother."

"Let me bring the boat over and you can help me unload it. It's kind of heavy."

"I'll take you over now," said Mark. He held his hand out like a butler. "Right this way, good sir." Then he turned back to Mama. "We'll see you back at the house, Mama." Jason and his party moved out toward the dock while Mama and her group continued toward the camp. Twony, still carrying Mama's bags, followed her. Jason was almost to the docks when a thought occurred to him. "Can I get my gun back, Robert?"

Robert looked puzzled for a moment, and then remembered. "Sure." He pulled the gun out of his waistband

180

and handed it to Jason, butt first.

"Thanks," Jason said, sticking it down into his pocket.

"Is that all you've got?" Mark asked, gesturing toward the revolver.

"I've got a thirty-eight aboard the boat."

"You'll need more than that. We'll hook you up."

They continued toward the dock where six men had resumed unloading supplies from the two boats. One boat was a white center console fishing boat and the other was an old workboat with a low cabin forward. Everyone helped put the supplies on to the dock, and then Mark spoke.

"If you guys get this stuff back to the camp, I'll take Mr. Jason and his family up to bring his boat back here."

"That's your boat?" asked one of the men.

"Yes, sir."

"Why is it...?"

Mark held up his hand and suppressed a chuckle. "We already covered that, boys. It's a night camouflage motif."

"Humph," another man said. "Must be a good one."

"It is," Jason said.

"He's going to let us have a generator out of the boat," Robert said.

"Oh?" another man said. "That's nice. Thanks. When you get back we'll help you carry it up to the house."

"Thanks."

Mark climbed into the white center console boat and motioned to Jason to do the same. Jason climbed in, followed by Brian and Julie. Despite its dirty and stripped down appearance, the boat seemed seaworthy. Mark started the motor as Robert and another man cast them off. Mark engaged the reverse gear and backed the boat out into the creek. Then he turned the wheel, shifted the lever forward and steered toward the small bay.

"Maybe we can get a bite to eat," Brian said. "I'm starving."

"Save your appetite for back at the camp. There'll be plenty of food. Good stuff, too." Mark winked. "You didn't think you could get away without being fed, did you? And you bringing a generator?"

"It's not a big generator," Jason said.

"It's ten times what we have now."

181

As the boat came into the small bay Mark steered right and headed toward the cruiser. The boat moved slowly through the water causing only small ripples on the glassy surface. Night was starting to fall across the salt marshes and Jason turned to see the sun as it fell below the horizon. Already one lone star shone overhead in the clear sky. The air still felt warm from the heat of the day, but the boat's motion through the water caused an apparent light breeze that made it comfortable. Behind Jason, on the island, he could hear crickets starting to chirp.

Mark turned his head to look at the setting sun. "It's beautiful, isn't it?"

"Yes, it is," Jason said.

"It's amazing the things we see once the television is off."

"Amen to that."

As they neared the cruiser Jason could see Valerie and Kathy on deck behind the transom. They stood still, their faces tense, and Jason could see Valerie's right arm held behind her. "Hey, Sweetie," he called.

"Where have you been?" asked she. "I've been worried."

"I met some friends. I'll explain later."

Mark brought the boat gently up to the swim platform and Jason, Brian and Julie climbed out. Valerie stepped back and placed the thirty-eight revolver on the cushioned bench. Jason stepped over to the captain's chair.

"We're going to go to that dock we saw," Jason said. "I think you'll like it there."

"Are you guys coming right now?" Mark asked.

"Yes, if that's okay."

"That's perfect. I'll head back and help you tie up."

Chapter Twenty-Three

"It's like we had a bomb lying dormant in our midst."

Fifteen minutes later Jason eased the cruiser up to the dock where Mark and the others stood. In the near dark of dusk he saw Robert make a comment to another man. The other man looked at the cruiser and chuckled. Brian and Kathy tossed the lines to them and they pulled the boat in, cleating it securely. Although Jason had explained everything to Valerie as they motored in, she still seemed surprised when four men climbed into their boat and gathered next to the generator.

"Ma'am," Twony said, with a polite bow of the head to Valerie.

"This it?" Robert asked.

"Yes, let me give you a hand," Jason said.

"We got it." As one man, the four bent down and lifted the machine to the starboard gunwale. There, two others from the dock, joined by two from the boat, picked it up and began carrying it across the causeway. The other two climbed out of the boat and followed the procession. Only Mark remained, waiting patiently on the dock.

"Do we need to bring anything?" Jason asked.

"If there's something in particular you need or want, bring it. Otherwise, just bring yourselves, and a good appetite."

"I've got that," Brian said.

"I feel like as guests we should bring something for the

183

dinner," Valerie said.

Mark gestured with his thumb toward the causeway. "Believe me, you already brought enough for many dinners."

"Well, let's go then," Jason said, sticking the thirty-eight in his other pocket.

They all climbed out onto the dock and Jason made introductions all around.

"I'm sure glad to meet you," Mark said, as they all headed up the causeway. "When we saw your boat anchored there we didn't know what to think. There's been so much craziness going on."

"Yes," Valerie said, "people think there's no electricity so there's no law."

"Don't I know it? We've got to be on our toes whenever a boat comes near."

"You haven't seen a red center console around, have you?" Jason asked.

Mark looked at Jason. "No, why?"

"He's a bad one." Jason briefly explained the events surrounding Billy's visits.

"Well, we'll keep an eye out for him," Mark said, his face serious. "He won't be welcome here."

"It's a hard balance, isn't it?" Valerie asked. "As Christians we're supposed to be hospitable, but then we've got to protect ourselves from people bent on doing evil."

"I know," Mark said. "It seems like the only thing we can do is to prepare for the worst, but trust the Lord that everything will work out."

"Take it one day at a time," Jason said.

"Yep," Mark said. "Sometimes one moment at a time."

Although the sky was completely dark now the pale colored causeway and road were easy enough to follow. All of the stars twinkled brightly and the breeze carried the aromas of the cooking fires in the camp. Jason's mouth watered as he caught the fragrance of grilling meat and he knew Brian and Julie must be famished. As he thought about food he heard the high-pitched rumbling of an airplane engine behind him. He looked back and could see a dark smudge flying over the land. Its lights were out and it seemed to be flying down the coast from the northeast to the southwest. Mark watched the plane too.

"Wow," Jason said, "we haven't seen too many of those lately."

"We've seen a few of them," Mark said, "but mostly out over the ocean."

They watched the plane as they walked. Then Jason asked, "Did the other planes you saw have their lights out like that?"

"Hmm. There was one in the daytime that was flying way out and low. The two other ones at night were closer in and had their lights out. They were heading north. Oh, and there was one really high, like a passenger jet, going south. He had his lights on."

"Interesting. We heard everything was grounded."

"Yeah. It makes you wonder if there's a lot of activity going on behind the scenes," Mark said.

Valerie sniffed the air and said, "Mmm. That smells good."

"I'll say," Brian said.

"Well, let's go get some," Mark said and they followed him into the camp.

*

The meal tasted better than any of them could have hoped. Shrimp boiled with a collection of savory spices along with fried venison cuts provided the meats. The vegetables included sweet potatoes, corn, and fried okra, as well as some fresh cucumbers and tomatoes. Jason relished a fish stew that had okra, rice and green peppers in it. Although a wide variety of dishes furnished the table, the quantities of each were small. Conscious of this, he took only a small portion of each item, and only allowed himself a second helping of the stew. The group he and Valerie sat with included everyone he had met earlier, plus several others. They sat in a variety of chairs in a rough circle near the large old house. In the center of the circle, on the ground, sat four camp lanterns, and Jason could smell the aroma of the Citronella oil burning in them. The odor discouraged the mosquitoes, but didn't eliminate them, and the hardiest came in to bite, usually in the center of the back. But no one around him complained about the mosquitoes, and he made a

185

conscious effort to ignore them.

Midway through his second helping of stew, Jason noticed Twony leading an attractive woman into the circle from inside the house. He led her to where Jason and Valerie were eating and held up his hand toward them.

"H-h-here they are, Ms. L-Lena."

"Thank you, Twony," she said. She smiled at Jason and Valerie. "I take it you're the folks who came in on the boat?"

Jason rose and held out his hand. "Yes. My name is Jason and this is my wife Valerie. Our kids are around here somewhere."

"I'm Lena," the woman said, shaking their hands. "I don't mean to interrupt your supper, I just wanted to come and personally thank you for the generator."

"Oh, it's nothing really," Jason said.

"Yes, we weren't even using it," Valerie said.

"Well, it's a life saver for us. We had one when we first came out here, but it broke down and wouldn't generate power anymore."

"Voltage regulator," Mark said, "and we haven't been able to find parts."

"We need it," Lena continued, "to keep the insulin cold."

"Insulin?" Valerie asked.

"Yes. We have a young girl, as well as one of our elders who are diabetic. We brought a large stock of insulin, but our generator broke down after the first day."

"We've been trying to trade for ice, but we can't always get it," Mark said.

"And it's expensive when we can get it," Robert said.

"And with ice we run the risk of freezing it," Lena said. "It'll last a lot longer if we can keep it cold."

"Lena is a registered nurse," Mark said.

"We're lucky to have her," Mama said, sitting nearby.

"I'm lucky to be here, Mama," Lena said. She nodded to Jason and Valerie. "I just wanted to tell you both, thank you very much."

"You're most welcome," Jason said. "Won't you join us?"

"No, thanks. Once that old refrigerator cools down we'll transfer the insulin to it. But I'll catch up with you later." She went back to the house.

Jason and Valerie sat and returned to their dinner.

"You see, Mr. Ribault," Mama said, "community is not just doing for others, but it's letting others do for you, as well."

Jason nodded, thoughtfully. He looked around at the faces illuminated in the soft glow of the lanterns. Twony had sat down to join them, his shotgun propped up next to him. "I guess living in a community is something a lot of us have forgotten how to do."

"A disaster like this is a tough time to learn," Mark said.

"It sure caught me by surprise," Jason said.

"It caught everyone by surprise," another man said.

"Not everyone," Mama said.

Jason looked at Mama. "You think some people knew this attack was coming?"

"The attack itself, no," Mama said. "I doubt if anyone but those Koreans knew about that. But some folks have been preparing for this crazy aftermath for years."

"Really?" Valerie asked. "How so?"

Mama spoke slowly and sounded tired. "Ever since I was a young woman like yourself, Ms. Ribault, I've been told of a great war which will come to this country. We were told that it would be a war between the Black Muslims and the Black Christians, and that the Black Muslims would wipe out the Black Christians forever."

"I've heard that, too," Mark said, quietly.

"Where did you hear that?" Jason asked.

"Idle talk, occasional threats," Mama said, "literature being handed out on street corners around town."

"I've seen those people," Valerie said. They wore suits and would hand out pamphlets to people in cars stopped at traffic lights."

"Did they give you a pamphlet?" Mama asked.

"No, I rolled down my window for one but they would turn their back on me. I knew they were Muslim, though, because later I saw a pamphlet on the ground where someone had tossed it out. I wish I would've picked it up."

"I think we all wish we would've taken them more seriously," Mark said.

"They sounded like a bunch of kooks," another man said.

187

"But they were deadly serious," Mama said. "All they needed was an opportunity."

"And our North Korean friends gave them one," Jason said.

"Is that what happened to youins?" Valerie asked. "They came after you?"

"In a manner of speaking," Mama said.

"The second night after Lights Out," Mark said, "two churches near ours burned down. Black Congregations. One of them was having a prayer meeting at the time."

"They burned the church while the people were inside?" Valerie asked.

"Yes," Mark said. "We got the message. That's when we knew we had to go."

"But," Mama said, "we can't know for sure who was responsible."

"I know who one of them was," Robert said, through clenched teeth.

"You don't know for sure," another woman said.

"I know for sure," Robert said. "He was hiding the next day."

"You went after him?" Mark asked.

Robert nodded grimly.

"Who?" Twony asked.

"If I said his name, you'd know him," Robert said. "But I won't say it here."

"So are all the people here from your church?" Valerie asked.

"Yes," Mama said, "most of them. The others are family members or people from the other churches."

"What made you decide to come out here to the island?" Jason asked.

"Well," said Mark, "like you folks, when we saw the craziness starting we figured we needed to get someplace safe."

"We could expect the looting and the mayhem," Robert said. "That just seems to come naturally these days."

"That's sad, isn't it?" another woman said. "We expected looting."

"Yes, it is," Jason said. "It's like we had a bomb lying dormant in our midst. All they needed to do was to drop a

188

few nukes on us to trigger the one that was sleeping."

"And our selfishness and greed would do the rest," Mark said.

"We did this to ourselves," Mama said.

"We did it?" one man asked.

"Time was when folks would put aside their differences and come together to get the nation going again, but not anymore. Now we have a whole generation of people who have no idea how a nation is created or maintained. They don't understand that each person puts something into it, and everyone gets some benefit out of it. They merely think it was always here, it will always be here, and that somehow it owes them something."

"If they ever saw life outside of this nation, they would value it more," Robert said. "I've been overseas. I know."

"There's no place like home," one man said.

Robert sat up sharply in his chair to face the man. "There's no place like the United States!"

"I can agree to that," Jason said, remembering the poverty in the Caribbean and the Middle East. "With all of her problems, America is the best thing going."

"Was," one man said.

Jason glanced over at the man and felt a cold hollowness in his chest. He let his eyes drift down to one of the lanterns. Was, he thought.

Mark rose to his feet. "I'm ready for some coffee. Anyone else?"

"Yes," Jason said, rising. "I need some coffee."

Robert rose and they followed Mark to one of the cooking fires where several camp-style pots were suspended over a fire by a wire mesh. At a table next to the fireplace stood a collection of coffee cups and Mark, using a rag as an oven mitt, picked up a pot and began to fill them. Robert produced a sack of sugar and a tiny pitcher of goat's milk and they added them to the cups, then they arranged the cups on a small piece of plywood and carried it back to the circle.

"You want coffee, Twony?" Robert asked.

"No," the young man said, "it makes me ha-ha-have to go to the bathroom."

"To some folks that's a benefit," Robert said.

"It don't take long to hit bottom," Mark said.

189

Jason chuckled and sat down next to Valerie.

"Thanks," Valerie said as she received her cup. "I'm glad you're back. I wanted you to hear what Mama was telling us."

"Mr. Ribault, I was just telling them about the news we heard today."

"Oh, yeah," Mark said.

"What news?" Robert asked.

"We got word today," Mama said, "of a big fight that occurred near Jedburg last night. It concerned that big food distribution center up near the Interstate."

"I know where that is," Robert said. "Who was involved?"

"As I heard it," Mama said, "one of our state senators and his deputized thugs seized the place in order to control who got the food. Word has it that they were bargaining with the power company to get power restored to certain areas before others."

"Oh, that's nice," one woman said.

"Which senator was it?" Robert asked.

Mama said the name.

"I don't understand," Valerie said. "There're some power plants still running?"

"Yes, most of the power plants were unaffected by the attack," Jason said.

"It was the power distribution network that was knocked out," Robert said.

"And now," Mark said, "as they're trying to reroute power to their local areas, these fellows want to be first in line."

"Or get their friends first in line," Mama said.

"Most of the workers have been living on site since this started," another woman said. "My cousin works at one. His whole family has been staying there with him since the second night."

"They've got plenty of power but little else," Mark said.

"As soon as they're out of fuel they won't even have that," Robert said.

"But who were they fighting?" Jason asked.

"Well," Mama said, "apparently those militia groups saw what was going on and decided to move in to stop it."

"Some said the senator had no legal right to make the seizure in the first place," Mark said. "Some were saying he violated his constitutional power."

"I doubt if they'll get the case heard in court anytime soon," Mama said.

"What happened when the militia moved in?" Jason asked.

"They came in and pushed the senator's people right out," Mark said. "Then they commandeered the site, putting themselves under the authority of the governor."

"And that's where the real crisis began," Mama said. "Since the governor has not been able to exercise full control over all of the Guard, the senator was able to enlist help from at least one of the units who were willing to take his orders."

"Man," Robert said, "talk about a constitutional crisis."

"Really," Jason said. "This is beginning to sound like a Third World problem."

"We were already moving toward Third World status before this Lights Out attack," Mama said. "The seeds of it were in our selfishness and greed and ignorance."

"At all levels of society," Mark said.

"Every time someone cheated on his taxes, stole from his company, or took revenge on someone," said Mama, "we moved a little further into the darkness."

"Righteousness exalteth a nation," one woman said, quoting from the Book of Proverbs, "but sin is a reproach to any people."

"So they called in the Guard units and that's when the fight started?" asked Jason.

"That's when the fight ended," Mark said. "They brought in armored fighting vehicles and walked over the militia."

"Probably Bradleys," Robert said.

Jason shook his head. In his mind he thought of a few people he knew who had probably fought for the militia. He slapped a mosquito on his neck and sipped his coffee.

"All that for food?" Valerie asked.

"Not hardly," Mama said. "Food, like religion, can be used as a political tool."

"Put both together and you have a very strong political tool," Robert said.

"How's that?" Jason asked.

"That food will not only be used to trade for electrical power," Mark said, "it'll be shipped to those makeshift Mosques."

"That senator has ties to Islam," Mama said. "The food given out at those temporary mosques is already cooked and prepared. You come in to eat food, like at a restaurant, and not buy food, like at a grocery store."

"And while you dine," Mark said, "you are treated to Islamic Indoctrination. A few of us went there the other day."

"How long do you think it will be," Mama asked, "before you have to recite the First Pillar of Islam to get fed?"

"Or receive a mark on your hand or forehead?" a man asked.

Jason shook his head again and stared into one of the lanterns. He thought of Jeremy and wondered how he was doing in the midst of all this turmoil. Is he safe? Would he have enough to eat tonight? He sipped his coffee and felt the warmth go down into his stomach, but it would not dispel the hollow cold in his heart.

"What's amazing to me is how fast all this is coming," Valerie said. "Who would have believed it?"

"Those people pushing for change feel they have nothing to lose," Mama said. "To them this is a time, not only to rise up against oppression, but to take charge in some new national order."

"And, while most folks are just trying to hold onto what they got while they wait for the mess to straighten itself out, these people are moving at full speed to take over," Robert said.

"How did you hear all of this?" Jason asked. "About the fight, I mean."

"We've been going ashore everyday to gather supplies or trade for stuff," Mark said. "We're in contact with other people doing the same thing."

"A lot of them we knew before Lights Out," Mama said.

"When we meet them we exchange news," Mark said. "Some of them have radios and they talk to others for trade or news. That's how we found out about the fighting."

"Isn't it unsafe to be traveling around like that?" Valerie asked.

"Sometimes," Mark said, "but mostly it's not as bad as you think."

"We stay off the beaten path," Robert said, "and only deal with people we know."

"People we can trust," another man said.

"What kind of things are you gathering?" Jason asked.

"Anything that can be useful to us out here," Mark said. "Food, gas, medicine,"

"Tools, weapons," Robert said.

"Farm equipment," one man said.

"Fishing tackle," another said.

"Anything we can think of that will be useful over the long term," Mark said. "We don't really know how long we might have to stay out here."

"Where do you find this stuff?" Jason asked.

There seemed to be a hesitation at the question. Mark looked at Mama and Robert before answering. "Sorry. I just don't want what I'm about to say to be misinterpreted." He looked over at Jason and Valerie. "My uncle owns a hardware store. When he heard that we were coming out here he let us come in and take whatever we wanted. He wanted to see that our family, and church family, would be taken care of. He stayed behind and he's one of our primary contacts for news and trade. We bring him shrimp or fish or venison and he uses it to trade with others for things we need."

"Hopefully before long," Mama said, "we'll be able to trade crops, too."

"That's right," Mark said with a nod. Then his face grew somber and he looked down at one of the lanterns. "Yesterday we found a new area to explore for necessary items. It looks like it had been a nice community, but it's abandoned now."

"Abandoned?" Jason asked.

"Yes," Mark said. "Now, I don't want you to get the wrong idea. We have no desire to take things that don't belong to us."

"Or things people might be coming back for," Robert said.

"But these houses," Mark said, "there's nobody in them. Some of them have been burned down, even."

"And all of them have been looted," Robert said.

"Yes," Mark said. "We found them left open, and no one around."

"Was there anything left after they'd been looted?" Jason asked.

"Well, that depends on what you're looking for," Mark said. "If you want stereos and TVs then you're out of luck."

"Asinine people," one woman said. "What good's a TV without electricity?"

"I know," Mark said, "but the good news is that the asinine people left a lot of things that are very useful."

"Canned foods, gasoline, gardening tools," Robert said.

"Medicine," someone said.

"Fishing tackle," another said.

"All the stuff we had mentioned before," Mark said. "We're just trying to get what we need until we are able to sustain ourselves. But like I said, we didn't want to take something that belongs to someone else."

"Nor did we want to let that stuff spoil and be of no use to anyone," Robert said.

"So before we took anything we came back to ask Mama what she thought."

"That's where I was today," Mama said. "I wanted to see what everything looked like so that we could know to do what's right."

"Mama decided that the right thing for us to do would be to bury the bodies first before we took anything."

"Bodies?" Valerie asked.

Mark sensed Valerie's concern. "Not all of the places had bodies, only a few of them. The rest either looked like they had been abandoned recently or hadn't been lived in for some time. We plan to go back tomorrow. You can come with us if you like."

Jason looked at Valerie. "What do you think?"

"You can go if you want," she said, "but I think I'll stay here."

"Mostly it's been the men going, anyway" Mark said.

Jason nodded, then he noticed several flashlights

194

approaching the circle from the picnic table area. The light beams wavered around erratically and soon Jason could tell that it was a group of young people, his three charges being among them. Some of them stepped into the circle while the others stood around it.

"Watch out for that lantern," Robert said to one of them. "Dad," a teenaged boy said to Mark, "we want to go walk on the beach and see if there are any sea turtles laying eggs. Can we go?"

"You better not mess with those sea turtles, Sean," Robert said, wearing his voodoo witch doctor grin. "They bite!" He made a biting motion with his teeth.

"We won't mess with them, Uncle Robert," the teen said. "We just want to see if they're out there."

"I want your chores done first," Mark said.

"My kids can help, too," Jason said. "I want them to help."

Mark held up his hand. "We would be honored if you all would consider yourselves our guests, at least for tonight."

"I don't mind helping out," Brian said.

"I'm sure you don't," Mark said, "and I appreciate the offer, but we've already got it organized for tonight. Tomorrow we'll put you on the list."

"You get a break tonight," Robert said, still grinning. "One night only."

"Dad," Kathy said, "can we camp on the island tonight?" "Sure," Jason said, glancing over at Mark, "if that's all right with you."

"Perfectly all right. Just find a place and pitch a tent." "Thanks," Kathy said, "sometimes it's too hot on the boat."

"You can stay in my tent," Sean said to Brian. "There's plenty of room."

"All right," Brian said.

"But first you've got to help us set up ours," Kathy said. "You can help them while Sean is doing his chores," Jason said.

"That'll work," Sean said. "It won't take me long. Then we'll head to the beach."

"We'll come, too," Kathy said.

"I want you to bring your rifle, son," Mark said. "Just in case."

195

"I-I-I'll go with them," Twony said.

"Dad, Sean has a twenty-two rifle of his own!" Brian said. "Semi-automatic!"

"Pretty neat," Jason said.

"If you kids are going to camp on the island," Valerie said, "then I need to help you dig out the camping gear."

*

It took nearly an hour for the Ribault family to break out all the camping gear and carry it to the intended campsite. It took another twenty-five minutes, longer than usual in the darkness, to set up the tent. Jason stood up and looked at the tent. "I take it you girls can furnish it yourselves."

"Uh-huh," Kathy said. "Thanks, Dad."

"You're welcome. I hope it's cooler for you."

"I think it will be," Kathy said. "They said there's always a nice breeze coming off of the land at night."

"That's true," Sean said.

"Dad, can we go now?" Brian asked.

"I guess so, but don't stay out too late. If you're coming with me then we need to get up early. And here, take this." Jason handed him the single action revolver. "Do you still have the other cylinder?"

"Yes, and the bullets," Brian said, patting his pocket.

"All right, be careful. I'm going to bed."

"We will," the boys said. "Goodnight."

"Wait for me," Valerie said to Jason, stepping up beside him. They bade goodnight to some of the others and then headed back to the dock, the moon casting a pale light on the path. As they left the clearing Valerie took his arm in hers.

"I guess we have the boat to ourselves tonight," she said, looking up at him in the darkness. Jason felt a squeeze on his arm. He looked at her darkened form, silhouetted against the pale gray marsh, and leaned forward to kiss her.

196

Chapter Twenty-Four

"Every one of them was beheaded."

The early morning air, cool and still, hung heavy in the mist-filled creeks of the salt marsh, muffling the quiet rumble of the boats' engines. Jason wore a long-sleeved work shirt over his T-shirt to help keep warm, but only denim shorts covered his legs, and running his hands over them he felt the tiny droplets of moisture clinging to the hairs.

He sat on the deck of the lead boat with his back against the starboard hull. Robert sat steering from the center console, the only seat on board, and concentrated on the water ahead. To Jason's right, in the bow, Sean and Brian each lay sleeping against a collection of empty containers and sacks that were covered by a tarp. Across from him on the deck sat Mark scribbling on a notepad. He wrote with great concentration and would pause every so often to study his work. He looked up to see Jason watching him.

"What are you writing?" Jason asked.

"I'm making a list of things we need to be on the look out for," he said. "There are some specifics, but mostly this is a general list. Canned food, baby formula, some machine tools, and the like, but I was trying to remember how many were still without bedding."

"What about winter clothes?" Jason asked. "It's going to get cold before long."

"I've got that," Mark said. "From the beginning we've

197

tried to approach this thing with a long-term view. We figured that if we planned short-term, and the situation dragged out, then we would be in trouble, but if we planned for the long term, then we'd be all right either way."

"That's the way to do it," Jason said. "Would you put down a short-wave radio for me? I lost mine."

Mark jotted the request on the notepad. "Got it."

"Thanks." Jason looked back at the other boat following slowly about thirty yards behind. "How long will it take to get there?"

Mark looked at his watch. "About forty-five minutes to an hour. You ought to try to catch a nap like those two." He said, nodding toward the bow of the boat. "I'm going to as soon as I finish this."

Jason closed his eyes and rested his head back against the hull and in a few minutes the sound of the engine and the water lapping the hull put him to sleep.

*

A little before eight a.m., the boat came alongside a wooden dock that stretched out over the pluff mud from a small park on the shore. The park, part of an upscale subdivision, featured some playground equipment and a picnic area with grills and tables. A pickup truck was parked on the grass and as Jason watched, two black men got out and began walking casually down the dock toward them. Mark waved to them as he and Jason tied the boats to the dock. Robert had switched on two FRS radios and handed one of them to Sean.

"Do you remember how to operate it?" he asked the teen.

"Yes, sir."

"Good. We'll call you boys when we're ready."

"We're not going with you?" Brian asked.

"Not at first," Robert said.

"We're going to check everything out," Jason said. "Then we'll call you when all's clear." He noticed the butt of the single action revolver sticking out of Brian's pocket and gestured toward it. "That's got the magnum rounds in it so no plinking. Self-defense only." Brian nodded.

"We'll fish while we wait for them," Sean said, pointing to the fishing rods in the stern of the boat. He clipped the radio to his pocket and the two of them went to retrieve the tackle. A teenaged boy from the other boat joined them.

The men from the boats headed up the dock. They reached the other men and Mark introduced them to Jason. Then they all continued toward the park. Like Mark's group they were each armed with a shoulder weapon and one or two side arms. One of the men from the truck noticed the butt of Jason's thirty-eight sticking out of his pocket.

"Is that the only gun you've got?"

"Yeah," Jason said.

"We're going to try to fix him up with something better today," Mark said.

"Good luck," the man said. "Everything's been picked over pretty good."

"It might not matter anyway," the other man said. "They're ramping up the gun-grab they started the other day."

"What do you mean?" Jason asked.

"The cops downtown have been going door to door rounding up all of the firearms they could find," said the man. "It started a few days ago in the streets. Now they're going house to house."

"But that's illegal," Jason said.

"Sure it is," said the man, "but when six or eight cops bust in the door, all armed with M-16 rifles and protected with body armor, see how far that illegal argument goes."

"I guess we're not supposed to protect ourselves," Robert said.

"Oh, no," said the other man, sarcastically, "you won't have to. The trusty police will always be there in every situation to protect you whenever you need them."

"And they bring the authority of the law," said the first man, "whatever that means anymore."

They continued up the dock in silence. As they came to the pick up truck Jason noticed a novelty license tag on the front bumper that read, "I fight poverty – I work!" Mark got in the cab with the two men and the others, eight including Jason, climbed into the bed of the truck with some shovels and a pickaxe. The man started the engine and drove slowly

199

through the small park and onto the main road of the subdivision.

Jason looked around at the new development and saw many lots that had yet to be built on and many more that had yet to be cleared. Most of the finished homes he saw were two stories and looked very expensive. They were clustered among a few cul de sacs and a side street that branched off of the main road. All of the houses looked either abandoned or not yet sold and only a few had not been broken into. Most of them looked undamaged but as they neared the front entrance the number of open doors and broken windows increased, as did the debris scattered across the front lawns.

The truck stopped several houses in from the main entrance and everyone climbed out. Riding in the back of the truck Jason had not been able to see the houses near the main entrance, but standing on the road he could see them now. The first seven homes had been burned almost to the ground and the rest of them had been vandalized considerably. At the elegantly landscaped entrance stood a truck riddled with bullet holes. Tire tracks marked the grass in front of houses. Mark stepped up to Jason and pointed to one of the last burned out homes.

"There were only four houses burnt when we first found this place," he said. "See those mounds in the front yard? That's where we buried the bodies we found inside. We had no way to know who they were so we decided that having them in the front yard may provide some identity to them, in case anyone ever asks." Mark looked into Jason's eyes. "Every one of them was beheaded. That's why we wanted the boys to stay behind until we went through these other houses."

Jason shook his head slowly. "I guess that's a calling card for them." He looked around thoughtfully. "So where do we begin today?"

"Well, the vandals seem to be working their way back from the main road, so I guess we need to keep working ahead of them."

"Do you think there will be bodies in all of them?"

"No, I don't. It looks like there was some fighting up here, but the rest of the neighborhood seems to have just packed up and left." Mark put his hand on Jason's shoulder.

200

"It's all right if you want hang back."

"No," Jason said. "I'm here to work. But I was just curious to have a look at the shell cases near that truck."

"Go ahead. We'll be starting with these next two, here, whenever you're ready."

"Thanks." Jason walked toward the beautifully landscaped median that formed the front entrance and read the name of the subdivision embossed on a rustic stone wall. Behind the wall a large oak tree shaded a terraced cluster of shrubs. In front of the wall and next to the truck he saw another fresh burial mound. At the end of the median nearest to him was a sign that read, "Have a great day!" The truck had come to rest half on and half off of the road and at right angles to the wall and there were brass rifle cases scattered in the grass. The splash of dried blood on the ground, the tiny streaks of silver on the pavement, and the locations of the various shell cases told the story.

The truck and at least one other vehicle had driven into the subdivision and had stopped at the main entrance. Whether they had started shooting at the houses from the street or had rushed the houses directly was unclear, but they clearly were well armed with AK-47 and M-16 assault rifles. Someone from this house had come out with a shotgun and had put up some resistance, even hitting one shooter at the truck, but the firepower of the intruders had overwhelmed him. Someone with a .357 Magnum had come in and dispatched the rest of the family inside, and then reloaded while standing in the front yard. They then presumably took what they wanted and fled the scene, leaving their dead comrade behind.

Jason winced as he looked at the variety of sizes of the graves in the front yard. Obviously, the entire family lay buried there and one of the mounds was small enough to contain a toddler. He stared at it and a sickening gloom began to rise from the pit of his stomach. He shut his eyes and clenched his teeth to stifle a groan, then took a deep breath and turned away from the scene. At one of the other houses up the street some of the men of Mark's party were already digging new graves. He dropped his head and sighed, then started down the street toward them.

It took until noon to bury the seven bodies found and judging by their positions it appeared that some of the homeowners had formed a defensive line for the neighborhood. They had been found in two groups and Jason could not tell if the defense had been successful or not, but the seven constituted the last of the unburied dead in the subdivision. The rest of the houses appeared to have been hastily abandoned.

Someone was sent to pick up the boys and when they arrived the group divided into smaller parties and began to overhaul the homes. Brian and Sean joined Jason and together they moved up the street. Over their shoulders they carried empty canvas sacks that would be filled with whatever canned foods or dry goods they could find. Sean carried a large cardboard box.

"It looks like this is a pretty nice neighborhood," Brian said.

"Yeah," Jason said.

"What's wrong, Dad? You seem bummed out."

"I, uh, just…." Jason searched for the right words, but could find none.

"Burying those bodies was hard on my dad, too," Sean said.

Jason nodded, and then looked ahead, trying to concentrate on the job at hand. At one house Jason saw a Ducks Unlimited sticker on the mailbox and said, "Let's try this one." They all walked up to the house where the front door had been forced open.

Inside they found a well furnished home. The elegant décor looked expensive, but a cluster of family photos along one wall revealed a lady's touch. There were some obvious items missing, but most of the room was still intact. A large painting of a salt marsh scene hung undisturbed above the empty television stand. On one of the end tables sat an ornate telephone and Jason picked it up and held it to his ear. He could see the wire plugged into the wall properly, but the dead line gave no dial tone and he replaced the receiver.

"Hey, Dad, come look in here," Brian called. Off to one side of the living room Brian stood inside the doorway of a den. Jason joined him and saw the head of a buck adorning the wall, along with a few other animals and birds above the bookshelf and above the fireplace mantle. In one corner a beautiful glass gun cabinet with an antique lock had been broken into, the glass smashed and every gun taken. The locked drawer beneath the guns had been forced open and all of the ammunition was gone as well.

"Well," Jason said, "I guess that's that. Let's go get what we came for."

The three of them went to the kitchen and began gathering food from the pantry and cabinets. Brian opened the refrigerator but closed it again quickly with a jerk of his head. "Whew! That sure stinks in there."

"Yeah," Sean said. "I can smell it from here."

"Let's forget the fridge," Jason said. "Brian, check that cabinet above the sink."

"Do we want stuff like this spinach?" Sean asked.

"Yes," Jason said. "Grab anything that's food."

It only took fifteen minutes to gather everything of value from the kitchen. They placed the sacks by the front door and then headed out to the garage. The only light here came from a window in a door that led to the backyard.

"Whoa," Brian said, "Nice." He walked over to an ATV and sat down on it.

"We need to find gardening equipment."

"Here's a rotor-tiller," said Sean.

"Now you're talking," Jason said. "Brian, give me a hand with this garage door. We'll roll it out to the street. Grab those gas cans, too."

They placed the tiller out by the road along with the gas cans and sacks of food, then went into the next house. After checking the phones and finding the same result they began gathering again. Once they had filled the sacks with food, three of them this time, they placed them in the living room by the front door. Jason stretched his back and worked his hands open and closed to relieve the tension.

"Wow," he said, "that was a heavy one."

"Yes, sir," Sean said.

"Where to, now?" Brian asked.

"Let's see what's in the garage," Jason said, and the three of them walked through the house to the utility room and into the garage. There were no windows here so Sean took a flashlight out of his pocket and switched it on. The beam was bright for its size, and Sean pointed it down at the steps as they went in.

"I wish I had thought to bring mine," Jason said.

"You can use this one," Sean said.

"That's all right. Just shine it all around the room slowly."

Sean did so and the first item to be illuminated was a gold-colored Jaguar XJ. Its metallic paint and chrome trim seemed to glisten in the flashlight's beam.

"Junk!" Brian said. "Look at that!"

"Junk?" Jason asked.

"He means 'phat,'" Sean said. The three of them stepped carefully over to the car. Sean illuminated the interior and Jason could see leather upholstery and burl wood trim.

"Man, that's nice," Brian said.

"I wonder why they would leave it," Sean said.

"It's a two-car garage," Jason said. "They probably left in their second car."

"I bet that one's a Hummer," Brian said.

"Most likely." Jason looked up from the car. "Let's continue looking around."

Sean shone the flashlight slowly around the room. The garage was immaculate and contained little. On one wall hung a rack that held snow skis and beneath it laid a large scuba gear duffle bag. Boxes labeled as Christmas items lined a long shelf, and next to them in the corner stood a large telescope under a cover. Jason felt a tug of temptation for the telescope, but quickly dismissed it.

"I guess they must get somebody else to mow their lawn for them," Sean said. "There's nothing here for grass or garden."

"They probably had a landscape company do it for them," Jason said.

"How do people get that kind of money?"

"I don't know," Jason said.

"I guess they must get a mechanic to work on their cars for them, too," Brian said. "There're no tools anywhere."

"Hmm," Jason grunted. "Let's go back."

The three returned to the utility room. Sean switched off

his flashlight and stuck it back in his pocket. "Weren't we supposed to be gathering blankets and stuff, too?"

"Yeah," Jason said. "I forgot about that. Let's see what we can find upstairs."

They passed through the living room and went up the stairs to the bedrooms. The first one appeared to have belonged to a young girl and the second had been a nursery. The master bedroom faced the back of the house.

"We need soaps and shampoos," Sean said, pointing to the bathroom. "I'll start here first."

"Good idea," Jason said, "Brian, look around the kids' rooms."

"What am I supposed to find in a girl's room?"

"There are girls on the island. Find something useful. We'll need baby things, too. I'll check this linen closet."

Jason found the linen closet well stocked and emptied its contents onto one of the larger sheets he'd laid out on the floor. He tied the four corners of the sheet and placed the bundle at the top of the steps. Sean came out of the hall bathroom with a plastic basin filled with toiletries.

"Well done," Jason said.

"Thanks. I guess I'll check out the master bath next."

"I'll go with you."

They stepped into the master bedroom and Sean headed for the master bathroom. The bedroom was beautifully furnished with an antique rice bed and matching dressers. A fine Persian rug covered the floor beneath the bed and the windows were decorated by a rich damask valence with matching drapes. A Venetian comforter covered the bed.

On an impulse Jason went to check the nightstand drawers. Finding nothing of value, he went to the bureau and opened the top drawer. After rummaging around the socks and underwear for a moment he found a modern web-style holster, black and made for a semi-automatic pistol. It even had a pouch for an extra magazine, but contained no gun. He checked the other drawers, then rechecked the nightstands, and then went to the walk-in closet. Opening the door he looked up on a high shelf and saw a small black gun safe with a key lock. He stood there a moment, trying to remember if he'd seen a cutting torch on the island, when he was struck by a hunch. He reached his hand up above the doorway and felt along the molding until he touched a flat piece of metal. He grabbed it and pulled down a small silver key. He inserted it into the lock and the door swung open. Inside the safe on a small shelf were several boxes of ammunition and beneath the shelf Jason could see the butt of a semi-automatic pistol.

He drew the pistol out of the safe and held it in his hands. It had a black polymer frame and a matte stainless steel slide and was very light. He turned it over in his hand and saw "40 S&W" stamped on top of the barrel. He dropped the magazine out and saw that it held fourteen hollow point bullets.

"Wow," Brian said. "You just found that?"

"Yes, in that safe." Jason replaced the magazine and stuck the gun into the holster. Then he reached up and handed the safe to Brian. "Put it on the bed, will you?"

Brian took it and the two headed for the bed. As the teen began to empty the safe of its contents, Sean came in with another basin of toiletries. He set it on the bed and nodded toward the gun.

"You found one, huh?" he said. "What kind is it?"

"Forty caliber."

"Is that a good one?"

"Yes," Jason said. "A lot of police use them."

"Dad, there're forty caliber rounds in here, and an extra magazine, but there's a lot of twenty-two rounds, too. Boxes of them."

"Well, look around. Maybe there's another gun somewhere."

Brian headed to the closet while Jason loaded the extra magazine, then he came out and looked under the bed.

"Here it is." he said and brought out a long, orange soft case. He laid it on the bed and unzipped it. Inside they saw a beautiful lever action rifle. It had walnut stocks, a bright brass receiver, and a long octagon barrel. Brian picked it up with reverence.

"Looks like you found your twenty two," Sean said. Brian held the gun to his shoulder and sighted along the barrel. "Man, I would love to have a gun like this."

"I think you should take it if you want it," Jason said. Brian took the gun from his shoulder and looked it over

206

closely. "It sure is a beautiful gun."

"I hear they're accurate, too," Sean said.

Brian nodded, but did not look up from the gun. He ran his fingers along the wooden stock and brass receiver thoughtfully, and then he took a breath to speak. "Dad, wouldn't it be considered stealing, me taking the gun?"

Jason pursed his lips and took a deep breath. He remembered the shotgun in the discount store on the first night of the attack and how he felt then. Everything was different now. "I've been thinking about that myself and I'm torn between two schools of thought. On one hand, if everything can be set right in a few weeks or so, and we can expect that these people who own these homes will be returning shortly after, then this would be stealing and I would have no part in it. But on the other hand, if things won't be set right for several months or longer, and these people won't be returning until then, all of this stuff will be taken by someone else anyway. If it's here, and will benefit someone, then that someone may as well be one of us. Besides, we don't know if things will ever be set right. And I doubt if these people are even coming back. I know I helped bury three outside who are never coming back." He paused. "I think the fact that we take only what we actually need, plus the fact that we leave everything else intact, and are respectful of what we find, plus the fact that we take the time and effort to bury their dead, shows our good intentions. We aren't just a bunch of looters. We're people in desperate need who are trying to survive this catastrophe."

Jason looked at both boys directly. "And I give you my word right now, with you two as my witnesses, that if this whole situation does set itself right, and we can go back to the way things were, then I will do everything in my power to square up with these people, and restore everything taken by me or my family. You can hold me to it."

Brian nodded, and then looked back down at the gun. "But do we really need a twenty-two rifle?"

"You will be called upon to hunt for food," Jason said. "There are ducks on that island, and other birds, as well as squirrels and rabbits, all of which can be taken economically with a twenty-two rifle. Not to mention that I would want you to have something for self defense that holds more than six bullets."

"They're not magnums," Brian said.

"No, but these hyper velocity ones are almost as powerful as magnums. And that rifle will probably hold a dozen or more." Jason grabbed a box of bullets and slid them toward his son.

"You might as well take it and enjoy it," Sean said. "If you don't, those hoodlums who burned down those houses will get it. Or they'll burn it down with the house."

Unconsciously, Brian held the gun close to him and nodded. "All right."

"Good," Jason said, patting Brian's shoulder. "Now, let's get all this stuff together, and then we'll head out to see what the others are up to."

Chapter Twenty-Five

"Islamic States of America"

Working with the other men of the group Jason and the
two boys helped with the backbreaking of loading all of the
sacks of food and supplies into the bed of the pickup truck,
filling it to the top. It amazed Jason that so much could be
gathered in so short a time. Mark and Robert had gone ahead
to assess some of the other houses farther up the street and
were not with the group, but as Jason paused to stretch his
back he saw them with another man walking toward the
truck. Mark carried a cardboard box and Robert carried two
sacks and they all had their guns slung on their backs. Jason
stepped over to them and took one of the sacks from Robert.
    "Thanks," Robert said. "Everything loaded?"
    "Yeah, pretty much," said Jason. "You guys didn't
happen to find any working phones, did you?"
    "Not a chance," Robert said. "But we did find a note."
    "Note?" Jason asked.
    "Yes," Mark said, "it was addressed to friends and
family and it said they were going to a local shelter. Oh, by
the way, I've got something for you in here."
    "For me?" Jason said. "Thanks."
    They reached the truck and the other men took the items
and put them with the rest of the goods. Mark set the box
down on the pavement and fished out at a gray, electronic
device. He handed it to Jason.
    "It's an electronic scanner radio," Mark said. "It gets

209

short-wave, too."

"Thanks." Jason took the radio and looked it over. It looked expensive and judging by the selector switch seemed to be able to receive every radio signal known to man. He switched it on but heard nothing.

"I found it switched on and the batteries were dead," Mark said, "but we've got plenty of batteries at the house on the island."

"Look, Dad," Brian said, "it's got automatic fine tuning."

"So it does," Jason said. "Thanks, guys."

"We ought to get going," said one of the men on the truck.

Mark nodded as he handed the box up to one of the men. They all climbed aboard and found places to sit atop the various bags and boxes as the truck drove slowly back down to the park.

After dividing the supplies with the two men who had brought the truck, they loaded everything into the boats and by noon they were headed back to Bulls Island. The work had been hot and exhausting and Jason could feel the skin on his neck beginning to burn. He drank a lukewarm bottle of water and Robert handed him a can of mixed fruit.

"Muzzle not the ox that treadeth out the corn," he said. Jason took the fruit with a nod of thanks and ate it greedily. Then he lay back against one of the sacks, jostling it until it was smooth, then let the afternoon drowsiness carry him off to sleep.

*

Four p.m. found the boats unloaded and everything brought to the house. Many people had come out to help carry the items, but not Jason's family. He inquired and learned that they had gone with several others to the beach.

"Dad, can we go?" Brian asked.

"Well, let's see if anyone needs help here at the house."

"We got this," one of the ladies said. "We know just how to organize everything and y'all will just be in the way."

"That's right," another said, "go down to the beach and

210

cool off."

"I'll go with you," Mark said. "Supper won't be ready for another hour or so."

"Well, let's go, then," Jason said as the four of them headed for the beach road. Brian and Sean walked quickly and had soon pulled ahead.

"I picked up some batteries for you," Mark said, holding a package out to Jason.

"Thanks." Jason took the batteries and inserted them into the radio as they walked. "There's a preacher I like to listen to." Jason said the preacher's name. "He seems to be on twenty-four hours a day."

"I like him, too."

Jason started to switch the radio on, but looked up the road and saw Valerie and Kathy coming toward them. Julie and Twony were walking together a little farther behind. Brian and Sean had come up to them and Jason could see his son eagerly showing off his new rifle. By now Jason could hear the sounds of the surf coming in through the trees. They continued walking and in another minute the groups had joined.

Valerie gave Jason a hug. "I'm glad to see you. I've been worried all day. How did it go?"

"Everything went well. Mark got me a new radio."

"It looks like a nice one."

"How was your day?" Jason asked.

"Good. We did some chores and then helped put the dinner on."

"I helped with the stew," Kathy said, proudly.

Jason raised his eyebrows. "Will wonders never cease?"

"Dad!"

"Just teasing," Jason said. "How was the beach?"

"It's beautiful," Valerie said. "The whole island looks perfectly untouched."

"I'd like to see it," Jason said. "I need my ocean fix."

"I'll go back with you."

"Twony and I will carry the stuff back to camp, if you want," Julie said.

"All right. Thanks." Valerie handed the beach bag and chair to them.

"Dad," Brian said, "Sean says the beach is a good place

211

to practice marksmanship."

"Yeah," Sean said, "you can see the spouts of sand and adjust your aim."

"Sounds good," Jason said. "You two head in one direction and we'll head in another."

"We'll see you guys back at camp for dinner," Valerie said.

*

Darkness had settled over the island by the time Jason, Valerie, Mark and the boys returned to the camp. Dinner was ready and after serving themselves buffet style they took their places in the circle around the Citronella lanterns once again.

"Mark," Mama called, "was there any news today?" After Mark related information about specific friends and family members, he said, "Jason got a new radio today." "Yes? Well, Mr. Ribault, what is happening in the world?"

"I haven't had it on yet," Jason said. "I could switch it on now, if you like."

"Please do," Mama said.

Jason set his plate on his lap and picked up the radio from the ground beside him. He switched it on and adjusted the tuning until he found a news broadcast in English. He turned it up so everyone could hear. Both the announcer and the correspondent spoke with British accents.

"But how could an attack like this be carried out successfully in area of such rigid security?" the announcer asked.

"The way we understand it from eyewitness reports, the attack came in two stages. The first vehicle, which some claim was an emergency vehicle, drove as far as it could into the compound and detonated its device there. It is estimated that the device was a one-half-kiloton nuclear bomb and it completely incinerated the security forces and their headquarters, along with the fences, walls, and checkpoints of the entire compound. That blast alone, which shattered windows as far away as the White House, might have been enough to satisfy the Islamic Extremists, but it was only a preliminary detonation. The second stage of the attack was carried out in a military style, all-terrain vehicle that actually drove up the front steps of the Capitol building, through the smashed front entrance, and onto the Rotunda. It was there that a second device, also believed to be a one-half-ton kiloton nuclear weapon, detonated. And as you can see, the entire dome and all but the very extremities of the two wings were completely destroyed."

"That's all that is left of the capitol?"

"Yes. It's hard to recognize, but usually from this vantage point the whole building stands out vividly against the sky. It's a disastrous end to a great building, which represented a once great, democratic people."

"It is indeed tragic," the announcer said. "Scott, thank you. And now for political analysis we turn to our political expert Dr. Norman Salisbury. Dr. Salisbury, what are we to make of these latest attacks and how do they fit into the big picture?"

"Well, as I see it, if the Lights Out attack was meant to bring America to her knees, as it were, then these attacks are designed to keep her from ever rising again. This latest attack, the first single attack using two nuclear weapons, constitutes the fourteenth terrorist attack using nuclear weapons in the last thirty-six hours. And there is surely more to come. The security infrastructure of the United States government has now completely broken down and the U.S. is quite vulnerable to whatever her enemies choose to throw at her."

"Has there ever been a link established between the initial attack carried out by the North Korean government and the subsequent attacks carried out by Islamic Extremists?"

"None whatsoever. It would seem as though the first was carried out as an independent strike, and the rest were conceived and carried out as the enormous opportunity presented itself. Thus far, there has been no evidence of collusion."

"Doctor, what can the American people expect now?"

"Well, in the short term, I am sorry to say, I think they can expect more attacks of this nature. And if we were to try to predict the most likely targets, the best we can do is to study what has been attacked already. There have been four nuclear attacks on government buildings, but I feel that these attacks were more symbolic than strategic. As in the case of this last bombing, an Islamic government operating under Sharia law has no need of a legislative assembly. And in the case of the three mega-churches destroyed by sub-compact nuclear devices, these were symbolic in the way that the churches were seen to be resisting the will of Allah. But they were practical targets as well, as each one had become distribution centers for food, medicine, and other necessary supplies, and the rising Muslim leadership wants the populace to see Islam as the sole provider for the people. And then, of course, there were the nuclear attacks carried out against the militia enclaves."

"The ones using single-engine, civilian aircraft."

"Yes. Those attacks were obviously intended to snuff out resistance to the rising political machine we now see taking shape. And then there were the attacks in the western states, which were intended to finish off the destruction of the electrical infrastructure in areas that were out of reach of the North Korean missiles."

"Why are there so few attacks against legitimate military targets?"

"I believe it's because they wish to keep the U.S. Military structure intact. It will be a valuable asset to the new regime."

"Dr. Salisbury, what does the long term picture hold for the average U.S. citizen?"

Dr. Salisbury hesitated a moment as he tried to gather his thoughts. "Hmm. Frankly, as much as I hate to admit it, I have no idea what to expect for the United States in the long term. This whole situation is unprecedented, possibly in the history of the world. And while it is inconceivable to imagine an Islamic States of America, we may be witnessing the birth of just such an entity. I suppose the average American citizen will have to adapt to this shocking new reality."

"And for those who cannot adapt?"

"Well, I suppose they will have to consider the offers of political asylum by many of America's allies. If I recall correctly Australia was offering amnesty to the first one hundred thousand U. S. citizens who can get there by plane or boat."

"That's a long way to go from a country without operational air or seaports."

"Yes, it is. Nonetheless, the offer is there."

"And a generous one at that. Dr. Salisbury, thank you so much."

"You're welcome, Diane."

"Islamic States of America," Robert said. "You've got to be frigging kidding me."

Jason turned the radio down, but said nothing.

"One nation, under Allah," one man said.

"With Friday prayers, and Burkas for all," one woman said.

"Well," another man said, "there's always Australia."

"How the hell am I supposed to get to Australia?" Robert snapped. "Huh? How is that supposed to help anyone?"

"I don't see how they expect to take control of this country, anyhow," another man said. "Even if they blow up a bunch of stuff, how can they take over a country the size of America?"

"Two reasons that I can see," Jason said.

"Do tell," the man said, with exaggerated interest.

"Well, first of all, most Americans don't care about anything anymore. Either they were too greedy to care about the country at large, or they were gung-ho about scrapping the whole thing for something different. We were ripe for take over."

"I wonder if the ones who wanted to scrap it," Robert said, "will be happy with what they get."

"Who knows?" Jason said.

"What was the second reason?" Mark asked.

"Choke points of power," Jason said.

"What?" Robert asked.

"Choke points of power," Jason repeated. "It was a concept started during the Russian Revolution, I think. They said that for a small group to seize control of the government from a large group, they have to seize the choke points of power."

"You mean like our communications?" Lena said.

"More like our military command and control structure,"

215

Robert said.

"Both, actually," Jason said, "and others."

"Food, fuel, and electrical infrastructure," Mark said, his voice somber.

"They're doing it already," one man said.

At those words the whole group became silent. Jason stared into the flame of the nearest lantern. Valerie put her hand on his back and patted it gently.

"Well," Mama said slowly, "no matter who is in charge when all this is over, we've got to figure out how to stay alive during all this mayhem with nuclear weapons."

"Yes," a woman said, "that radiation is dangerous, isn't it?"

"It'll cook your skin right off you," Robert said.

"This far away?" one man said.

"How far is far enough?" Robert snapped. "That radioactive dust can be blown by the wind hundreds of miles, and still come down and kill people."

"I was talking to a man on Isle of Palms," Jason said, "who said he was taking pills to protect him from the radioactive fallout." He turned to Valerie. "What was the name of those pills he was taking?"

"I didn't talk to him," Valerie said.

"No, but I told you about him," Jason said. "It was potassium something."

"Iodide?" Lena said.

"Yes," Jason said, turning in his chair to face her. "Potassium iodide. He said the iodine fills up the pituitary gland so the radioactive particles can't get in. He said that would prevent all the cancers from starting."

"We don't have any pills like that," Lena said, "but we do have plenty of iodine. We've got a large stock of it in the house."

"Can you drink it the same way?" Mark asked.

"No," Lena said, "but you apply it to the skin and it can be absorbed that way."

"Well, maybe we should start doing that right away," Mark said. A murmur of assent passed through the group.

"We should think about a shelter of some sort," Robert said, "to protect against any heavy fallout. I know you've got to have so much dirt to shield you."

216

"You can't dig around here without hitting water," another man said.

"Perhaps," Mama said, slowly, "we should begin exploring alternate sites for settlement. We are remote enough for now, but we can't know how long it will last."

"Are you thinking farther up the coast, Mama?" Mark asked.

"Yes, but I wouldn't want to get too close to Georgetown."

"Cape Romain is getting pretty remote," one man said.

"How far is that?" a woman asked.

"It's on the other side of Bulls Bay," Mark said.

"Isn't that a wildlife preserve?" Valerie asked.

"Yes," Mark said. "This island is part of it, too."

"I don't think these Muslims care a flip about wildlife preserves."

"Mama," Mark said, "if you like, I'll send a team up to Cape Romain tomorrow to scout around for a new settlement site."

"I think that would be best," Mama said, "but first, I think we need to pray."

The group became silent and bowed their heads as Mama began to speak.

"Father God, we come before you, Lord, with anxious and heavy hearts. We come to you, Lord, gravely concerned for our nation and its people. We don't know how long these attacks are going to last, nor how far America is going to fall, but you know, Father. You knew from the beginning that this nation would rise in righteousness and collapse in iniquity. You knew when it would occur and who would be affected. There is nothing that surprises you, Heavenly Father. We know that to be true. Furthermore, we know that you are near to those who seek after you, and you will cover them with your divine protection. We are like a bird escaped from a gin. The snare is broken and we are free."

Around him Jason heard murmurs of assent that increased in frequency and rose in intensity. He heard phrases such as, "Yes, Lord" and "Yes, Lord Jesus" and "Hallelujah," and others. He could hear the passion rising in the hearts of those around him and he was stirred by it.

"You promised in your Holy Word, dear Father God,

217

that though a thousand fall by our side, and ten thousand fall by our right hand, that it will not come nigh us. Precious Lord Jesus, we stand on those promises, we abide in them. Your words are life in us. This grievous news from afar will not frighten us, nor cause us to doubt. We are yours, Lord Jesus. We belong to you, and by your hand we stand, and no other. Nothing can separate us from the love of our everlasting and Almighty Father. Glory to you forever, Holy Father."

By now everyone in the group was shouting phrases of "Glory" and "Hallelujah." Some were standing, some were clapping and some were crying. Jason set his plate and the radio down on the ground and stood up. He began to clap softly and whisper, "Glory to you, Jesus." As strong emotions welled up in him, tears brimmed in his eyes. Mama, now standing, continued, her voice piercing the gloom, "We worship you, Lord, and magnify your Holy Name. No matter what happens to us, Father God, we will praise you, and lift you up, and sing praises to you, because of who you are. You are high and lifted up. We praise you and give you all the glory. At the name of Jesus every knee shall bow and every tongue shall confess that Jesus Christ is Lord, to the glory of God the Father. Blessings, and Glory, and Honor, and Power be unto the Most High, who sits upon the throne forever. And to the Lamb, who is worthy of all Praise and Glory and Power and Honor forever, and ever and ever! Hallelujah! Hallelujah! Hallelujah!"

Jason held his hands up and was weeping openly now. He felt as if he were in the very presence of God himself and all of his fear and worry and tension melted away. God was at the center once again, where He always needed to be, and Jason let the heartfelt, wordless praises gush forth from his soul to a receiving, loving Father. And he felt that love in return.

As the moment began to subside, Jason lowered his hands and bowed his head. His heart and mind were still focused on God when he felt a touch on his arm. He opened his eyes saw Valerie standing, her eyes wet with tears. She exchanged a glance with him and took his arm in hers, then closed her eyes again.

As the emotion subsided they both took their seats once

again. Jason reached down for the radio and considered turning it up, but decided against it. He felt that it would hijack the moment, so he switched it off. Jason looked up and saw that others had joined them, now standing around the circle of chairs. Twony was among them, and standing next to him was Julie and Kathy and Brian. Sean, too, was there. Looking at his children caused a tug of regret that Jeremy was not there among them.

"Boy," Robert said, "I needed that."

"Me, too," Mark said. "God is good."

"All the time," Lena said.

"It's been a long time for me," Jason said.

"We always need to keep God at the center of our lives," Mama said. "We were made that way. And the Lord inhabits the praises of his people."

"Mmm-mmm," Jason said, nodding his head slowly. "Yes, He does."

Chapter Twenty-Six

"America as we know it may never be restored."

"It's absolutely unbelievable," said the radio preacher. "Here was the statement issued earlier today by the so-called Al-Mahdi from his Army headquarters outside of Damascus. He said, and I quote, 'The failure of the U.S. government to protect its own people is unforgivable. It deserves to be overthrown. The American people deserve better, and Allah will help the American people in this great struggle for liberation.'"

Jason shook his head in the darkness. He sat on the dock next to the cruiser, the slotted non-slip surface quickly growing uncomfortable. Adjusting his position, he leaned back against one of the pilings and looked up at the stars.

The radio preacher continued. "Now, if that isn't a blatant attempt to foment subversion, I don't know what is."

"It sounds like it to me," the preacher's guest said. "Similarly, it sounds a lot like hypocrisy. You can't tell me that he didn't know those nuclear attacks were going down."

"He may have even planned the attacks himself."

"I wouldn't doubt it," the guest said. "And then he has the audacity to condemn the U.S. government for allowing the attacks to happen."

"Later in his statement he goes on to praise the efforts of many leaders in the U.S. who are working hard not only to feed people and restore power, but who are vigorously opposing the terrorist activities of the American militia

220

movement. He mentions several names and all of them are prominent liberals."

"Of course they are," the guest said. "The liberals in this country have been working to erode the values and principles of the United States for forty years."

"And that brings me to an important point. If this catastrophe would've happened forty years ago, it would've been bad, but in no way would it have been unrecoverable. At that time Americans would've united and would've worked to help each other to get us back on our feet. But after forty years of eroding our values and creating an entitlement culture, I don't think we're going to get back on our feet."

"I agree entirely," the guest said. "If all we had to deal with was the Lights Out Attack, and nothing else, then we may have been able to bounce back. We may have even had the power restored by now."

"I believe that," the preacher said.

"But with the rioting and looting and subsequent attacks, and reprisals against American citizens seeking to defend themselves, I just can't see it happening."

"We may get the power restored eventually, but America as we know it may never be restored." Here Jason heard the slap of a hand against a tabletop. "This nation has walked out from under God's protection, and the liberals and atheists led the way."

"And now we will all pay for it."

Jason heard footsteps coming onto the dock from the causeway. He leaned over to the side and looked around the piling he sat against. In the starlight he could see the figure of a man standing at the end of the dock. He had stopped walking as Jason had leaned over to look.

"Is that you, Jason?" Mark asked.

"Yeah," Jason said, returning to his former position.

The footsteps continued. "Man, you scared me." Mark stepped up next to Jason. "I didn't think anyone was out here and when I saw the light on that radio I didn't know what it was. Has Miss Valerie gone to bed?"

"Yes," Jason said. "I just wanted to hear if there was any more news from today. Valerie doesn't like to hear the news too much. It upsets her."

"Sometimes it upsets me, too," Mark said. "Hey, let me grab my flashlight I left in the boat and I'll join you, if that's all right."

"Certainly."

Mark leaned into the white open boat and picked up a large flashlight. Leaving it off, he placed it on the dock and sat down, his back against the piling opposite Jason. "So, what's the news?"

"Not much new," Jason said. "That Muslim messiah is ranting about the U.S. again. Same old favorite theme."

"The Al-Mahdi," Mark said, speaking the name with an Arabic accent. "He'll be coming over here before it's over."

"That Isa character is supposed to be coming over next week, and they're ready to embrace him. When I first turned the radio on, they were talking about how some of the larger denominations are telling the people that Christianity has had it wrong all these years. Jesus was really rescued from going to the cross and they put Judas there instead."

"That's Muslim teaching," Mark said, "but the scriptures say otherwise."

"I know they do. And so does common sense. Jesus' own mother and some of his disciples were there with him."

"Not only that, what would be the point of sending anyone to the cross if not for the remission of sin, as foretold by the prophets?"

"Without the shedding of blood there is no remission of sin."

"Of course," Mark said. "And when we accept that Jesus died to pay the penalty for our sin, and we make him our Lord, all our sins are forgiven."

"Absolutely," Jason said. "Then I hear this nonsense from these denominations and I wonder what they have been studying and believing all these years?"

"Jason, we are in a time of great dividing, of polarization. We have been dividing for many years now. It's like the voltage is being turned up on the two poles of some great magnet and everyone is being attracted to one side or the other. There is no sitting on the fence anymore. Jesus is coming and each one of us is either in or out, either with Him or without Him."

"It's like there's a separating of religion from true

222

relationship with God."

"Exactly," Mark said, "but that's been Jesus' ministry all along. Come out of your religion and embrace God. He alone can save you."

"It was religious people who killed Christ."

"That's right," Mark said, "and if we don't survive this period, it'll be religious people who kill us, too."

Jason nodded slowly. "I guess it won't be long before that Mahdi feels that he has enough support and power to conquer."

"If he hasn't got it already," Mark said. "And when he starts, any group that holds out against him will have no hope, except through God's direct intervention."

"Like Israel," Jason said.

"Especially Israel," Mark said.

Jason looked up at the stars, cold twinkling in the still air. "I've always believed that if we stay under God's authority, we'll be protected by Him. It always seemed the United States was a huge zone of protection in the world. But now that zone is getting pretty thin. How long can it hold out?"

"Jason, bad things can happen to anyone, even people who are under God's authority. In those times we have to trust that God is in control, and that he has a purpose in mind. Only He can bring good out of suffering. In those times we need to cling to Him more closely than ever."

Jason nodded in agreement. He looked at his friend in the dark, but could only make out a widening at the piling opposite him, silhouetted against the moonlit marsh. "Remember when I started crying today?"

"Yes," Mark said, "and it was nothing to be ashamed about. I cried there myself the day before."

"Part of the reason I cried was because of what had been done to those bodies. It's bad enough to say you're in a war and are really killing unarmed civilians, but what they did was totally wrong."

"Some folks on the radio are saying that it's the militia groups who are destroying these neighborhoods."

"The militia groups don't cut off people's heads," Jason countered.

"I know," Mark said, gently. "That was my point."

223

Jason took a deep breath. "The other reason I cried was because I saw a car that looked just like my son's car, same color even, but different wheels."

"I didn't think Brian was old enough to drive."

"He isn't. I mean my older son Jeremy. He chose to stay behind with his girlfriend's family."

"I see," Mark said. "Have you heard from him since you guys came out here?"

"No. That's one reason I went ashore today, but all the phones are still dead." Jason shook his head. "Seeing that neighborhood did a number on me. What if they attacked the neighborhood where he is staying? How can I know if he is all right?"

"Man," Mark said, "I'm sorry. If I was here and Sean was back home in all that mess I don't think I could stand it."

"I'm not sure I can stand it."

"What are you going to do?"

"I'm thinking about planning an expedition of my own," Jason said. "I'm thinking of going back to my truck and taking it home to find him. If I can just know he's all right, if I can just know he's somewhere safe, then I can stop worrying and let him go."

"When would you want to go?"

"Maybe tomorrow."

"Hmm. Maybe it would be better tomorrow night. My friends tell me it's a lot less hassle traveling after dark."

"The ones we saw today?"

"Yes. But they live near that subdivision. They don't go near a larger town during the day. Too many idle people hanging around and too much chance of getting stopped. And they said they would never go near Charleston or the North Area, night or day."

"I'll bet."

"Where's your truck?"

"At Shem Creek."

"Well, if it's still in good shape you can take Highway 17 to 41, and go through Moncks Corner. Those are all country roads."

"There's even a bypass around the bulk of Moncks Corner." He nodded thoughtfully. "That's what we'll do. I'll go to the house and check it out. Maybe we can pick up some things we may have forgotten."

"Sounds like a plan," Mark said. "You think Valerie will agree with it?"

"I think so. I'll talk to her in the morning."

*

The next morning Jason discussed the plan with Valerie over breakfast.

"All of us would go?" she asked him.

"No. Just me, and you, if you want to go. Mark said he would like to go to check on family members near Strawberry. He said Robert would want to go, too."

"Well, I would want to go," Valerie said. "There are some things I would like to get from the house. When?"

"Tonight. We would probably leave here late afternoon."

"I'll be ready."

They spent the morning with the kids helping out with the various chores around camp. The afternoon they spent on the beach. Mark sent a team of men in one of the boats to investigate the area around Cape Romain, but he stayed behind.

They stripped the cruiser of everything not essential to the trip. Several people from the camp, including Mama, gathered to help.

"Why are we taking everything out of the boat?" Kathy asked.

"It will prevent theft while we're gone," Mark said. "They can't steal what isn't there. Besides, it will free up some room for anything we may find to bring back."

"Put the food in the house with the rest of the camp's food," Jason said. "The other stuff you can put under the tarp next to your tent."

"How much gas have you got?" Mark asked.

"The tanks are full, and I have one five gallon can left in the engine compartment."

"How many empties do you have?"

"Five."

"Good," Mark said. "Maybe we can trade for some gas while we're there."

225

By late afternoon the boat was ready for the trip. Mark and Robert brought aboard a forty-eight quart cooler filled with shrimp and ice along with a thirty-six quart cooler filled with iced gator tail.

"Trade goods," Robert said.

"Gator tail?" Jason asked.

"Of course!" Robert said. "Fried gator tail and grits. Mmm-mm-mm."

"Yes, sir," Mark said.

"Huh!" Jason said. "You guys have been holding out on me."

"What time do you want to head out?" Mark asked.

Jason looked at his watch. "Any time now, I guess. I'd like it to be getting dark just as we enter the harbor."

"Sounds like a plan," Mark said. "Let's do it. Robert, hand me my stuff on the dock there, will you?"

"Mr. Ribault," Mama said, stepping over to the boat's side. "I feel I should tell you something."

"What is it, Mama?"

"Where you are going, you will need the Lord's protection. As you carry a weapon, you get the weapon's protection, but if you leave it behind you will get the Lord's protection. And that's much better."

Jason's face grew solemn. He thought about the police gun grab that he was told about the day before and nodded. "Thanks, Mama." He leaned out of the boat and lightly hugged her delicate frame. Then she backed away as Kathy and Brian stepped forward.

"Dad," Kathy said, "I have a bad feeling about this trip."

"You're just nervous," Jason said. "I'm nervous, too, but it'll be all right."

"But what if you don't come back?"

"We will. In the meantime you'll be in good hands." Jason patted her arm. "But if you're still worried, pray."

"I will," Kathy said. She leaned forward to give him a hug across the gunwale. Then Brian gave him a hug.

"We'll be back before morning."

"All right," Brian said.

"Cast us off, will you?" Jason started the engine as Robert climbed aboard. Valerie stood next to the transom and received the stern line.

"Robert," Jason said, "would you go up and get that bow line from Brian?"

"Got it, Boss," Robert said as he climbed onto the foredeck.

"Boss?"

"Yeah. You're the boss on this boat."

"Does that mean I get to throw you to the alligators?"

"Gotta catch me first."

Jason nodded silently and put the boat in reverse. Everyone waved as they backed out into the creek, and then they waved one more time as he moved forward and away from the dock and on to the small bay.

"We're going to be up late, aren't we?" Valerie asked.

"I would think so," Jason said.

"Then I'm going to take a nap."

"All right," Jason said, kissing her as she went below.

"Do you want to take a nap?" Mark asked. "I could take the wheel."

"No, thanks. I'm too keyed up. Besides, I took a long nap on the beach earlier."

"You didn't get burned, did you?"

"I was under a tree. But I love the sound of the ocean. I could fall asleep to it anytime."

"I know what you mean," Mark said. "If you like, I could show you the shortest route to the ICW."

"By all means."

Chapter Twenty-Seven

"I wonder what they're all waiting for."

Mark showed Jason the route and soon they were entering the Intracoastal Waterway. Jason steered left toward Charleston and increased speed and in a little over an hour and a half they were passing the Isle of Palms Marina. Jason slowed as he came into the no wake zone and all three men began studying the boats with great interest. Then Jason raised his hand to point at one of the docks.

"See that guy with the cast net? He is the one I told you about."

At that moment Billy was preparing the net for another throw and he looked up to see the cruiser approaching. He recognized Jason at once.

"Oh, hey, friend," Billy said with a friendly wave, raising his voice to be heard across the space of water. "We came back out for another visit, but couldn't find you. Now I see why." He nodded to indicate the mud paintjob.

"We saw you come back out for us," Jason called out. "And if I ever see you out there again I'll shoot you on sight."

Billy's face darkened. "Is that so? Well, it's a good thing for you my friends aren't here with our boat."

"It's lucky for you they're not," Mark snapped. "We already heard about you, and now that I know what you look like I give you this warning. Don't come snooping around out there. If you do you won't come back."

228

"Oh," Robert called out happily, "but please come out anyway. We've got a new sport for you to try. It's called 'Alligator Chase.'" And with that he made an exaggerated biting motion and sound with his teeth.

Billy said nothing, but stared after them as they moved away down the channel.

"I guess he don't want to play," Robert said.

"I guess not," Jason said. He increased speed again and continued down the ICW.

At the Isle of Palms connector bridge they looked up to see several men gathered behind what appeared to be a barricade erected at the highest point of the bridge. Several men looked down at the cruiser and one of them held his assault rifle up to show that he was armed. Jason waved slowly and then deliberately looked away, concentrating on the water ahead.

They came to the Ben Sawyer Bridge that connected Sullivan's Island to the mainland. The drawbridge mechanism was the type that swung the span around on a central axis and Jason saw that it was open, effectively cutting off the road. At the island side of the road another barricade had been erected and several armed men stood watching them. Jason chose the channel that ran along the mainland side of the bridge. One of the armed men shouted out to them as they approached.

"Where're you headed?"

"Town," Jason returned.

"What's your business?"

"Nothing that concerns Sullivan's Island," Jason said without looking over. He could feel the eyes and gun muzzles directed at his back, but they continued up the channel past the bridge without incident.

Before they entered the harbor they came upon the abandoned sailboat that lay in the creek between Sullivan's Island and the salt marsh of Mount Pleasant. It lay against the mud bank standing almost upright and the shadow of the mast stretched out long across the water. Jason pointed it out to Mark.

"I love that style of boat," he said. He traced the outline of the hull with his finger as he spoke. "I like the way the top of the hull curves down and then back up again to that sharp

229

bow. It makes it look like a clipper ship. Isn't it beautiful?"

"Yes, it is," Mark said. "How long do you think it is?"

"Probably fifty feet." Jason studied every line of the craft. "If I was ever able to buy any sailboat I ever wanted, I'd buy one like that."

Mark smiled at his friend. "Why don't we go over to it and have a look?"

"You think we should?"

"There's nothing stopping us."

"All right." He slowed the cruiser and steered for the creek. Robert got up on the foredeck and made ready with the line.

The companionway door opened and Valerie came up with a yawn. She looked around at the marsh and then saw the sailboat. "We're not there yet?"

"Not yet," Jason said. "I want to get a peek at this boat while we wait for dark."

"Is this the one we saw on the way out?"

"Yes." Jason reversed the engine to slow the cruiser and watched as Robert cleated the line to the sailboat and climbed aboard. Then Jason shut the engine down and followed Valerie and Mark up to the foredeck and onto the yacht.

"Man," Robert said, "lots of room on this boat."

"Yes, sir," Jason said. "Let's see if we can go below."

"They all stepped forward and down into the center cockpit. Finding no lock on the hasp, Jason slid the companionway open and looked inside. The interior was dry and well kept. There was no evidence of it ever having been flooded. Even the cushions looked pristine. Jason stepped down inside and Valerie and Robert followed him. Jason went to the chart table and found charts from many parts of the world. He opened the electrical panel and found it to be dry and well labeled.

"Look, Jason," Valerie said, "a gimbaled stove!" Jason looked and nodded his approval. "This definitely is a blue water boat."

"Did you see the master stateroom? It's like a hotel room."

"And there's a ton of storage space," Robert said, holding open a deck cover hatch. "Every one of these is a storage locker." He replaced the cover and lifted another. "Oh, well, this one is to a tank. It says 'Potable Water.'"

They moved around the rest of the boat and saw a forward V-berth for two. Aft of that they found a head with a separate shower and opposite the head was a narrow compartment that held three bunks. Aft of the cockpit was the master stateroom.

"Pretty impressive," Robert said. "Do you plan to pay with cash or credit?"

"Cash, please," Jason said, "but I'll have to wait until payday."

From beneath the cockpit there came a clicking sound. "What was that?" asked Valerie.

"That was me," Mark called from the cockpit. "I was trying to see if the engine would start, but I guess the battery is dead."

"We could hear the bendix engaging," Robert said.

"There's not much juice left," Mark said.

Jason climbed back into the cockpit and sat down next to Mark. "It sure is a beautiful boat."

"Sure is. Did you notice the registration on the bow?"

"No."

"It expired back in March. This boat's been abandoned. And maritime law says it belongs to anyone who claims it."

Jason looked around the deck. "We could just take it?"

"Sure. It's not attached to any mooring or dock. It's not even anchored. Some storm probably broke it loose and set it adrift."

"But why wouldn't anyone else claim it before now?"

"Who knows? Maybe it broke loose recently. Maybe the owner lives out of town and doesn't know it's adrift. He sure didn't care about the registration. And in any case, it's unlikely he'll be coming back for it now."

Jason looked around the boat again thoughtfully. "You think so?"

"If you had this boat out here waiting for you and all this mess was going on, wouldn't you come out to get it?" Jason nodded and Mark continued. "This boat is a floating home, a safe and mobile home. And if you want it, I say you should take it."

"You mean we could keep it?" Valerie asked, coming up

through the companionway. She took a seat next to Jason.

"Looks like it would be all square."

"That's great," she said. "We've always wanted a boat like this."

"I know."

Robert came up through the companionway. "How would you float it off?"

"There's a way to do it," said Jason, looking around at the creek. "It's actually easier than you think with sailboats. The tide's going out right now, but if we came back early in the morning when it is up I think we could do it. We'll see." He looked up at the sky. "In the meantime I guess we should continue our journey."

Robert slid the companionway shut as the others climbed back into the cruiser. Then he climbed down and cast off as Jason started the engine and backed out into the main channel.

*

They entered the harbor just as the sun set behind the city of Charleston. The church steeples of the peninsula seemed to be reaching up to pluck the last of the converging beams of gold. As Jason made his right turn toward Shem Creek Valerie touched his arm and pointed.

"Look," she said.

Jason turned and saw Fort Sumter still guarding the harbor, its American Flag snapping in the breeze as it caught the last rays of the sun. Beyond it to the south the sky was already turning dark and the ensign stood out in sharp relief. As he watched it he felt an indefinable longing.

"I wish I had my camera," Valerie said.

"I wish I had a time machine," Robert said.

"I guess they don't take it down at night?" Mark asked.

"They're supposed to," Jason said. "It's not lit up. I guess no one comes out to lower it at dusk anymore."

"It'll just have to stay up all night," Robert said. "Just like in the song."

Jason nodded and turned his attention back to his steering. As he watched the darkness fall across the harbor, a feeling of eeriness rose within him. Beside the soft glow of candles in many of the windows along the battery the city was completely dark. Even the State Ports Authority dock, normally lit up at all times, was black and the unlit cranes raised up from over the water formed jagged traps for an unlucky aviator. Only the channel markers and buoys in the water were lit up as if nothing had happened.

To the right, the darkened town of Mount Pleasant glowed with candlelight in some of the windows. The solar powered lamps on the docks began to glow warmly, as oblivious to the disaster as the channel markers. Jason could find only two houses burned down and concluded that at least this side of Mount Pleasant had been spared the brunt of the mayhem.

They rounded the last of the docks and entered Shem Creek, as dark as the rest of the city, except for two shrimp boats whose engines were idling and whose decks were lit up as normal. Men worked on both decks and none seemed to take notice of the cruiser. As they passed the shrimp boats Jason could see that the icehouse was partially lit up and men were working there as well, dressed in hip waders and carrying flat shovels.

They moved past the shrimp boats and Jason saw the fancy house with the large sport fishing boat, but the house was dark and silent and the boat was gone. The restaurants, too, normally a cacophony of light and sound, brooded dark and silent, except for a few small groups of people who had gathered on the docks to sit and talk.

They passed under the low bridge and soon came to the boat yard and landing. Jason eased the boat beyond the dock and let the current push him toward it. Valerie and Robert climbed out and tied the boat to the cleats as Jason shut the engine down and put the key in his pocket. He looked around.

At the town homes across from the boat yard he saw people sitting on lawn chairs. They were talking quietly and some had citronella candles burning. Jason looked at the row of docks on the creek and saw the same thing. On the dock closest to the landing a couple sat staring at the cruiser in silence, a candle flickering between them. Jason waved but they did not wave back.

"I wonder what they're all waiting for?" Valerie asked.

233

"Probably waiting for the lights to come back on and everything to get back to normal," Robert said.

"Good luck," said Jason flatly. "Here, take these coolers." Jason and Mark passed the coolers up to Robert and Valerie who placed them on the dock. Mark began to climb onto the dock when Jason stopped him.

"Where're your guns?"

"I stashed them below. Valerie helped me find a good spot."

"You're not taking them with you?"

"Normally I would, but when Mama says something like she told you back at the island, I run with it." Mark turned and climbed onto the dock.

Jason stood on deck a moment. He could feel the reassuring weight of the pistol against his elbow and he thought about what Mama had said. He looked at the others who waited patiently. "Hold on a moment," he said, and went below. Once out of sight of the people in the town homes he removed the gun from his belt and stashed it in the lower drawer under the sink. Then he went back on deck and locked the companionway behind him. Once on the dock he lifted the larger cooler with Robert and led the group to the parking lot.

Jason took a deep breath and braced himself as he stepped around the corner of a privacy fence and looked into the parking area. But he exhaled in relief when he saw the truck still there and intact. The small round door to the fuel tank left open and the gas cap hanging below it seemed to be the only things amiss.

"Looks like they got your gas," said Robert.

"Yeah. Let's see how much."

Jason opened the tailgate of the truck and they slid the coolers onto the bed. Then he opened the driver's side door and sat down inside. Turning the key, he watched the gauges as they rose to their normal positions, but the gas gauge stayed at empty. "Looks like they got it all," he said. He switched the key off and got out.

"I'll get the one from the boat," Mark said.

"Bring the empties, too," said Jason.

"I'll help you," said Valerie.

"Let's get this trailer unhitched," Jason said to Robert.

They unhitched the trailer and rolled it into the next empty space as Mark and Valerie returned. Mark poured the contents of the last five-gallon can into the truck's tank as Valerie put the empty ones in the bed beside the coolers. Then they all got in the cab and Jason started the engine.

"How much did that give you?" Mark asked.

"Just under a quarter of a tank," Jason said. "But that should be enough if I drive economically. I'll have to go the Interstate, though. It's the most direct route and we won't have enough to take the back roads."

"Let's do it."

The drive through Mount Pleasant proved uneventful and the only other vehicles they saw were two police cars in a parking lot on Coleman Boulevard. They parked with their driver's sides together talking and took no notice of Jason's truck. The bridge was free of traffic and Jason drove at forty-five miles an hour, his most economical speed. He anticipated a long glide down the far side, but when he got to the top a sight caught his eye that nearly made him slam on the brakes. Ahead of him, covering almost every one of the eight lanes congregated a mass of people. They appeared to be young people from the poor neighborhoods of Charleston and in the headlights Jason could see that the majority of them were armed. They looked up at the truck as it approached and most were turning to face it.

Instinctively Jason began to slow down. His mind was rapidly weighing his options, and one of these included turning around and retreating into Mount Pleasant. But then the crowd suddenly began to part. Everyone moved aside to make his lane clear.

"Don't stop," Mark said.

The lane continued to widen until there was at least half of a lane on each side. Jason's speed had fallen to twenty miles per hour and he glided easily between the two groups of people. Every one of them seemed to stare in fascination at the truck, and they continued staring until it was past. In his rear view mirror Jason could see the gap closing as he increased his speed to forty-five again.

"Remind me to change my drawers when we get to Strawberry," Robert said.

"That makes two of us," Jason said.

235

"I wonder what made them get out of the way like that?" Valerie asked.

"They must have seen something," Mark said, exchanging a glance with Jason.

Chapter Twenty-Eight

"I'm looking for my son."

The rest of the trip proved uneventful. They saw a few vehicles on the interstate and several more as they got on to Highway 52, but nothing like usual weeknight traffic. In one parking lot they saw a delivery truck that had been converted into a rolling cantina. A side panel was raised where the food was sold and several tables were set up nearby. Attached to the truck were floodlights and a Spanish menu was written on the upturned panel. Dozens of Mexicans were either standing to buy food from the truck, sitting at the tables eating, or standing in groups talking peaceably.

"Their lives haven't changed much," Robert said. No one answered him.

They drove to the tiny town of Strawberry. They had agreed that the first stop should be to trade the iced food before checking on Jeremy and Robert directed Jason to a large doublewide trailer where several cars were parked. Mark and Robert greeted the group gathered near the front porch and introduced Jason and Valerie. Then the coolers were brought forth and the haggling began in earnest.

"Only two cans?" Robert protested. "That's only ten gallons!"

"I know," said the man, Robert's cousin, "but do you know how hard it is to get gas anymore?"

"But this is shrimp!"

"I know it."

237

"And I'm throwing in the gator tail for free."

"You can keep that."

"We don't need it," Robert said. "We've got more than we can eat now." He glanced at Mark. "But of course, I know someone else who would want it. I know he's got gas, and he would want the shrimp, too."

Robert's cousin made no reply.

"All right," Robert said, "you all have a good night." He gave a nod to Jason and Mark, who each took a handle of the larger cooler. But before they could lift it the man raised his hand.

"Hold on. I'll fill three of them for you, but that's really all I can spare."

"It took two to get here and back," Robert said. "But I'll tell you what, make it four and I'll give you the coolers, too."

The man agreed, and soon they were on their way again, heading north towards Moncks Corner.

"I'll need one of those cans to get us back," Jason said.

"I know," Robert said. "Did you see that tank he had back there? I should have pushed him for five."

"You wouldn't have got it," Mark said. He faced Jason. "Where to now?"

"Let's go to my son's church. He's staying in the parsonage behind it."

Jason headed back toward town. He soon turned down a side road into a lower middle class neighborhood, slowing as he drove past houses where people were gathered around outdoor braziers or charcoal grills. Kids ran playing in between the groups and Jason saw several shotguns and rifles leaning against cars or trees, all within easy reach. A few looked up and waved as Jason drove by, but most just watched them pass.

At the end of the road Jason made a left turn onto another street, this one nearly deserted, and after they passed several houses the church came into view. Not the church building exactly, but rather what was left of it. Jason's heart sank and a feeling of nausea began to grow in his stomach as he stared in disbelief at the burned out structure of the church building. He pulled into the driveway and stopped the truck, the headlights illuminating where the front door had

238

been. The entire front of the building was gone, as were most of the sides, and a pile of charred rubble was all that remained of the roof. Only the rear wall remained, scorched and cold and dead.

Everyone stared silently for a few moments, then Jason drove to the far end at the small parking lot, following the asphalt driveway that led to the back of the building. There, illuminated in the truck's headlights, stood the remains of the burned out parsonage.

Jason stopped in front of the house and shut the engine down. They all got out and stood staring at the blackened debris. The fire had happened only a day or so ago for the charred remains still hissed in the cool night air and gentle wisps of smoke could be seen rising over the ruins, like ghosts hovering over a graveyard.

Valerie clutched his arm in disbelief and the action made him shudder. A tide of pain and confusion rose within him, choking his breath, and blurring his vision with tears.

"No, no, no," he repeated in a whisper. Next to him Valerie began to sob.

Just then a voice crackled out of the night air behind him. "Look here, what're you all doing?"

Jason turned around and saw the head of an older man above the privacy fence that separated the property next door. The glare of the headlights illuminated a scowl on the man's face and Jason could not see his hands.

"I'm looking for my son," Jason said, struggling to get the words out. "He was staying with Pastor Rick and his family."

"Jeremy?" The name rang out like the clear note of a bell.

"Yes, Jeremy."

"He went with the family to a shelter after the fire. We would have put them up here, but I already have a house full."

"What shelter?"

"The one they set up at the high school," the man said. "But I don't know if they'll let you in, it being after curfew and all."

"Thank you." Jason turned to Valerie and saw the anxious tears in her eyes. He gave her a quick hug, then they all got back in the truck and headed out to the main road.

*

The school, set back from the road, loomed dark and silent against the cold starlight. A dim glow shone through a glass doorway near the gymnasium where a few dozen cars were parked. Somewhere in the distance a generator hummed. Jason drove up near the door and parked the truck.

"There's Jeremy's car. I see it," Valerie said. "It's behind that van."

They all got out of the cab and looked. "That's his all right," Jason said. "Same ding in the bumper. Let's go." Inside the door a wide hallway, rigged with temporary lights, served as an entrance to the school. Two long tables sat against the side walls and upon these were arranged a variety of pamphlets. Some had been provided by the government and featured topics such as *Disaster Preparation and Recovery* and *Procedures for Applying for Government Aid.* Some forms were available, as well. The rest of the pamphlets seemed to have been provided by some religious organization and featured topics such as the *Five Pillars of Islam* and *Preparing for The Month of Ramadan.*

At the far end of the hall two men sat at a long table. One of them, a college-aged white man, wore glasses and a knit Rastafarian cap and was writing in a notebook. Next to him a middle-aged black man worked on a crossword puzzle. They both looked up as Jason and the others approached.

"Excuse me," Jason said politely, "but I'm looking for my son, Jeremy Ribault, and I was told he was here. Could I speak to him, please?"

"It's after lights out here," the young man said. He spoke with a New Jersey accent. "You'll have to come back in the morning."

"Sir," Jason said, "we've come a long way to see him. I haven't spoken to him since the Lights Out Attack and I just want to know if he's all right."

"Come back in the morning."

"Can't you even tell us for sure if he's here or not?" Valerie asked.

240

The older man slid several sheets of paper over toward the young man. It listed names and addresses of refugees, but the young man merely placed his hand over it. "I'm afraid I can't give out that kind of information," the young man said, his voice ripe with contempt. "Besides, it's after curfew."

A flash of anger rose up in Jason. With clenched teeth he leaned forward and clutched the young man's shirt collar. Then, with one motion Jason leaned back and lifted the young man out of his seat and over the table, scattering the papers and notepad. The young man hit the floor with a deep grunt. As he lay on his back, Jason, still holding him by his collar, leaned over him to speak.

The older black man stood up immediately and took a radio from off of his belt, but before he could raise it to his mouth to speak, Mark snatched it out of his hand. "I'll hold on to this for a few minutes, if you don t mind."

The young man's face became a mixture of astonishment and fear as he stared up at Jason. The father's face purple with bridled fury.

"Now listen to me," Jason said. "I know my son is here. I've seen his car outside. What you're going to do is call him out here so I can speak to him. Do you understand?"

The young man nodded hurriedly. "I'm not supposed to call him out here because it's after lights out, but if you want I'll take you to him."

Jason nodded and released the man's collar. He straightened up and held his hand out. The young man hesitated a moment, then took Jason's hand and lifted himself from the floor.

The young man gathered up the papers and began shuffling through them on the table. "What did you say his name was?" Jason told him and when the young man found the name he said, "Follow me."

"Robert and I will stay to hold the fort," Mark said. Jason nodded and followed the young man down a side hall. The man took a small flashlight from his pocket and led Jason and Valerie inside the gym door.

Despite the openness of the pitch-black gymnasium, the warmth and stifling humidity made the air seem very close. Around him Jason could hear people snoring or whispering

241

quietly and at several places he could see tiny pen lights illuminating open books. Several of these winked out soon after they entered.

Jason's eyes followed the young man's flashlight beam as it wove its way down the aisle, flashing over the ends of sleeping bags or small piles of personal belongings or an occasional set of bare feet. The smell of a dirty diaper mingled with the odors of sweaty shoes and the sickly, sweet smell of unwashed bodies. The gloom and the heat and the aromas seemed to close in on Jason and he fought off a sense of claustrophobia. He despaired at the thought that his son has been in this dungeon for days.

The young man's flashlight beam stopped at a place where a comforter had been spread out on the floor. Next to it, and separating it from the adjacent sleeping areas, were stacked a few cardboard boxes and books, arranged like some unfinished rampart. The flashlight beam illuminated the comforter and upon it Jason saw his son Jeremy lying flat on his back. He wore a tank style T-shirt and a pair of gym shorts and he had no pillow for his head. Next to him laid Ruthie, similarly attired and holding Jeremy's hand. A tiny pillow lay under her head.

Jeremy rose up on one elbow and brushed the hair out of his eyes with his hand. He squinted into the light and said, "What's going on?"

"Someone to see you," the young man said.

Jason went down on his knees and leaned forward into the light. Jeremy's eyes opened wide and he drew in a sharp breath of surprise. He sat up and reached his arms around his father's neck, hugging him tightly. Jason heard his neck pop and felt a small stab of pain at the awkward embrace, but he didn't protest. Instead he reached around his son's wide shoulder with one arm and returned the embrace.

"Oh, God," Jeremy sobbed. "I prayed so hard that I would be able to see you again and…." His words were lost as his weeping began.

Valerie knelt on the comforter and shared the embrace. By now all three of them cried and Jason leaned back to let Jeremy hug his mother. Ruthie sat up, her eyes wet with tears.

Jeremy regained some of his composure and spoke in a

whisper. "You were right, Dad. You were so right."

"No, son, I wasn't right. I just did what I thought we had to do."

To the right of them another light came on and Jason could see Pastor Rick and his wife Darlene sitting up on the next comforter. "Is that you, Jason?" he whispered.

Wiping the tears out of his eyes, Jason nodded and waved.

To the left of them an annoyed, "Shh!" flew out and the young man bent over to speak. "I need you guys to come out in the hall to talk."

Without a word they all rose and followed the young man's flashlight beam out of the gym, Pastor Rick's flashlight bringing up the rear. As they entered the hall the young man shut the door behind them and headed for the table again. The older man had stood up when the door opened, but at a hand signal from the young man he sat again and returned to his crossword puzzle.

"Boy, it's much cooler out here," Darlene said.

Robert and Mark stepped over to the group and Jason introduced them. Mark was still holding the radio.

"These are our new friends we met out on the island. This is Mark and Robert." As they all shook hands Jason said, "This is Pastor Rick and his wife Darlene, and this is my older son Jeremy."

"Linebacker, huh?" Robert said.

"Sometimes," Jeremy said.

"And this is Jeremy's girlfriend Ruth. Rick and Darlene are her parents."

"Uh, Dad," Jeremy said, hesitantly. "I've got something to tell you." He glanced at Ruth, and then back at Jason. "Ruthie and I are married now."

"Married?" Jason said.

"Yes," Jeremy said, taking Ruth's hand. "When the fire happened, and the nuclear bombs started going off, we sort of felt like everything was about to end, and we wanted to face it together. Pastor Rick married us. I hope you're not mad."

A smile began to spread over Jason's face. "No, I'm not mad, not at all. We had anticipated it, but we just didn't know when. I'm sorry we missed it."

243

"I am, too," Jeremy said, his eyes tearing again. "I wanted for you guys to be there most of all. We tried to get a hold of you, but...." His voice trailed off.

"Forget it," Jason said, his face beaming. "It's all right now. Besides, congratulations are in order." He hugged his son again and then hugged Ruthie. Both of them were damp with sweat.

"We took photos of the wedding," Darlene said. "I know you'd like to see them."

"Yes, I would," Valerie said.

"I have some chairs, if you guys want them," the young man said, carrying several folding chairs with the older man.

"Thanks," Jason said. They all took the chairs and sat down.

"So what brought you back into town?" Rick asked.

"Well, when all the stuff started really hitting the fan, we too began wondering if this was the end," Jason said. "I never could get a hold of you, either, and we just had to find out if you were all right."

"We're alive, but not exactly all right," Rick said.

"Was anyone hurt in the fire?" Valerie asked.

"No," Darlene said, "We were at someone else's house when it happened."

"I saw the lovely reading material," Mark said, nodding toward the entrance.

"Oh, yeah," Rick said. "And that's just the start of it. We've had an Imam in here every afternoon holding Islamic Awareness classes. Then he gives us the latest news, with a Muslim perspective, of course. He told us today that members of the Islamic Freedom Action group intercepted a nuke on its way to another attack. The Mahdi praised their success at foiling a viscous plot, and called on all extremists to suspend their activities. He said they want to take control of the U.S., not destroy it."

"That's nice," Mark said. He shook his head in disgust.

"Nicer still," Rick said, "is him coming to speak to the U.N. You remember which city the U.N. headquarters is located, don't you?"

"Good grief," Jason said, "Imagine having him on our soil."

"Are they ready," Valerie asked, "with water and

244

electricity and all?"

"They will be," Rick said, shaking his head slowly. "I'm telling you, I think it's all over for us."

Everyone sat quietly at those words, until Mark broke the silence. "Not much of a honeymoon, is it?"

Jeremy and Ruth shook their heads.

"You should come out with us," Robert said. "It's a lot cooler out there, with plenty of food, and lots of room to get away from things when you want."

"Where are you staying?" Rick asked.

Mark took a glance over to the table where the two men were sitting and then lowered his voice. "Up by Bulls Bay, on the island."

"I think you're going to need to go further than that," Rick said, gravely. "When this Imam found out I was pastor, it was one veiled threat after another." He looked around the group, making eye contact with each one of them. "These people will brook no competition. Once they realize you are out there, and they will find out eventually, they will come out and eradicate you. You will have to leave the country."

"And go where?" Robert said. "We don't even have passports."

"I don't know where. I hear Australia is taking people."

"Pastor Rick," Mark said, "we have a large group of people. We're limited in how far we can go."

"Hijack a freighter, whatever it takes, but get out now."

Jason thought about the sailboat. "We could cut out a few more sailboats. I could teach you how to sail."

Mark shook his head. "It was like pulling teeth to get some of our people out to the island. I can't see getting them out on the ocean in a sailboat." He grimaced. "No, I think we'll make our stand out on the islands. It won't be long before we're self-sustaining. Then we can lay low and wait it out. Jesus has got to come back sometime."

"Very soon, I think," Rick said. He looked at Jason. "You have a sailboat now?"

"Yes. We're going to float it off the mud when we get back."

"Would it be big enough to get to Australia?"

"With a little luck, I think so."

"Would you take Ruthie with you?"

245

"Yes. But I'm sure we could make room for you guys, too."

Rick shook his head solemnly. "No. Our place is here, to preach the true Gospel for as long as we can."

"I don't want to leave you behind," Ruthie said, her voice choking with emotion. "I won't."

"You must," Rick said. Darlene took his hand.

"No." Ruthie began crying.

"You must. I have a calling here. But if we all die here, then our entire family is lost, cut off. If the Lord Jesus comes, then it won't matter, but if he delays, then I want to know that I have grandchildren somewhere who are safe, and happy, and are learning about the one true God."

Ruthie got off of her chair and hugged her father. She was weeping openly now, as was Darlene. They all three stood in a sobbing embrace. Jason looked at Valerie and saw she was crying, too. He clenched his teeth to stifle a groan. Mark and Robert kept their eyes to the floor, respectfully silent. Jeremy stood up and joined the embrace.

"Take care of my little girl," Rick whispered, hoarsely. Jeremy nodded.

After a few minutes the embrace was broken and everyone sat back down. Mark waited for the sniffles to subside and then spoke.

"You folks are welcome to come out and stay with us. There's plenty of room, and we could always use another preacher."

"Thank you," Rick said, "but we need to stay in town. We're going to try to keep the congregation together as long as we can. Of course, it's been hard since the church burned down."

"Take our house," Jason said. "We won't be using it. It's out in the country so there's lots of room for parking, and it's likely to escape notice for awhile."

"And there's plenty of room inside for meetings," Valerie said.

"Yes," Jason said. "We were going to head over there before we went back to the island to get some last minute things, but, after that, it's all yours."

"Let us donate it to your ministry," Valerie said.

Rick looked at Darlene who nodded silently, and then he

nodded, too. "All right, maybe we'll take you up on that."

"The entertainment has got to be better than what you're getting here," Mark said.

"I know that's right," Robert said.

"Could we come now?" Darlene asked.

"Absolutely," Jason said. "We've got the pickup truck. There's lots of room."

"Just give us a minute to gather our things," Rick said. "We'll just gather it all in the comforters. There's not much."

"We lost everything in the fire," Darlene said.

"Need a hand?" Jason asked.

"No, we got it."

"Here, you'll need this," Mark said, handing Jeremy a flashlight.

"Thanks." The four of them disappeared through the door.

Mark and Jason began gathering the chairs and Robert helped them carry them to the table at the entrance. The two men looked up from their diversions.

"All done?" the young man said.

"Yes. Thank you very much."

"Where do you want these chairs?" Mark asked.

"Just up against that wall, there. That's fine."

Soon Rick and the others came out carrying their bundles. The young man looked puzzled.

"What's going on? Hey, you guys can't check out without permission."

"You going to start that again?" Robert said to the young man.

"They're checking out right now," Jason said. "If I need to sign anything, just put an 'X' down for me."

Everyone except Mark headed out the door to the truck. He stood waiting for them to climb in and for Jason to start the engine. Then he placed the radio on the floor and turned to go.

"Gentlemen," he said, walking through the door, "I bid you a good night."

The two men stared after him in astonishment.

Chapter Twenty-Nine

"Things will never get any better. It's all gone."

It relieved Jason that they did not find their house burned
down, but only broken into and looted. Using Mark's
flashlight they found their way through the open front door
and into the interior of the home. They lit some decorative
candles that Valerie had been saving for the holidays as well
as a few tea lights.

"Now we can see what's left," Jason said.

"Look, Dad," Jeremy said, "there's the stuff you and
Brian bought that night."

Jason looked and saw the poster board and plastic
discount store bag full of school supplies, now relics of
another world, another age. He turned to Valerie. "Do you
know what the kids wanted us to bring back?"

"I have a list," Valerie, her voice somber said.

"Are you all right?"

"Yes, it's just a weird feeling to know that someone has
been in our home and has gone through all of our things."

"I know what you mean," Darlene said. "If you like I can
help you gather up what you need."

"That would be a great help," Valerie said. "Thanks."

"Is there anything we can do?" Mark asked.

"Uh, yes," Jason said. "Would you mind checking all of
the doors and windows to see if everything is secure? I don't
want a return visit."

"I'm sure no one would come if they saw candles lit,"

248

Rick said.

"You never know," Jason said, exchanging a glance with Mark.

"Would you like us to open the windows to let some fresh air in?" asked Robert.

"Yeah, that'd be great, but only where the screens are intact," said Jason. "I don't want to fill the place with mosquitoes."

"I guess I need to see what's left of my things," said Jeremy, and he and Ruthie headed for his old bedroom, leaving Jason alone with Rick.

"What can I help you with?" Rick asked.

"Let's go into the study. I need to gather all of our important papers and things. You can have a look at my Bibles and Christian books. I have a lot. Maybe there are some things you can use."

"It's more than I have now."

"And by the way, if you can get a generator you can use it to run the well pump. We're not hooked up to city water out here so you won't have to wait for the all clear to use the water."

"That sounds good."

They took their candles into the study and Rick looked through the bookshelf while Jason went through his desk and file cabinet. Jason was amazed at how many documents he had collected throughout the years, now almost all of it entirely useless. He tried to concentrate on important family records as well as professional training and experience records, documents that would help him get a job in Australia, or wherever else they ended up. When his wastepaper basket became full Rick fetched a garbage bag from the kitchen.

"You can leave that stuff on the floor if you like," Rick said. "I'll get them up tomorrow."

"No. I'm not going to leave a mess for you to deal with."

"Are there any books here you want to take with you?"

"I'll have to look." Jason leaned back in his chair from the file cabinet and let out a deep sigh. Rick turned around to face him.

"Kind of overwhelming, isn't it?"

Jason nodded and leaned forward to rest his forehead in

249

his hands. "Not just this paperwork, though, but all of it. How did it happen? How did it all fall apart so fast?"

"Well, it really wasn't all that fast. It had been brewing for decades."

"I guess so."

"But there's one question that keeps nagging me. I think about it all the time. Where was the tipping point?"

Jason looked up at Rick. "The tipping point?"

"Yes. Where was the point where America was lost? At what point did we actually give it away?"

"You mean concerning the decisions that were made after the Lights Out Attack?"

"No, much earlier. Do you remember the story in the Bible about when King Saul disobeyed God's instructions?"

"Yes. The Prophet Samuel came to him and told him that obedience was better than sacrifice."

"Correct. But he also told him 'this day the kingdom is rent from your hands.' Now, Saul was still king for several years after that event, but it was on that day that the decision was made, and nothing would change it. A series of events started after that day that would eventually put David on the throne of Israel. But Saul had lost it that day. As I think about the situation we are in, I find myself racking my brain to see if I can pinpoint the moment where we lost it all. Was it some election, or a certain law passed, or a court case decided? Or was it just some action of the people that started an irrevocable chain of events that led to our downfall?"

"I could think of a lot of possible answers."

"Me, too. But which event was 'the one'? That's the question that eats at me."

"Maybe it has to do with an apathy that set in among Christians," Jason said. "Some point when there was more of us thinking about our own comfort than of the things that matter to God. I know that I used to give out cartoon Gospel tracts to people, or leave them in places for people to find. You would be amazed at the change of atmosphere that would occur in the workplace. I've worked in some pretty rough workplaces, too. But the change of atmosphere would allow conversations to start. But you would be shocked to see how hard it was to get people to buy in to something as simple as that. I mean, most Believers would be involved in

Christian works, but some of those works seemed to have only a marginal payoff for the kingdom."

"Or they expected to have some possible payoff in the future."

"Yes. They felt so sure that they were fulfilling a God-given calling." Jason paused a moment. "But I shouldn't judge. What they were doing was between them and God. I just thought there were simple things everyone could be doing that would pay off now as well as in the future."

"I know what you mean. I know in our congregation it was so hard to get people to volunteer for just about anything. It was always the same few people doing everything. I tried to tell them that if we do nothing, then we deny the power of God and his Word to change people's hearts and lives. I got an 'Amen' every time, but few would show up."

"Maybe your tipping point is found somewhere in all that."

"Maybe."

They sat quietly for a few moments and Jason thought he heard someone crying. He looked at Rick and it was evident he heard it, too. They each took their candles and headed for the bedrooms.

In Kathy's bedroom they found Valerie sitting on the bed crying. A stack of photos of Kathy's childhood lay on the floor before her and a small pile of Kathy's school artwork lay across her lap. Darlene sat next to her on the bed, her arm around Valerie. She looked up as they entered.

"What's wrong?" Jason asked.

Valerie shook her head, but continued to cry a few moments longer. Then she collected herself and took a deep breath. "I'm sorry. I didn't mean to break down like that, but we've had so many memories in this house, it just kind of caught up with me." She looked up at Jason and began tearing again. "Our children were raised in this home."

Jason got on one knee before her and took her hand. "Do you want to stay, after all? We could change our minds."

Valerie shook her head. "No, it's not that. We have to go. There's nothing for us here now. It's all gone." She sat quietly, trying to compose herself. "It just crept up on me, that's all." She fought off the tears once again.

251

"I'm sorry," Jason said.

Valerie nodded. "Me, too."

Rick spoke softly. "We would like you folks to consider this house your own, still. And if this situation ever settles out, and things get better, you would always be able to come back and live here again. It'll still be your house."

"Things will never get any better," Valerie said. "It's all gone." The finality of her words silenced the rest of the conversation.

It took a little more than an hour for them to gather up the last of their things. Jeremy had the most to bring, having gathered so little the first time he left home. They loaded the truck and said their goodbyes. The parting was hardest on Ruthie, who at one point had convinced Jeremy of staying, but Rick and Darlene would have no part of it.

"You are to leave your parents and cleave unto your husband, and become one flesh. You belong with him now," Rick had said. Darlene stoically agreed and together they convinced Ruthie to get in the cab of the truck.

Jason shook Rick's hand. "Thanks for taking care of Jeremy through all this."

Rick nodded his head toward Ruth. "I expect a return favor."

Jason nodded. "You got it. I gave you the information about radiation sickness, right? And the papers about the house?"

"I got them. Thanks."

"You know, I'm sure they'll have the post offices up before long, and mail delivery. We'll correspond as soon as we can."

"Yes, they'll have everything up and running again, set up their way."

"No doubt."

"Thanks for letting us have the house."

"It's the least we could do. You're still in the fight and we're running away."

"You're not running away. You're preserving a remnant."

Jason nodded and hugged Rick. Then he hugged Darlene.

"Write as soon as you can," she said.

"We will." Then Jason joined the others in the truck. He started the engine and drove out onto the street. As they pulled away he took one last look at the house and saw Darlene collapse into Rick's arms, sobbing uncontrollably.

*

The trip back to Shem Creek passed without incident. They did see one group of cars traveling in the opposite direction on the interstate, but the truck continued unnoticed. Coming over the bridge they saw the glow of several large fires around the Charleston area, but the bridge itself was clear of all foot traffic, and they saw no one on the roads in Mount Pleasant. Jason backed the truck down to the boat landing and everyone got out and loaded the supplies into the cruiser.

Mark went with Jason to park the truck one last time. As they walked back Jason said, "I wish I could get something for that truck. It's a shame to just abandon it there."

"Maybe we can trade it for a load of diesel fuel for that boat, as well as some gas," Mark said. "If you want, I can ask around."

"Please do."

When they got back to the dock everyone was already waiting in the boat. Jeremy ran his hand along the muddy gunwale.

"Killer paint job, Dad," he said. "I'm glad the fine people of Mount Pleasant didn't get to see it in the daytime."

"Young man," Robert said, wearing his voodoo grin, "you don't have to care what they think in Mount Perfect. Besides, the mud makes the boat look genuine."

Jason shook his head. "Genuine. That's a word I wouldn't have thought of. Let's cast off." They released the lines and motored out into the harbor.

The water of the high tide had flooded the saw grass by the time they reached the sailboat, but in the dim light of early dawn Jason could tell that the keel still held fast in the mud of the creek. Robert took the wheel of the cruiser while Jason and Mark climbed aboard the sailboat. Valerie came aboard as well to inspect the storage capacity.

Jason unclipped the halyard from the boom and tied a

253

long piece of rope to it, then he turned to the cruiser. "Jeremy, take this line and make it fast to one of the cleats on your stern. Robert, when he gets that tied, I'd like you to ease away from us until you take up the slack."

"Roger dodger," Robert said.

Jason turned to the companionway and called out, "Valerie. We may be heeling over a bit, so watch yourself." Then he turned back to Robert. "All right, now, take a strain and we'll see what happens."

Robert eased ahead on the engine and the cruiser moved away into the darkness. The halyard grew taut until it began to pull against the top of the mast. The leverage of the mast, combined with the hull's buoyancy acting as a fulcrum, lifted the deep keel clear of the mud. Once clear the cruiser towed the sailboat sideways until it floated free in the deep water at the middle of the creek. Then he put the cruiser into neutral and Jeremy untied the line. Jason retrieved the line and retied it onto a cleat at the bow of the sailboat.

"I take it you want a tow?" Robert asked.

"Yes, at least until we get past the Ben Sawyer bridge. After that, I'll try to sail her. We'll need some wind, though."

As it turned out they ended up towing the boat all the way to the small bay at Bull's Island. The night had been calm, but even if there had been wind the waterways were too narrow for Jason, unfamiliar as he was with the vessel. They had passed both bridges without eliciting a response from either set of guards and they saw no one at the Isle of Palms Marina. Although the boat towed easily, it still made for a long trip and they did not anchor until after eight a.m. Jeremy released the towline and urged Robert to hurry to the dock. He had seen Kathy and Brian waiting there, and Jason watched as his son hurriedly climbed onto the dock and hugged his sister and brother. Jason's heart was touched to see the affectionate reunion. Ruthie got out of the boat and was likewise received. Jason heard a squeal of delight from Kathy when she heard about the marriage.

The sailboat's keel was too deep to allow it to tie up to the dock so Robert had to return to pick up Mark and Jason and Valerie and bring them over. The kids waited for them and Kathy hugged Jason as he stepped onto the dock.

"I waited here all night for you," she said. "I was worried when you didn't show up before sunrise."

"You waited all night on the dock? Did you sleep?"

"Yes, but it wasn't very comfortable."

"I guess not."

"So, what's with the new boat?"

"Let's talk about it over breakfast. I'm starved."

*

"Australia?" Kathy asked. "Why Australia?"

"Many reasons," Jason said, between bites of food. Mama and many of the others gathered around their picnic table to hear their adventures as they ate.

"First," Jason continued, "Australia has opened her doors to any American who can get there. That boat gives us the means."

"Would we get to see the zoo where Steve Irwin worked?" Brian asked.

"I'm sure," Jason said. "And we'll take a trip to the Hillsongs Worship center."

"And eat a kangaroo steak," Robert said without looking up from his plate.

"I hear it's delicious," Jason said.

"But..." Kathy said. She hesitated, then said, "I don't know. I guess I just can't get used to the idea of leaving America, our home."

"You never even voted," Brian said.

"Why don't you shut up? I'm not asking you," Kathy said.

Jason put down his fork. "I know how you feel. Honestly, I do. But believe me when I say that America as we knew it is gone. It's not coming back."

"Dad is right," Jeremy said. "The America you and I grew up with is over. When the lights come back on, you will see something totally different."

"I don't want to live in a country run by a bunch of Islamic Fascists," Jason said, flatly. "And you don't either, believe me."

"But you're an American," Robert to Jason said. "And a veteran, to boot! How can you decide to leave America and

255

live someplace else?"

Jason looked at his friend. "America is a dream, an ideal. It is all about freedom to choose your own path and prosper accordingly. It's about choosing your own faith and letting others choose theirs, proselytizing instead of beheading. America was about reaching for the stars, and the highest that is in men. I will always be that kind of American, but that America is gone now. We were losing it before all this happened, but it's gone now for sure." He looked around at everyone. "The best an American can do when America is gone is to go find someplace else to start."

"Australia?" Robert asked.

"Australia, or somewhere else on the way."

"Furthermore, young lady," Mama said, soothingly, "don't look at us and wonder why we aren't going. We've already found sites on another island and we will begin moving too, even this week. But mark my words, if that place becomes dangerous, we will move again, even overseas if need be."

Kathy nodded.

Mark put down his fork and wiped his mouth. "Thanks for breakfast. I needed it." He turned to Jason. "So, you're going to give the boat a shakedown cruise today?"

"Yes. And make whatever repairs need to be made. How about you?"

"Well, as tired as I am, I feel the need to go join the others to make another haul in that neighborhood. If you don't mind me taking the cruiser."

"Not at all. I told you, it's yours now. Just please give my battery on the sailboat a jump start before you go."

Mark nodded. "And since you refused to supply your new boat with food from the house, this haul today will all go to you."

"You don't have to do that."

"It's the least we can do, as a trade for the cruiser, I mean. Besides, you're going to need it out on that ocean."

"Let's quit talking and move out," Robert said. "There's lots of work to be done."

"I want everyone in our group to go sailing with me. I want everyone to be familiar with sailing that boat."

Chapter Thirty

"They know we're out here."

The shakedown cruise went as well as Jason could have wished. The boat had two complete sets of sails, along with a spinnaker and a storm jib. He took her through her paces, even going offshore, and found her to be stiff, dry, and weatherly. Everyone was attentive and eager to learn the working of the rig, even Ruthie who had never been on a sailboat before. Jason felt disappointed that Julie had decided to stay ashore.

They all got a chance to rest as they motored back through Bulls Bay, an engine test being part of the shakedown. The ladies sat on the cushions while Brian attached his bell to the mast. Jason let Jeremy take the wheel.

"I'm wondering, Dad," he said. "How are we to navigate in the open ocean?"

"I found a sextant onboard," Jason said. "I'm not very good with it for shooting stars, et cetera, but I know how to find our latitude at noon and I have a watch set to Greenwich Time."

"Will that be enough?"

"If it was good enough for Sir Francis Drake and Captain Cook, it'll be good enough for us. They both went around the world on that kind of navigation." He patted his son on the back. "Ease back on the throttle and come alongside the raft. Brian, take the boathook and grab the raft's mooring line. Valerie, stand by to let go the anchor, if

257

you please."

They anchored the sailboat where they had left the raft moored. As soon as all was secure the kids petitioned to go ashore.

"Why not?" Jason said. "You guys did well today. Liberty call commences now."

The four young ones cheered and climbed into the raft. Jason began to restow the lines and sails and watched as they motored ashore. Valerie came up on deck through the companionway.

"Where are they going?"

"Liberty call."

"Are they bringing the raft back?"

Jason's face registered his surprise. He looked toward the raft and saw that it was over half way to the dock. "I guess not. I'm sorry. But Mark and the others will be here in a little while. They'll give us a ride back."

"All right, then you can help me get the storage lockers ready below."

They worked in the galley and after a short while they heard a voice alongside.

"A-a-ahoy! Request perm-m-mission to come aboard."

Jason came up on deck and saw Twony and Julie in the raft next to the boat. "Of course! Come aboard." He gave Twony a hand up, then the young man helped Julie aboard. "You sound like a real sailor."

"Y-y-yes, sir. My dad was in the Navy."

"Is Valerie here?" Julie asked.

"Sure." He turned to call down into the galley but saw Valerie coming up the ladder.

"I'm right here," she said. "Oh! Hello."

"Hi," Julie said. "There are a few things I wanted to tell you." She waited as they sat down on the cockpit cushions, then said, "First of all, I wanted to thank you all for taking me in back when all this started. I don't know what I would have done if it weren't for you guys."

"Well, you're family," Valerie said. "You know that."

"I know. The second thing is this. I was talking to Mama today and she helped tie a lot of thoughts together for me and, in a nutshell, I accepted Jesus Christ as my Lord and Savior today."

Valerie and Jason both got on their feet and cheered and both hugged her in turn.

"That's excellent!" Valerie said. "I'm really happy for you!"

"Me, too," Jason said, beaming. "Welcome to the Kingdom!"

"Thanks," Julie said. "I owe you guys a lot for that, too. Your love and example and words were showing me the way the whole time. Thanks, again."

"Well, thanks for telling us," Jason said. "That makes my whole day."

Julie nodded, and then her face grew serious. "There's one more thing. I've been thinking it over, and," she looked down at the deck, "and I've decided that I will not be going with you. I feel that I need to stay here with, with Mama and everyone."

"Are you sure?" Valerie asked.

Julie nodded. Jason saw Twony touch her arm tenderly and watched as she stole a glance at the young man, and he knew. His heart was happy for her.

"I hope you're not disappointed," Julie said. "I feel like I owe you all better than that, but I really feel like I should stay."

"You don't owe us anything, Julie," Jason said. "As a matter of fact, you've been a major help, more than my own kids sometimes."

"I guess if you've already made up your mind then that's it," Valerie said. "I'll miss you, though, for sure." She hugged Julie again.

"And d-don't you worry about her safety," Twony said. "I'll…" he caught himself, "we'll take good care of her."

"We know you will," Jason said, sadness growing in his heart. He moved forward to hug the young man. "We know you will." Then Jason hugged Julie. "We'll miss you, daughter. We'll try to keep in touch."

Julie nodded and began to tear up. Jason offered her all of the camping gear on shore and anything else she thought she might use. She thanked them, and then said she needed to return to camp to help out with the supper. Jason offered to take them back so that he could bring the raft back to the sailboat.

259

When they came alongside the dock the two young people climbed out. They offered their thanks for the ride and were moving out onto the causeway when Julie turned and came back to the raft, her face in tears again. Jason stood up and stepped onto the dock just as Julie gave him one last hug. She hugged his neck tightly, but that was all she hugged. It was an innocent church hug between a brother and sister in the Lord.

"Thank you," she whispered, hesitating to find the right words, "for not giving in to me back there in the forest. You don't know how much that means to me now."

Jason now began to tear up. He nodded and whispered, "It's all right. I'm glad it worked out the way it did." Then he added, "I love you, my sister."

"I love you, too, brother."

They broke the embrace and Julie turned to rejoin Twony at the causeway. Jason saw them take each other's hand. He got in the raft and motored back out to the sailboat.

*

At four p.m. Jason awoke to the sound of a helicopter flying nearby. After he and Valerie finished their work, they had decided to take a little nap during the heat of the day. Valerie slept in the master stateroom with the windows open and Jason slept on the cushions in the cockpit. He sat up and looked around and saw the aircraft away to the northwest, toward the mainland. The executive style helicopter seemed to be orbiting something in the marsh, flying only a few hundred feet above the ground. As he watched, it turned and headed for the sailboat.

Valerie came up on deck and stood next to him in the cockpit. They both watched as the helicopter came and began to circle the sailboat's position. It had a gray and pale blue color scheme and Jason could see no military markings on it. The passengers inside were invisible behind the dark tinted windows. They could feel the wash of the rotor blades, and Valerie reached up to keep her hair from blowing in her eyes.

"Who are they?" she asked. "Coast Guard?"

Jason shook his head. "No, Coast Guard choppers are

orange. I don't know who it is." He waved to the helicopter, but got no acknowledgment.

After circling a few times around the sailboat it flew off in the direction of the camp. It circled there several times, at one point very slowly, and then made a pass over the beach. Then it turned southwest and flew along the coast headed toward the city.

As they watched the helicopter disappear they heard the sound of boats approaching at high speed. They looked toward the main channel and saw Mark and the others coming in fast. Mark, in the cruiser, veered off toward the sailboat while the other two boats headed for the dock. He came alongside and Robert tossed Jason a line. They tied the two boats together and Mark and Robert climbed aboard.

"Was he flying around here?" Mark asked.

"Yes," Jason said. "He flew around us and then went around the camp."

"Man!" Mark said.

"Who was he?" Valerie asked.

"I don't know, but I have a bad feeling about it," Mark said, looking off in the direction the helicopter had taken.

"What do you think they want?" Jason asked.

"I don't know, but they know we're out here now, whoever they were."

"I don't like it," Robert said.

Mark turned back to face Jason and Valerie. "But anyway, we did get a good haul. This boat is loaded with food, and I hope you like it. We got mostly dry goods and cans. There's not much meat, but you can take some of our salted meat from the house."

"Rich folks don't eat meat out of cans," Robert said. "But we did find some tools for you to get fresh meat with." He pointed to the stern of the boat where two large deep-sea rods were propped next to a large tackle box.

"Oh, man. Thanks," Jason said. "The boys are going to love those."

"We traded your truck for two drums of diesel fuel. They're in the other boat. They'll bring it over as soon as they unload the other tools and stuff."

"Excellent. Thanks."

"And for you," Robert said, "I brought this." He reached

261

into his back pocket and pulled out a hand-held GPS receiver. He handed it to Jason.

"Oh, man! Thank you very much. We were just talking about this earlier."

"It's not fancy, no maps or anything, but you won't need'em out there anyway."

Jason shook Robert's hand. "Thanks, again, man."

"You're welcome. I don't really want you to go, but if you must, you might as well not get lost."

"All right," Mark said, "I think we need to get this stuff aboard your boat right away. Mama will want to talk about that helicopter. Where are your kids?"

"I let them go to the beach."

"Okay. I'll start handing the stuff up from the cabin to Robert, Robert can hand it to you, and you can hand it to Valerie down below here. Valerie, if it starts to come too fast, just stack it up for now."

They worked quickly to get the supplies, mainly sacks and cardboard boxes, aboard the sailboat. As they were handling the last few containers the workboat came alongside from the dock. Jason looked over and could see the two drums of fuel in her stern and appreciated the backbreaking work to get them into the boat.

"Hey!" the man in the boat called, "Mama wants you to come ashore at once."

"What about the fuel?" Jason asked.

"I'll get it in the right tanks," the man said. "You all just go ahead."

Without a word the three clambered into the cruiser and headed for the dock.

*

"Is that similar to what you saw, Mr. Ribault?" Mama asked.

"Yes, ma'am."

"And you saw no markings of any kind?"

"There were some small letters or numbers, but I couldn't read them."

"I see," Mama said, nodding her head slowly. She took a deep breath and kept her eyes toward the ground. Everyone

262

around her waited patiently for her to speak.

"What did you fellows find at Cape Romain?"

"The brush is pretty thick around the outer part of the island," one of the men said, "but it thins out under the canopy of the trees. We found some likely places to dig for water, but there were no clearings like there are here."

"That may be a blessing," Mama said. "Was there a decent landing?"

"We found one good one on the backside of the main island, deep water close up to the bank. We could rig a board to walk on."

Mama nodded again, considering. "That's good. Thank you." She turned to Mark. "I suppose there's nothing else for it. We need to get over there as soon as possible."

"Do you want us to move tonight?"

"I see no other way. If they don't return then we can come back, but if they do return I want us to be gone. I want there to be no trace that we were ever here."

Mark nodded, then spoke to the crowd that had gathered. "Okay, I want to get the word out to everyone. We pack up and head out tonight. Everyone is responsible to get their own things to the dock. We'll begin ferrying them over in an hour."

"We can help," Jason offered.

"Mr. Ribault, I suggest that you folks prepare to leave, as well," Mama said. "We don't know who these people are."

"Yes, ma'am. But all of our supplies are already aboard and Valerie is stowing them away right now. My kids will get our personal things aboard and after that we can help pack or carry things."

Mama nodded again. "That will be much appreciated."

*

Once Jason had gathered the kids from the beach and had informed them of the plan, they went into the camp and broke down the tent and other gear for Julie. They gathered all of the personal gear that had been sitting under the tarp and took it down to the dock where a small crowd had already gathered. Mark was helping to load one of the boats,

263

and Jason and the boys stepped up to help.

"How does it look over there?" Jason asked.

"It's rough, but maybe we won't have to stay for very long," Mark said. He placed a box into the boat. "The mosquitoes will be bad."

"Maybe they'll settle down with winter on the way."

"I hope. Are you guys needing a ride out to the boat?"

"No. Just give Valerie a yell to bring the raft. I'll send the girls out with our stuff, and the boys and I will help pack the stuff in the house," Jason said. "How about your things, do you still need to pack?"

"No. My stuff is already taken care of."

"I'll see you later, right?"

"Oh, yeah. After we get everyone over we will come back to cover the tracks, hide the fireplaces, et cetera."

"All right, I'll see you then. Thanks for telling Valerie."

Mark winked at Jason as he helped an elderly man aboard the boat.

Jason turned to the young ones of his group. "Kathy, they're going to send for your mom and the raft. Get this stuff aboard the boat. Boys, come with me."

"When will we get to eat dinner?" Jeremy asked.

"Yeah," Kathy said. "I'm hungry."

"There're sandwiches at the house. Come and get one when this stuff aboard."

*

Darkness had fallen long before the last of the people had been taken over to the cape. Jason and his family helped pack the rest of the supplies into the boats while others straightened up the campsite. When the last of the men had come to the dock and the last of the things had been loaded aboard, the engines were started. Mark spoke to Jason.

"Tie the raft to the stern and I'll take you out to the boat. It's getting choppy."

"All right, thanks." Jason did so, then joined his family on the open boat. Brian stood next to Sean talking quietly. The cruiser and the workboat pulled out into the creek and moved away into the breezy darkness. Mark followed after them, but steered toward the sailboat anchorage.

Jason looked up at the clouds racing across the sky. He could taste the salt spray carried on the wind. "You know, I hadn't thought of it until now, but we won't be able to tell if a hurricane is coming."

"Keep tuned in to the radio," Mark said.

"What about you guys?"

"We've got Mama. She says her joints always hurt when a blow is coming."

Jason nodded. "Internal barometer, huh?"

"Yes, sir," Mark said. "But speaking of storms, how are you going to handle that Cape Horn weather I've heard so much about?"

"Well, it'll be the middle of summer by the time we get down there, so it won't be bad. But then again, we might go down around Africa and across the Indian Ocean."

"Which route is shortest?"

"I'm not sure," Jason said. "To tell the truth, I'll have to check on the map."

Mark nodded and brought the boat alongside the sailboat. The boys tied the boats together and hauled the raft on deck. The kids said their goodbyes and then climbed aboard. Jason could see that Brian was trying not to cry. Valerie thanked Mark and wished Sean well and then climbed aboard with the others.

Once everyone else was aboard, Jason gave Sean a hug. "Take care of yourself, Sean. And look out for your old man."

"I will."

Then Jason turned to Mark. He looked at his friend for a moment in the darkness, then leaned forward and hugged him. Mark returned the hug tightly. After a few moments they broke the embrace.

"Mark," Jason said, struggling with the words, "thanks for everything."

"Man, thank you."

"I feel like," Jason paused, "I feel like you've been my best friend all of my life."

"Me, too, brother."

"This really sucks."

"Yeah, but you know what they say, 'here, there, or in the air.'"

265

Jason grimaced. "That's right." He turned to climb aboard the sailboat, waiting until the rolling of the two boats brought the two decks close together, then jumped across. Once aboard he turned around and leaned over the gunwale. "Tell Robert I said, uh…." he stammered.

"I will," Mark said. "Godspeed, my brother."

Jason saw Mark wipe his eyes. "And you, too." Then he turned to his boys already waiting on deck. "Cast off."

The lines were untied and Jason heard the boat's engine RPM's increase. He saw Mark wave one more time as the boat pulled away into the windy darkness.

Jason sighed deeply. "All right, stand by to weigh the anchor."

"We're not waiting for the tide?" Valerie asked.

"Not with this wind in our favor. I want to be far past the twelve-mile limit by the time the sun comes up. Untie the gaskets on the main and stand by to set the sails." Jason reached down into a pouch next to the wheel and took out a bundle. He kissed it lightly and handed it to Jeremy. "Hoist this up to the top of the mast, please." Jeremy took the flag and stepped forward while Jason took the wheel. "All right, heave around on those halyards. Brian, pull up the anchor. Shift colors, underway."

The United States flag raced up the mast and got to the top ahead of the sails. The mainsail and jib were adjusted, filling with a sharp crack and the vessel began to heel over as it gathered way. Jason steered southeast, away from the dark land and out into the boundless ocean.

The End

266

"Pass the Word"

One of my greatest hopes for this novel is that its message would get out to as many people as possible, and that this nation would get back on track with God before it's too late. But if that were no longer possible, my next hope would be for God's people to prepare themselves for whatever may come. I've spoken to many people from all walks of life who also feel that bad times loom on the horizon for America and are preparing in various ways. Some are collecting seeds and planting gardens, others are exploring ways to become energy and water independent, and still others are collecting firearms or gold. But too many have given no thought to life beyond our present circumstances. If the message of this novel resonates with you, and if you agree that the United States of America should always be "One Nation, Under God," then I invite you to pass this book to others, along with your recommendation. Word of mouth is the most powerful form of publicity. If we can get the word out, then maybe things can turn around. If not, then surely each of us will want our family and friends to prepare for whatever may come. I've included a bibliography, complete not only with my resources for writing this novel, but with information on how people may prepare for the worst.

I also ask you to pray for the message in this book, and that it would reach as many as possible. Sometimes we must lose something, or have a vision of losing it, before we realize its true value to us, and our nation is no exception. Pass copies of this book along to people in your Bible study or home group. Give them to staff members at your church. Provide them to your youth group. Give them to your unchurched friends. Talk about the ideas in the novel, and how to prepare. By doing so you are sharing in this important work, one that clearly presents the message of Salvation. And as Keith Green once said, "We're responsible for this generation of souls all over the earth." Thank you and God bless you for your support.

Sincerely,
James Howard

Bibliography –

Books –
Holy Bible, KJV
From 9/11 to 666 by Ralph Stice
Jerusalem Countdown by John Hagee
Final Move Beyond Iraq by Mike Evans
Student Handbook: Medical Self-Help Training Course Part 1 by the U.S. Government Printing Office: 1961 O-601828

Websites - (links available on my website www.apenforhisglory.com)

Nuclear War Survival –
www.nukalert.com
www.ki4u.com
www.physiciansforcivildefense.org/
www.wnd.com/news/article.asp?ARTICLE_ID=51648
www.youtube.com/watch?v=Dobys9s9f2w
video.google.com/videoplay?docid=-1528313029232126903&q=duck+cover&hl=en
www.archive.org/stream/AboutFal1963/AboutFal1963_256k
b.mp4

Power Grid –
http://en.wikipedia.org/wiki/Electric_power_transmission
http://www.cbsnews.com/stories/2003/08/14/national/main5
68370.shtml
http://www.geni.org/globalenergy/library/national_energy_g
rid/united-states-of-america/index.shtml
http://www.encyclopedia.com/doc/1P2-20105.html
http://science.howstuffworks.com/blackout.htm

Islamic Messiah –
http://en.wikipedia.org/wiki/Mahdi
http://www.jfednepa.org/mark%20silverberg/wahhabi.html
http://www.joshuatreevillage.com/601/laryabra.htm
http://en.wikipedia.org/wiki/Ahl_al-Bayt
http://www.wnd.com/index.php?fa=PAGE.printable&pageId
=44480
http://en.wikipedia.org/wiki/Jesus_in_Islam

http://www.joelstrumpet.com/?p=19
http://www.stpaulsbiblechurch.org/mahdiwatchpage.html